Family Secrets Book Six

Howling Winds

By

Rebekah McClew

Dedication:

Thank you for taking the time to dive into my books; I sincerely hope that you enjoyed them so much that you'd be tempted to reach for another one, like how it's impossible to eat just one potato chip!

Chapter One
Finding Sydney

As far as I can say. I have always hated the dark. No time in my life had I ever thought it was a good thing to be sitting in the bottom of a hole, where you have no clue where you are, sitting in the dark with people trying to kill you! Lucian might have been able to see well enough, but I had still been partially human, so my eyesight wasn't as strong as his. Feeling along the wall, trying to stand up had been rather difficult because of the slippery floors. It had been much colder and wetter down here. Our main priority had been to get out of this massive maze we were lost in. As much as Lucian tried to be positive after what felt like a week of being stuck in here. I started feeling as if I would never get out to see my wife Rose or daughter Larissa again.

"I'm beginning to think this tunnel is never going to end. It's either that or we're about to find some seriously deep water soon. I'm sopping wet!" I hated complaining but after being caked with mud, not an area of my body hadn't been covered with it, my hair was thick with mud from falling in it.

Lucian didn't have the same problem that I had, he was only dirty from the knees down.

"Jacob, I don't think you're going to like what I found just ahead, let me check it out first otherwise we might have to go back the other way. There was one more tunnel we passed before taking this one. I'll be right back." His voice drifted off, not that I could see him leaving.

I could hear his footsteps as he stepped into deeper water as the splash hit, he was gone checking out the rest of the way. At least I didn't have to wait long before Lucian made it back rather quickly.

"How bad is it?" I only guessed it had been him or at least hoped it had been since I couldn't hear anything other than Lucian walking out of the water.

"I promise you're not going to like it. It's cold, wet, and goes a distance but it is a way out. You'll need to hold your breath for a long time. I can swim you out if you want. It's pretty dark in there even for me." Lucian was rather blunt and to the point.

I didn't exactly like the sound of that when Lucian says it's too dark for him then I know it's not good.

Reaching out, I tried to feel where he was. Lucian grabbed for my hand helping me up. Walking blindly trusting Lucian that he knew where he was going, holding onto his shoulders as we went into the water. As soon as the water reached waist deep, Lucian told me when to hold my breath. At that moment he went under, taking us both out as quickly as he could. Lucian had been a much faster and stronger swimmer than I was. I knew for what he had swam, it would have taken me much longer not that the darkness helped at all. It was no different than the rest of the tunnel.

I felt the colder air on my skin as we emerged from under the water. Opening my eyes I could see that we were not far from the beach, sliding off Lucian's back we both swam for the side. The water was rough but not where I expected it to end up. We wound up in the lake on the far side of the city, I never knew the tunnels could go out this far. Climbing up the side as I watched Lucian struggling with a broken arm, he was still faster than I had been. I knew it was more out of stubbornness than anything. His arm was going to be messed up after this. Stopping long enough to straighten out his arm using my spring jacket even though it was wet trying to tie it around his arm for added support, even though he complained about how goofy it looked and not the pain.

"Rose would kill me if I didn't at least try something to keep your arm halfway normal looking." Smiling at him Lucian knew Rose was very protective of both of us.

Not moving around too much, at least it had been late at night and dark, and no people in sight or we might have had others staring at us thinking it was strange we went for a swim at the beginning of winter. Looking around I wasn't sure where to start other than maybe head home. Who knows where Luther brought Sophie, and no one knew where Sydney and the others disappeared to?

"I'm staying out, but you should go back and at least let Rose know how everyone is, especially Charlie. I'm sure he's worried about where Sophie is right now, not that I like the idea of telling him the truth. That she's with Luther. I'm going to try to pick up on their scent while you head back. If I hear anything I'll call you." Looking down into his pocket pulling out what should be the now mud-encrusted, wet cell phone, smiling Lucian seemed rather happy.

6

"Good thing Rose made you keep it in a plastic case protector, don't feel so geeky now do you?" Lucian gave me a slight shove that almost sent me back over the side again.

"Yeah but I have to use it now that it's still working. I think until I dry off. I'll leave it in the plastic protector." Putting the cell phone back in knowing Lucian's history with cell phones was never good, he had broken, smashed, and lost so many already.

"I'm pretty sure you should come with; Nichole could set your arm better. I'm sure by now she's had enough practice from raising you." We started to walk through town when other people were standing outside of a nightclub.

Finding less crowded routes proved more challenging than we had anticipated.

"I don't want to risk having to come all the way back out here once we finally make it home. Plus, the trail could disappear completely once the snow starts falling - right now we just have to deal with the freezing cold. I can't afford to waste any time on this trip." Even I couldn't argue against that logic.

We hadn't even made it halfway across the city. There were a lot of events going on tonight but then we were used to living far out in the middle of nowhere. We could get going much faster, sadly here in the city, there were so many people. A lot more than we cared for.

At least along the water, there hadn't been anyone. I almost wished we had followed it down further. It was going to take forever to do this by foot, sadly both of us had been wishing we were still in the tunnels running, it would have been easier to hide. But then guessing from where we had been they were not the regular city tunnels we ran through. They had been tunnels built underneath the city-owned tunnels. They kept an eye on this entire city not letting anything escape their attention, even though most vampires who did not want to get caught or noticed would never live near here unless they were trying to blend in. I couldn't help it, but I was missing the countryside and much smaller towns.

"You're heading my direction, so I'll stick with you, at least until the edge of the city and then I'll take off." Not a moment before I said that Lucian had a rather strange look on his face.

I knew that look all too well when he found something he was looking for. Starting to walk faster, I kept up keeping an eye on those who might be watching or around to ambush us.

"It's Luther's scent. He's headed this way but he's with someone other than Sophie." Getting tired of walking there had been a motorcycle parked on the curb.

Messing around with it, Lucian whispered to me, 'borrowing it for a while, they can find it later' as he got it started, I hopped on the back before he could take off, otherwise, I was going to be stuck walking through the city on my own. Even though it would have been a lot safer compared to the way Lucian drives. I may have been adventurous however I wasn't dangerous like Lucian had been. Holding on hoping not to fall off the bike as he shot through traffic, even being honked at several times while weaving, we got ahead of the traffic as he was still following the strange scent. It hadn't been the direction we planned to go. We wound up on the much further end of the lake, but then at least there had been fewer people up here. I planned on traveling north and straight across and dropping down south again to go home. We already rode on the motorcycle for a few hours staying most of the time following along the water's edge, if we hadn't been dirty before from all the mud we had certainly been kicking it up now as we followed back roads and two trackers. Not sure how much further we would need to go until Lucian had driven into a small side road stopping to look around. Getting off the bike and setting it aside. I followed Lucian very closely in case others might show up. I was sure we wouldn't be surprising them with how loud the motorcycle had been.

"You don't have to come. I don't even know if he's still here?" Lucian had never once taken his focus off from the trail he had been following.

Something I wished I had been trained to do, someday I'll have to convince Charlie to teach me.

"I'm already late getting back, what's a few more hours?" Besides, I didn't want to get back and explain why I left Lucian to himself.

Walking down to the beach there had been no way of following footprints with so many already down here other than the smell that stayed in the cold damp sand which made it much more difficult. We kept following it for a good hour until we left the beach walking through the woods. Stepping over broken branches or dead trees that had fallen as we went further into the woods where it was getting thicker. It seemed strange that he would carry Sophie through here.

"The thing I don't understand is the other set of scents that I'm picking up. Sophie and Luther came through here but as we get up here Sophie leads to the left with the other person as Luther heads back towards the water. Sophie's scent is just as strong as the others, so she's not being carried. She's walking willingly, so at least we know she's okay for now." Lucian stopped in his tracks.

I wished Charlie could have been here also; he could have followed at least one set of tracks while we followed the others. Then I thought that should be it, taking my phone out of my pocket, it had been caked with mud as well, now dried on solid to the protective case. Ever since Lucian lost so many cell phones. Rose got tired of trying to get a hold of a new one so now, we all have cases to keep the phones safe. It had taken a few times before Charlie answered his phone.

"Hey Charlie, we have a problem. It's kind of hard to follow two trails when they're going in different directions. One has Sophie going in one direction with someone we don't know who it is and Luther in the other direction. Lucian and I are following Luther's trail, I'll leave a mark here so you can find Sophie's trail even though it's heading west, you might pick up on it. We are much further up north than I thought we would be." After giving him the directions we took off after Luther, even though Charlie told us to stay put.

We marked the spot where we stood by tearing off a piece of fabric from the corner of Lucian's shirt leaving it tied tightly to a small branch. At least Charlie knew what Lucian was like, we wouldn't have to explain why we didn't stick around. One thing we found was that no matter how much the mortal world changed, Luther still hadn't. He still insisted on traveling by foot refusing to use modern conveniences as much as possible.

Now that we were not that worried about anyone being out here to see us, we ran as fast as we could through the woods, I could barely keep up with Lucian and keep him in view, when he set his mind on something he couldn't be stopped. I did my best to keep up with my brother-in-law. Slowing down, I could guess either we were getting closer, or Lucian saw something.

"The trail is getting stronger, and I don't like who's with him, this isn't good." Not that he looked worried, Lucian was more upset rather than sad.

"Who's with him? Should we turn back and look for Sophie with Charlie for now?" Shaking his head answering no, we kept walking towards the direction that was troubling him.

We walked down to the sand again, which I was hoping the trail would have left the water area even though the air from the water felt extremely cold, and I was still cold myself. At times like this, I wished I had been a full vampire, at least the weather wouldn't affect me as much as it does, but then again I couldn't trade my other options. We had gone quite a ways until Lucian stopped. I didn't have to worry about passing him since I finally caught up to him. Shaking his head I could only watch as he now looked even more worried than before.

"The trail ends here for some reason. For a short distance, she walked with him and then stopped here. The trail completely ends. She transported him somewhere. Why would she risk coming back here unless he found Sidney or figured out where she would go?" There was no sign of a struggle, no blood or anything to suggest that she opposed being there with him and both trails were the same as in age for the time.

Now there wasn't anything to follow or hints since they could be almost anywhere. We both turned and headed back to where we were supposed to meet up with Charlie. While we waited I called Rose to find out what else was going on at home. Lucian said he wasn't going far; he wanted to check around in our area. That he would be right back. Nodding in agreement I waited for Rose to answer the phone.

"Where are you? Everyone is looking for Sophie, she's missing, and Charlie took off without warning. Andrew and Goseck are heading off with him. Several are leaving for their homes. But keeping alert in case they hear anything. Where did you two go? Larissa started school again yesterday with Amanda and Savannah." I was trying to think how exactly to word things so that I wouldn't worry her too much.

"Not to worry, I think we might be heading back soon. We're waiting for Charlie. I called him not too long ago on the cell phone and he said he was on his way to meet up with us. As soon as he gets here, I'll head home except it's going to take a while. I was almost thinking of stopping at Lorah's apartment in Chicago. It's in the city, then I would take off from there for the rest of the way. I think we are in upper Michigan. The compound wasn't anywhere near where we had guessed. We left Chicago to head up far north along the water. Anyway, I'm getting pretty tired, so I better get going or I'll never make it. Unfortunately, I don't have transportation so there are a lot of places I'm going to have to walk instead of run." I knew it was going to be a long way back.

Lucian agreed he was going to wait for Charlie to figure out what to do next.

"Lorah can come to pick you up, she's working at her old job already. She should be able to get you. I'll call her and she can find you along the water if you follow down until you hit the border." Looking over at Lucian I could see the worry in his eyes that I felt concerned about leaving him here behind even if Charlie was coming.

But then at the moment, Charlie was going to be more worried about tracking Sophie than anything else not that he didn't care about finding out what happened with Sydney and Luther. He would certainly find it interesting, but he would even acknowledge there wasn't much we could do right now if there were no clues as to where she was. Then there was the look I was worried about as he started to look around. I knew Lucian was thinking of doing something.

"Rose, how badly do you need me to come back home? If you have everything handled I think I would like to follow Lucian around a little more." As I watched him formulate some idea in his head he hadn't heard me ask Rose for more time.

She agreed to this at least, she knew we were alright, and I promised to check in again soon. Closing the cell phone and placing it back in its protective case, I stayed waiting for the others to show up.

"So, what's the plan now?" As I looked at Lucian hoping he was going to share his plan since he was known for ditching others.

Close as he had been to Charlie and Lorah, he's ditched them in the past.

"I thought you were heading back home. Is Rose alright?" Looking concerned.

"Yeah, she's fine. Anthony and Nichole are helping her with the publishing company even though now at this point it pretty much takes care of itself. Larissa is busy with school. She's let the forestry office where we worked know that we won't be coming back. She told them we had family obligations. So, I'm assuming from the look on your face you've decided what you're doing next?" Giving me his usual smile I knew we were about to fall into hell again.

"Before the others object to what we are about to do, let's take off. They can find this spot. They have the coordinates, and they're still marked. I don't feel like waiting

13

here for them." Taking off again this time we followed the water only passing a few homes and other smaller areas along the water.

It had still been a lot faster to travel along this way as the sun started to come up. We had to find a place for Lucian to stay until we could travel in the tunnels again. Instead, we made a straight line to Lorah's apartment which would at least be safer for us to wait until the sun went down to move around. Out of the corner of my eye, I could see a movement that had been rather quick as I realized it was Lorah herself heading home. As soon as we had come close to the city we slowed, thankfully she lived close to the border rather than directly in the larger part of the city. Following her into the apartment, we were not the only ones who had thought about coming here. Goseck, Andrew, and Charlie had already been here. Charlie lowered his hand with the cell phone as he saw us walking in behind Lorah.

"I was trying to call you on your phone, did you lose it already? Jacob yours wouldn't work either. I kept getting the answering machine instead. We were already heading out here since Lorah said she heard the news about the old compound. We were going to check it out but now that you're here, you can bring us to where you saw the place except unfortunately we are going to have to wait a while. Andrew and Goseck were going to get started earlier and I planned on catching up to them.

"We still have our phones, they're turned off. We figured we would wait here. We didn't think you would make it in time before the sun was up and possibly stay somewhere until you could." Looking at Lucian I figured it was better if I answered since Charlie would have figured it out too easily that Lucian was up to something.

14

I started explaining to Goseck and Andrew how to get to the spot, we had to figure out how to ditch Charlie so he wouldn't try to follow us back to the tunnels even though Lucian was better at ditching him than I was.

While the others were talking in the kitchen with Lorah, she was watching us. We tried to speak quietly to each other. We knew Lorah had been eavesdropping, not that she was sharing it with the others. Taking out his cell phone from the protective case, he texted a message as I had pretended to get a call from Rose wondering when I was coming home. Instead, I pretended that I was taking off from Lorah's now and would be home in about a day. No one else thought anything of it since it hadn't sounded out of the ordinary. I was so tired, and I would have preferred getting a chance to sleep, but I knew if we were going to do this then I had to take off. At least it wouldn't take Lucian long to join me. Waving goodbye to everyone. I walked out the door. All I knew had been that Lucian expected me to take off for one of the closer storm sewer drains and we hoped we would find one that connected to the hidden tunnels again. Pulling out my cell phone to see what he had texted me. I followed the direction I was given and exactly near the water had been a drain letting water out. Climbing down into it. I waited for Lucian to catch up.

Reading over the text it simply said, 'enjoy sitting in the storm drain feeling wet and cold till I get there, ha, ha." Leave it up to Lucian to make a joke out of the situation.

I knew he could move a lot faster than me but then who knows maybe with the two of us we can avoid what he's been getting into so far? Surprisingly I didn't have to wait as long as I thought I would. Just after an hour, I could see

15

Lucian dropping down into the tunnel behind me with a huge smile on his face.

"How did you take off so soon without them seeing you?" I was going to have to take lessons from him now.

"Not a problem, Lorah distracted them while I slipped out the window from her bedroom. At least she's on the ground floor so they didn't hear me land. As soon as I hit the ground I ran for it." Taking the lead, we didn't wait around as we followed the tunnels back in.

We hoped we wouldn't run into Alana, but we did hope to find some clue as to where Sydney would have taken off to. She must have dropped her trainers off first before she met up with Luther, unless that had been a surprise visit from him. But then where were the others and why was there no sign at all of a struggle? They could have only vanished from the area if she took him willingly to transport somewhere. Not that I was looking forward to walking through the cold water. It would have been better if we could have done this in the summer, but then you can't exactly plan for these things. As good of an idea as this had sounded like. I was beginning to wonder if we were making the right choice. After all, Sydney was on her own now and didn't seem like she was coming back to the family or Lucian. Not that I wanted to let him know what I was thinking, but I highly doubted I was the only one thinking this anymore.

Similar to the tunnels we were already in earlier, these were either muddy or filled with water up to our knees. As we worked our way through. I followed closely to Lucian hoping not to lose him. At times he would race faster but then I think he was rather tired of the tunnels also. As we made our way deeper, we found a tunnel leading upward. Part of it had collapsed leaving only a small hole to squeeze through. I wasn't looking forward to telling Rose that her brother was squished because he figured he could get through a small hole. As soon as he passed through I followed next. What I hadn't been expecting had been the large room we wound up in. We could only guess this had once been an escape route or a quick tunnel leading into the city. As we followed it out now into drier hallways there hadn't been anyone around. We kept walking until we found where we were. We had been down the hallway near the picture where Luther had torn the water away from the picture which trapped us in here the first time.

It felt so strange walking around the old compound with no one else here or at least we hadn't come across anyone yet. I wasn't sure if it had been a good or bad thing if we hadn't run into Alana, instead of going the way we ran the last time when we got lost, not wanting to risk getting stuck in the main hall. We had gone in the direction that Lucian thought might have been Sydney's chamber while she was living here. We guessed we were in the right area, there was a steel gate going across the small hallway closing it off from the rest of the area. Looking through we could hear voices, but we hadn't seen anyone yet. Heading back down the hallway the way we came, we went into one of the rooms we passed once we heard footsteps coming toward us. Not wanting to go too far, we could hear the person unlocking the gate to get out. Lucian swept around the doorway catching up to the person as they turned to face him, he then knocked them out.

As Lucian dragged him into the first room he came to. I pulled the gate closed trying to make it look as if the lock had still been closed. Following behind into the room Lucian was busy tying the person up hoping to give us enough time to look around. The room looked basic but nothing we were looking for. Looking back out into the hallway to make sure no one else was following out after him, we kept listening at the various doors we passed only opening a few on the way. We heard a lot of talking behind one as the voice belonged to Alana. She was still around. Going into the room next to hers we had found Sydney's room. At least the walls had not been too thick to hear through.

"Where do you think they went? It seems like Maddie should have been back already unless Luther was able to kill her?" The one voice that sounded concerned, we hadn't recognized but the other had been Alana.

"Doesn't matter, as soon as we locate either Luther or Dorina we have some hope of preserving the power from Sydney. As soon as we do, I'll teach her for taking the power from me, no one gets in my way. This was supposed to be all mine. She's a worthless human; she has no right in our world. She never should have been given power like that. I only set the stone up to preserve itself until I came for it, why did it never come to me?" As we heard crashing we could only assume she was angry throwing things around.

While we listened to the two of them making plans on how they wanted to track down Luther, they picked out his usual haunts. He was known for showing up even though it would take a while to track him, they still had more leads than we did.

"First we need to check this warehouse he stays around. We might have a better chance of finding him there since he likes hiding there. He finds more places to hide. I can't blame him, it's harder to get around without being noticed unless you know the place well. I should have known better than to trust a vampire to do a simple little task. He's far too confident, that's what's going to get him in the end.

18

There's no way Sydney would trust him to rule with her. He has to be up to something and convinced her." Not that either of us had liked the sound of that.

Maybe there was more to it, maybe she was cooperating to keep Sophie safe? Searching through the dressers there had still been a couple of shirts left but nothing she couldn't live without. In the corner, Lucian picked up a small box, the same one we had seen Nikolai holding as he had left with Sydney. At some point, she must have come back to her room. Smiling to himself, at least Lucian knew she was given his gift. Not much else had been left other than a few small crystals that Lucian felt like taking in case we could find some way of tracking them down. Wanting to take off before the others get a head start on locating Luther we were starting to leave. No one was in the hallway, we also wanted to take off before they realized the person was still missing. Leaving the door open a crack that way they would at least find him and possibly let him out. We had taken off running. We hadn't found what we were looking for but then maybe if we found Luther, we would find out where Sophie had been taken to and why possibly Sydney was with him.

At least one of the places hadn't been too far from here. There had been a warehouse nearby that he supposedly liked hanging out at. The only difference about this place had been only vampires had gone there, once in a while, a human might get invited or wander in, but it had been strictly private. Taking the tunnel back the way we had come seemed easier than trying to find the exit heading out the other way and possibly running into someone. At least now we knew that Sydney and Alana separated, and most had either followed Sydney with her into the new place or just took off again on their own. Apparently if what we heard had been correct, Sydney's trainers were no longer teaching her, they were co-ruling with her. With several guards, it seemed a lot more solid than this place had been. But then this was only a temporary place until Alana could figure out how to get the power out of Sydney and take control of it again.

Navigating our way through the city was a pain since we were both on foot trying not to catch attention, but then one nice thing about larger cities, most people were busy with their problems, than to worry about a couple of people walking along the road. Not that we had been too familiar with this area. We looked around where the empty warehouses were rumored to be. Separating once we found a few. I had checked a couple while Lucian was checking out the others. Not finding anything I had taken out my cell phone to call Lorah.

"Has Charlie left yet?" I was curious if he had, now that the sun was setting.

"You just missed him Jacob, and yes, he plans on kicking you boys when he gets a hold of you. He's not mad but he's tired of getting ditched. He feels there's something you're not telling him." Lorah was smart for figuring it out not that we wanted to share our plan for now.

"There is more but we can explain that later, do you know of a warehouse down here in Chicago that vampires only hang out at?" I knew Lorah liked attending parties and if there had been one, she had probably been to it.

"There is one, but it only operates on the weekends and by invite only, there are a few new people that show up but only if they come with someone invited. I usually go in with Jessica. She's friends with the owner; you're not tracking down Luther are you? I thought you were searching for Sydney?" Now Lorah seemed worried, before she was fine with us looking for Sydney, feeling it would be safe but after seeing what Luther did to Lucian, she didn't want to risk anything worse happening.

"We are not looking for him exactly, we are looking for someone that hangs out at the club." I was trying to make an excuse not that I had ever been very good at convincing people, but then with Lorah having experience with Lucian, I was sure I wouldn't be able to convince her.

"If you want. I'll take you this weekend, but I'm not going to have you two going in there alone. It's not a safe place if they find out you're looking for Luther, he has a lot of friends there that are rather protective of him." At least agreeing with Lorah, it would get us in.

The faster we could exhaust our leads the earlier we could go home, even though knowing Lucian he may just stay in the city anyway until he found out more about where Sydney had been. He told me he was tempted to make his presence known and she might come looking for him. Feeling it was a bad idea. I was glad to persuade him from it in case she wasn't able to do so yet.

I was about to catch up with Lucian when I turned around expecting to see him standing behind me when I saw the last person I thought would be there. Reaching out in an instant, we vanished and reappeared in front of my home. Rose had no idea we were here yet. As she put her finger to her lips to tell me not to speak. Then in a flash, she disappeared. Taking out the cell phone, I called Lucian right away.

"Where did you go, I can't find you. I've searched every building. I thought you might have gone in and gotten caught or something?" Lucian was concerned but more worried if he had to explain that something happened to me to Rose.

Not that she was a tyrant, she's always been patient, sweet and an incredibly loving person, we both knew how angry she could get when we acted like adult children. She tended to bottle her emotions, unlike Lucian who put them out on display.

"Just stand still. I think you're about to get a surprise at any second, it should be her." I wasn't sure what else to say but then I hoped she didn't separate us to have something horrible happen to him.

But then as she appeared to him, Lucian said he would call back later.

"You need to stop looking for me. You're only going to end up getting hurt further." She seemed rather worried but then what could she possibly fear?

If she needed help Lucian wanted to be available to protect her.

"If you need protection I can help. I found your trail and it led the same direction where Sophie separated and went off with someone else. Do you know who she is with? Why did your path end at the same spot with Luther, did he surprise you?" Watching as she had a nervous look on her face, Lucian knew he wasn't going to like her response.

"Sophie's fine, she's with Maddie. They had an agreement when she lived with her that she needed to keep, as soon as they are done they should be back. Besides, I need her, and Maddie is a part of it. Luther was only supposed to make it look like Sophie was being held against her will so that Alana wouldn't figure it out. He was never supposed to hurt you, he was there to grab Charlie, and we knew he would come to help you. I know you won't understand everything right now, but I can't tell you everything. I'm safe right now, so don't worry, but I can't be with you. I have too many things I am responsible for. I was going to ask you to assist me, but I know you would never want to be permanently away from your family. It would endanger them if you tried to see them, things need to be different now. This is a choice that I've made. I know at the time I slipped into it without having a choice and I couldn't remember the truth, but I have regained my memory. Unfortunately, I remember you, and I wished I hadn't. It would have made it so much easier." Sydney let out a sigh.

Soon as she said that. Lucian felt sick to his stomach.

"Where is Sophie right now? Why can't we know how to help her out? Is Charlie going to be able to see her? Did Luther talk you into this? If you want, you can walk away from all of this. I can help you." He didn't want her feeling trapped, but he also wanted her to know she had options.

"Lucian you would have no life; I like being in the position that I'm in right now. I miss Goseck and especially you, but I know you wouldn't be happy. Luther isn't a danger to me; he's a major power behind this also. Just trust me, things are fine but you're going to have to stop searching for me. Life isn't the same anymore. I'm not in a position I can treat you differently. I am not the same person anymore." A single tear dropped from her eye as she tried miserably to explain to me.

Neither of us seemed to know what to say to each other.

"So, I don't get to see you anymore? This is really what you want? Don't you want to see Goseck again or the rest of the family?" Not that I wanted to hear the words I knew I would hear, but then I also heard words I had been worried about.

"I only came to stop you from searching for me before something happens to you. Sophie and Charlie will be home soon. Sophie had been out for a reason when the others had to hide. She was helping me get my memory back, but I also know how to control and release the power inside of me. I was setting up the future for the life stone when I visited my old friend Beth. She had just moved away so I spoke with her roommates; I never knew she had a twin sister; I was able to close that chapter of my life. There are a lot of things going on beyond you and me. I know you want to see me; to be with me, but it's just not the way things are going to work out. If you love me, you will stay away." The last few words she had barely been able to speak as her voice lowered to a whisper.

"If you truly want me to leave you alone then I will, but I don't believe you want me to. I wish I knew more. I feel like I'm being left out of so much. There must be something I can do to help. It's fine if this is what you want but it shouldn't be where you must give up everything. We can find a way of making it work." Lucian was trying to search for something, some way of handling this even if she wanted to be in power.

Lucian was sure there had to be a way of supporting her without giving up his family.

"You're not going to like what I'm about to do. I can't have you there. Just trust me and stay away." As soon as she said that she disappeared leaving me there wondering what exactly it was that she was worried that I wouldn't like?

I wished there was a way of finding out. At least for now until I can find out more. I intended on staying with Lorah. At least she had space and wouldn't mind me joining her for a while.

Chapter Two
Starting lessons

Not long after taking off from the compound with Luther. Sophie never knew anyone to be so strong even as a vampire herself, Luther had still been stronger but then over the centuries he had more of an upper hand knowing exactly how to prevent another vampire from escaping, not that she wanted to risk it. Knowing he could go back and hurt her family. She hoped by going willingly she might find out what he wanted. What she wasn't expecting had been the other person who had been following them, she assumed she was working with Alana, trying to get her back from Luther until he suddenly stopped when they were far enough letting Maddie catch up, now turning Sophie over to her, he took off towards the water saying he had another person to catch up to.

"Maddie, what promise did I make to you? What do you need me for? I won't help Luther if that's what I'm here for." Sophie hadn't been too sure why she was brought here.

At the last, she had been whisked away watching her grandsons being left behind with a dangerous woman and another young woman who she had taught as the guardian of the stone, no longer the confused person she used to be but now a very powerful person. Sophie was no longer sure if it had all been a good thing or not, now that the power could be used dangerously if Sydney decided to go that way and there would be no one to stop her.

"Trust me, it's not a promise you needed to vocalize. After all, if I had kept you with me all those years ago, instead of handing you over to that family. Katherine would have done you in and you wouldn't be standing here having a family to worry about. I knew exactly what I was doing all those years ago. Didn't you ever wonder why the fact Katherine was a vampire dropping off a recruit, never raised suspicion? I couldn't exactly risk Alana knowing which side I was working on, after all, I used to be her protégé. It's a rather unique relationship between those who have been changed. You always have that permanent link to the one who changed you, even if you hate that person." Starting to walk, Sophie followed her, she wasn't sure why she was walking away from her if she had expected help.

"Luther was supposed to have Charlie here already but then we hadn't expected him to have so many with him, let alone not be at home. He was protecting that grandson of yours. Luther didn't get a chance to separate him yet, don't worry he'll join us soon. Dorina, or rather Sophie, you're my best student yet, even I must be humble and admit you happen to be better than I am with potions. Also, the favor isn't directly for me, it's for your student. I tried talking her out of it, after all, who doesn't want so much power? She felt she could trust you. But first, we must get to where we need to go; of course, we need to cover our tracks. It won't take long for others to find ours." Maddie took off in a shot trusting that Sophie would follow, which she had since she wanted to know which student was asking for her help.

She taught so many over the years even though Sydney had been the only one that came to mind. At least she knew Maddie wasn't working for Alana in this matter or she wouldn't have staged it back there with Luther to set up this whole thing.

It took us a while to get to our destination. We had run so far north. I was beginning to wonder if we would ever stop. For the last several months I hadn't seen my family even though I wondered how they were doing. They were all I thought about while sitting in a dark and wet cell. I hadn't seen or heard another voice for quite some time. Alana had been keeping me there hoping I would help her perform some magic for her. She wanted the power source taken out of Sydney even though I knew she intended on using it for herself. This time I wondered if Sydney wanted it or if this was going to be another trick? I could understand not wanting to live with such a strong power inside of you, the power never allowed the host a chance to relax, let alone how many would come after you trying to harness the power.

We had gone up much further than I thought we would until I recognized the area as we were going in the direction of my old cabin and the last carriage that I used while living as a gypsy. The old carriage sat behind the broken-down-looking cabin, looking as though it was in rough shape, except I had known that was intentional. I figured no one would mess with the place if they thought it had been abandoned and dilapidated so badly. No one would know where I hid my things other than possibly Maddie. She was the one who originally taught me to be so creative at concealing things I didn't want others to find. Exactly as I had guessed we skipped the cabin heading right into the carriage. Opening the door, she had at once gone to my stash of crystals taking them out placing them on the table, then headed for the bookcase pulling it forward and sliding off the back to reveal tiny vials and bottles of already mixed potions and dried herbs.

Pricking her finger Maddie mixed some of her blood with a few of the potions that I stored. As they mixed a light smoke started from it coming out of the mortar. Chanting something in a low tone as she poured the mixture over the crystals as they absorbed the liquid. Cleaning off the rest of the table and placing the crystals on the side table now only one crystal remained.

"However, you prefer to do your magic you do so, but practice on one crystal at a time. That way I don't have to keep mixing them. I may be able to create low power energy and harness it, but it takes a stronger sorceress to be able to take it out, let alone control it. I can control this because I'm already connected to it; this power has my blood signature in it; however, I need you to practice taking something out that you do not have a connection to. This lesson makes it easier since I wasn't the one who blooded you, your connection to my blood won't be there." Walking over to the door Maddie looked as if she was still expecting someone, either that or nervous someone she didn't want to show up?

"You still haven't told me why you want me to do this? Alana is a powerful sorceress, why doesn't she try to create her power? She could probably do this very easily?" I still felt confused about why all of this had been going on.

What did she want with a basic vampire venom mixed with mist removed from a crystal? There wasn't much energy from it let alone a power that could harm anyone unless you wanted to change someone without having to be there, to blood them yourself?

"I'm here for Sydney. She asked that you do this for her, and I cannot tell you why right now, that is something she wants to speak to you about when she gets here. Right now, she has other things she has to tend to first. I hear Charlie coming, as soon as he's here. I'll leave the two of you alone. Funny how no one sees Sidney coming, yet if you were to just listen, the power makes an interesting sound. As for Charlie, he's only here to keep him quiet, he draws far too much attention when he's looking for you." Continuing to watch out the door for signs I could see her smile as someone was now outside walking up the steps.

Maddie took a step back to let Charlie and Sydney inside. Charlie looked relieved when he saw me walking over immediately.

"Are you alright Sophie?" Not worried about what else was going on Charlie always seemed to put myself or the rest of the family first.

We watched as both Maddie and Sydney stood at the doorway. Sydney had been the first to speak.

"There's a reason I need you to find a way to take the power out of the crystal and still control it without losing the power itself, it needs to be relocated into another object as soon as it's taken out. When you're able to do that. I have a much stronger power that I need you to remove or at least partially remove. I'll explain more of it later but for now, I need to get back, Luther is waiting for me." As they both stepped out they hadn't even bothered closing the door.

Charlie walked closer looking out, both girls disappeared leaving no one guarding the place.

"No one's out there. We can escape. You don't have to do this; I don't know what they expect but nothing is holding us here." Charlie sounded optimistic until he tried to take a step out of the carriage, it had been as if he hit a solid wall that wasn't there.

29

"I didn't think she would leave us unguarded or that it would be that easy, Maddie used to have a protection spell that would be able to keep others from attacking us while some of the others slept or we stayed in an area that we might not have been welcomed. Sadly, it can also be used as a prison of sorts keeping those in that you don't want out." Sitting down now, looking over the crystal that lay on the table.

Picking it up and looked it over more closely. I wondered what power they were talking about unless they were hoping to harness Sydney's power but then she said they might want to split it, perhaps there would be more out there with the same power. That could lead to even more danger.

"Are those more crystals? I thought they were destroyed. What did she ask you to do with these?" Walking over Charlie picked up one that had been on the dresser with several others looking it over with curiosity.

"I think Sydney either plans on giving up her power or splitting it, sharing it with another not that I know who she would do that with? Luther cannot use it; he's a vampire and so is Maddie. She's separated herself from Alana so now she needs to guard herself against her. Alana is extremely angry that she left her and took the power with her since Alana wanted to gain control over it, which is why I thought Sydney wasn't a part of it until Maddie took me here. Sydney explained a little of it. I wished I could have talked to her to find out what exactly she is planning." Not that I wanted to do this if it meant spreading such a strong power around.

But then who would inherit it? Did she have someone or a few in mind that she wanted it to go to? Closing my eyes I had hoped I would be able to find the other guardians except I couldn't find anything outside of this room.

Noticing my frustration Charlie came over placing his arm around my shoulders.

"We've been through worse, eventually this will be over. Other than what they asked you to do, is there anything else you can do with those things?" I knew what he was thinking, not that I hadn't already thought it myself.

Sadly, my crystal ball wasn't left in here. They only left certain herbs and oils being careful not to allow me too much freedom, otherwise, I probably would have come up with another way out or at least a way to close Maddie's protection spell. At least I might as well see what they left me with. Getting up, I walked over to the cabinet taking out all the herbs that had been left. Any small utensils and other objects that I could find. As I separated them. Laying out each item on the table. I could see out of the corner of my eye Charlie leaning against the wall smiling as he watched me.

"What are you smiling about?" His smile was infectious, I couldn't help but smile back at him.

"The sweet young curious girl who exposed me to the world beyond my window, the one I fell in love with so many years ago, and now here you are, and I still get just as excited when I see you. There is no other rush as strong as how I feel when I look at you." No longer leaning against the wall, Charlie walked over to me as I stood near the table setting the herbs down that had been in my hand.

"This isn't exactly the place to be getting fresh with me. Are you sure you want to be stuck with me for an eternity?" Even though I knew the answer, I still loved hearing it.

Leaning against his chest as Charlie hugged me.

31

"An eternity would only be unbearable if I didn't have you." Holding me rather tightly close to him, kissing me on top of the head.

Centuries ago, when I lived with my sister Laila, I never once would have thought this is how my life would have turned out. Leaning back a little, I didn't want to spoil the moment, but I had to ask.

"What am I going to do about Sydney? I don't even know how Lucian is coping mentally or physically after Luther grabbed me. He was stuck back there with the rest of them along with Jacob. Alana kept me hidden for so long. I never would have wound up out of that cell she had me in if it hadn't been for Maddie, and I don't know if I should trust her or not?" Leaning back into Charlie, I had always felt safest with him.

Maybe that's why Maddie let me have him here. She knew I wouldn't do anything until I knew my family was safe.

"Don't worry. Lucian and Jacob will be fine, I last saw them at Lorah's apartment so they made it out alright, the boys can take care of themselves. They were worried about you when they saw you get taken away with Luther. I had to admit it when they called me to let me know what was happening, it scared me knowing he had you. I am just as confused about all of this as you are, except you don't have to worry about it, at least you won't be dealing with this alone this time." As comforting as his words were, I knew I had to do something, even if it was only a backup to keep us safe.

Just in case something had gone wrong. Not wanting to let go of Charlie. I reached out picking up the single crystal looking at it. I wondered what I would be able to do with it but then it hit me exactly what I should do. The only way I would get any idea what was going on. I had to find Sydney or Maddie to see what they were doing; I might not be able to find anyone outside of here intentionally but by looking through the crystal. I might be able to see them as I would have with my crystal ball.

Moving away from Charlie. I sat back down in the chair as he wrapped his arms around me still standing directly behind me as I gazed into the crystal. The blood had swirled away from the mist looking thicker than it had before almost knowing what I wanted. As I watched, a small form started to show. I could see the shape of two people. Continuing to stare into the crystal the images became much clearer as the two figures moved around, they were walking among mortals almost as if they were looking for something or someone. Moving faster in the crowd, it looked like they spotted whoever it was they were looking for. As they seemed to approach a young woman, they had walked into a building and Maddie turned to face me, almost as if she knew she was being watched shaking her finger in a disagreeing motion and the whole scene went black.

Whoever the human was, they were out searching for someone, and I could only guess it was for the power, not that the stone had worked that way before. It would have gone to the next in line, not that Sydney had any family left. It had been why it went to a distant relative of the other guardians rather than a direct descendent since there hadn't been one. A bit of a drawback when you have that much power it eliminated the ability to have time to have a family. Taking a piece of paper, I had written a spell on, then set it on fire. I placed it into the small cauldron on the table watching it burn. Then placing the crystal over the cauldron balancing it I watched as the smoke escaped from the crystal leaving the blood to drain out into the cauldron. Not exactly what I had planned on doing however it was a start. The white smoke hovered in the air as I wondered how I would capture it again. Not that I wanted exactly to do what they asked. I hoped I might be able to do something else with it. Not that I planned that far ahead.

Then it had hit me, it would be a lot easier to split the power versus taking it out completely. The lesser power could be taken in much easier than removing the entire power. Not that I was sure what other gifts Maddie had, but then I would also be bound to her somewhat. I knew Maddie used to get visions; she might still, however, she had stopped talking about them. Not sure how Charlie would take it. I decided to test it by opening my mouth. I had breathed in as the now smokey mist inhaled as I breathed. I could feel how worried Charlie became when I had done that not that he liked me risking myself, he always thought there should be another way, however, over the last several years. I had been used to testing things out and hoping for the best. It was the way I learned to live when I first became a vampire, trial, and error. Closing my eyes. I could now see Sydney and Maddie talking to a rather frantic-looking girl who didn't seem that she liked what she was hearing, almost looking for a way out. I could not only see but also feel her panic feeling.

The three of them stood up from the table, they were talking as the girl walked out of the building rather quickly. Sadly, the vision and feeling didn't last very long. I could only guess it had lasted maybe about twenty minutes before it dissipated. Unfortunately, we would have to wait until either Maddie or Sydney were to come back here since most of the herbs I needed to absorb or make the power last longer were not here, but then I wasn't sure if taking power from another would entirely stay permanent to whatever took it in?

Moving my hand I accidentally bumped the crystal a little as it slipped into the cauldron, creating a huge billow of white smoke to come out covering the crystal as the blood itself hadn't disappeared, it simply dried, casing itself around the crystal now absorbing into it. Looking at it, I couldn't see any of the characteristic swirls of blood moving around inside of it.

Grabbing another crystal. I repeated the same motions except for this time I left the smoke hanging in the air as I reached in touching the dried blood, the same smoke had billowed out surrounding my hand absorbing into me as it had the crystal, only with myself it had done it much faster. This time the sensation hadn't gone away but then I wasn't sure if it would have been the same if Maddie had simply bitten me herself. I guess I wouldn't know until they let me know which power they were talking about. Not that I was sure I could take Sydney's power out from her. The crystal had been very different and nothing like what I had been taught. The woman that taught me many years ago had passed on the knowledge knowing I would still be around, that it would never be lost. She taught me many things about wanting certain parts of history to be preserved.

Standing up and walking over to the couch in the far end with Charlie, he sat back as I leaned against him resting there, thinking over the past and then feeling worried about what was to come. Pulling in his arms wanting to be held even tighter. I always felt safe with Charlie. I hope I can help continue to keep him safe as well as the rest of our family. We sat there for several hours neither of us wanting to move, still staying there when I heard the characteristic clicks of the charm being removed as Sydney walked in. I expected to see

35

Maddie come walking in with her, except it had been just her this time.

"I didn't get a chance to talk with you earlier. I had to find someone. Maddie told me that you already found us earlier, so I guess you were working on the spells and crystals?" As Sydney asked she looked overseeing that there were still a few crystals left.

"Sydney, you know that I cannot help you until you tell me what you're planning on doing, even if I didn't know what you were doing. I couldn't make the right potion or spell if there isn't more information to go on." Standing up, I had walked over to her hoping she might say more.

But then I also wondered how much she had remembered especially with my training her.

"I know you're wondering if I remember you and the last several years. I can hear your thoughts, not sure why, but then I had always heard Lucian and Goseck, so I guess it shouldn't surprise me that I can hear yours and Charlie. I have decided that normally the stone when it was no longer needed, would have been hidden away or at least been in a safe place until it was needed again. The only problem is that it can't go anywhere while it's inside of me. This is far too much power for one person to have, and if for some reason. I ever become corrupt, which I could do very easily, there isn't any way for anyone to stop me. Even Luther for as long as he's been around knows that. I have searched everywhere and spoken to so many, even the past guardians who trained me, informed the only way of taking it out now would mean I would need to die or have it removed. If only a part of it can be removed that's still better than nothing. But I don't want anyone knowing it was only partial. I know I can trust you with this and it's why I chose you." I could tell from the way

36

that Sydney never once hesitate that she had given this a lot of thought, even though I wondered what Luther had to do with all of this.

"What does Luther get out of this?" Charlie had been the one who voiced what I was thinking and Sydney had to assume we would both be wondering about this.

"Because of his experience, family history, and the fact that so many vampires respect him, he is serving as one of the leaders of the new order along with Jaron, Jordyn, and Roman. They would help represent shades, like Nikolai, Luther would represent the vampires. We have many who work for us well. We have made our location so that humans cannot accidentally walk into it or discover for some reason that we happen to be there. I understand that taking the power out from me may put you in danger because vampires cannot handle it, however, I am hoping you might be able to figure out a way of harnessing it so that it will be able to be put into something or someone. We have a mortal who is well worth the risk if it needs to be transferred. I'm leaving her here with you and me to be trained, so it's time for Charlie to leave for now." As Sydney said this Charlie was about to object when Sydney simply touched him transporting him elsewhere, leaving him there and taking off before he even had a chance to say anything other than to feel shocked that it happened so fast.

Not taking any longer than she needed to, Sydney had popped back to me to finish discussing what she wanted. Standing in front of me she had a worried look however still seemed confident unwaveringly so that she knew exactly what it was that she wanted to be done.

"As I said before, I realize this power might not be able to be taken out of me completely and this could present a danger to you, but I know you won't try to take off with it or do something with it. Right now, you're the only one I trust to do this. I know there's the possibility that I could die. Not that I want to, but I can't keep living this way either. I must change something. So, it's a risk I'm willing to take. I hate making you do this but as I said before, you're the only one I trust." Walking over, she sat down on the couch next to me almost pleading with me.

"There should be another way than risking your life, perhaps we can try to fool others by making it look as if the power has moved on or that you don't have it anymore?" I was trying hard to figure out something even though I was more concerned with her life right now than I had been with mine.

"I'm sure Alana will be watching; she will know if I still have it or not. Sadly, I think once it's gone she would come after me out of revenge anyway, so it might not matter if I survive with it. I'm almost thinking it would be better if I had died with it." Her last few words had trailed off as I understood what she meant.

Even if she did get rid of the power there would always be those who didn't know if she had it, coming after her trying to get it. Even with an attempt of passing it on, there was the danger of the other person being attacked or simply those who wanted revenge. I couldn't help but wonder what Luther had told her of his opinion of all this?

"Has Luther offered any of his advice about this?" As I mentioned his name she looked up at me with tears in her eyes.

"What's the point, when I've lost so much? At this point I would rather die, I've tried believing that I wanted this, after all, when I didn't remember anything I did and I can't say I don't like the position of power, but I am worried that I could lose control and who's to stop me? More important, do I want those who I care most about to be the ones who must stop me? Luther thinks I should stop focusing on the past, let everything go, and move on with the future. He feels I should split the power with another human and keep it secret while I stay in power with him. He wants more than partnership and if Lucian were to find out it would kill him, the sad thing is, I know what my relationship was with him, and it won't ever be like that again. It's not safe, besides, there's another problem that no one else knows about." Holding her hands in her lap fumbling nervously with them not wanting to let go of the information.

I could pretty much guess it just from observing others over the last several years.

"I'm guessing that over the last few years that you were not with us and couldn't remember your past, you started a relationship with Luther. I hadn't said a word to Charlie about it however I thought it might be a factor." Now at least I understood more of her dilemma.

But then I also understood the tendency to change when so many of those around you can get corrupted so easily, which is why Nikolai had kept such a close eye on her looking over her, but then I had been the only one he shared this with. She had been his favorite and most promising student so far.

"It's not like I need the power anymore. I'll have such a strong group behind me, especially when everyone finds out who else is in the coven. Luther's family isn't dead, they had only lost one member, they simply went underground to get away from the world for a while. Valafar, Seth, Sakarabru, Adhene, Charity, Desmond, and Lilitu are all still here.

They've only decided to come out because Damar has become active. So, there's more reason to spread out my power for the safety of everyone." I hadn't been too familiar with the ones she listed other than hearing general rumors.

They had run the original order and were known to be quite dangerous if they chose to be, but why appear now just because of Damar? Usually, his group preferred never to get involved unless someone bothers them or there was something they want. What could they possibly want since they never had a problem with the old order before? Unless they had heard about Sydney's power, something I need to run by Charlie, since he was more familiar with the Damar clan. As far as I can remember there had only been seven members in his group, always keeping it rather small. There had been Angelita Voss, Kristopher Vondrak, Lucius Delgado, Pollux Moretti, Regulus Delarosa, Reyes Moreau, Ruby Vondrak, all related to Damar in one way or another.

"This won't be easy to hear and I'm sure my grandson won't like the fact that I am saying it. I agree with having a way to keep you from getting corrupted, not that I want to see it come to this, I have a plan and hopefully, it will even fool Alana as long as it works right." I had been thinking about this for the last year when I first heard rumors.

As much as I knew that Lucian was angry about them. I had felt there was a grain of truth in them and now I knew the truth. Even though this would make him unhappy, after all, for as long as he has lived now, she was the first and only one he had fallen in love with.

"Which human had you picked and what particular reason do you think this person is ready for this, after all, remember what you're having problems with, the other person will also." I hoped she gave solid thought to this even though I knew Maddie to be a good judge of character.

I don't know why I doubted her earlier. I think I was nervous not knowing what was going on.

"I've been watching this girl for a while, she kept showing up in the crystal and then I started seeing her places. Maddie said it's either that she is following me herself or she is naturally drawn to the power of the stone. She's not related in any way, but she seems to have the personality of many of the guardians. That and she is also the daughter of my old best friend. My friend was married for only seven years, then died in a car accident. When I found out she had a daughter. I wanted to find out what happened to her, so I searched for her. She's already had a hard life, but I believe she can handle this." At least she had a reason for watching this girl, I wouldn't have felt so comfortable about it if the girl had found her first or had been around for some other reason.

Over the next several weeks. I drained small portions of Sydney's blood hoping this would do it allowing the blood to breath in the container, not allowing anything to touch it yet. Luther had stopped by to see how Sydney was doing. For a man that spent his entire life on his own neither answering to anyone or waiting for anyone, his vulnerable side had shown when he had seen how weak Sydney was. I had to admit to myself that he had a lot in common with Lucian. I could see how she would be attracted to him.

Now that there was enough, I had put it into a crystal. Most of it went into one and then the smallest amount to test had gone into another hoping it would be as temporary as the vampire venom had been of Maddie's. We had to wait a few days for Sydney to regain enough strength, she had flashed herself to get Nikolai and to bring him back. We tested the small crystal with Nikolai and as I had thought, it only lasted for a very short time. The only other way I could imagine would be for the power to remove itself from Sydney if she were bitten. I hoped she would survive and not die from it revolting against her.

Sadly, we wouldn't know this until the time had come; if it had come to that we were going to leave it as the last option and for Charlie to perform, since I had yet to do it myself. Charlie had much more control and experience. So, for now, we only had this choice. We had to find the girl again and try it out. I hoped once it was in her system it would last longer or even more permanently than the vampire venom had. At least Sydney agreed to involve Charlie again, she knew he wouldn't risk someone's life, however this time with everything else that she had told me, he would understand there hadn't been another choice. At least now I understood the urgency and secrecy. As Luther had made it very clear when he was here, the Damar clan planned on bringing on the ritual summoning of the bones of darkness. A very serious dark magic that would threaten the way of life for everyone, especially the mortals, we may not be able to cure the world or prevent all its tragedies, however, we can prevent those beyond human control to try to keep them safe, after all, we used to be humans ourselves at one point. However, first I wanted to find out from Lorah what her boss in the human world Valafar knew about all of this.

Chapter Three
My beginning, a new guardian

Fresh out of high school. I hadn't made plans other than wanting to take a year off before I started college. I moved into a little cottage along the lake giving myself some time to relax, figuring my ordinary life would pretty much stay this way. I had a rather small group of friends that I used to hang out with, however, now with me taking time off, many of them had gone ahead, starting college. Working part-time at the local grocery store gave me plenty of time to swim, hike, and do other things that I used to enjoy as a child, or at least had done while both of my parents had still been alive. Not something I could ever forget, being so young I could remember it as if it happened yesterday. I was fourteen when the usual babysitter sat out in the living room watching television as my friends and I were in my room goofing off, talking about the boys at school and what we were going to do.

We all heard the phone ring, then a few hours later, each of the girls had been escorted home by their parents leaving me in my room alone. Not even my babysitter would explain why they had to leave on such short notice. My parents had taken a trip, just the two of them figuring I would be busy with school and friends. They wanted to take some time off from work and relax leaving me in the care of someone who they felt was capable. It wasn't until the day after all of this happened that I had been picked up by my aunt, her eyes were bloodshot. I knew something was wrong. She rarely stops speaking. When we were at the house with her husband, they sat me down to explain that I would be living with them. That I could finish school in the same area but for now, would be with them until more permanent arrangements could be made. I knew then that something happened to my parents. Then the news hit, they explained they had been struck by a drunk driver, and neither of them survived. Both my aunt and uncle waited for me to react. I hadn't known how to?

Most people would have burst into tears, after all, I was capable. I cried when my hamster died so why not for my parents? I loved them and even looked up to them. I even wanted to be as intelligent as my father and loving as my mother had been, but for some reason, I never shed a tear. I simply stood up and walked to my room closing the door behind me as I sat for several hours in the dark just staring at the wall, I felt broken. All through high school permanent arrangements never had been made. I simply went home or hung out with my friends. Once the time for college had come after graduation, my aunt had been angry that I wasn't going right away. I simply announced it was time for me to move out on my own, that college would be waiting for a year. Not that they could do too much when my taxicab had come to pick me up. As soon as I had finished explaining my plans to them. I moved into the cottage that had been put in trust for me, a place my family and I used to go for summer vacations.

No one had been out here in years since the place looked like a mess with slimy brown stuff on the windows and the sides of the wood panels were just as dirty. Opening the door before I could walk in. I could feel the years of spider webs that had built up with dust. It had only taken me about fourteen hours before I decided to crash on the floor with my new blanket that I had brought with me. First thing in the morning, I would have to go buy a mattress since there were only springs on the bed. Finally, being set up with a lot of time on my hands. I started hanging out at the bars and not that I liked any of the guys there, they were usually drunk and stupid, so I started reading a lot of books which is where I had met my first date.

He was a rather handsome-looking man, a little overweight but certainly friendly enough. We found we liked the same books and had come back here for the same reasons, just to let go of life for a while before we had to face too much of reality again. I had to admit what attracted me to him first, had been his voice, it sounded so sultry. He opened doors for me and quite frankly treated me like a queen. So why didn't I feel satisfied? The sad thing, I had written a list of his qualities, he had all the qualities that I should be looking for, he was dependable, honest, trustworthy and most of all, he cooked! Not just macaroni, he could cook specialty foods. I wasn't sure if he had his place when I met him or not, but after a week of dating he had just not gone away, he moved right in with me. Finally, I went out and picked up a dog, and yes I still had the guy.

He had even started working with me at the grocery store, which I guess I shouldn't have minded, after all, there weren't very many places to work around here in a little town. After a while, he became my manager, it wasn't easy working under him. I did my job, but he started to knit pick over everything I did, his excuse had been he didn't want to show me special favor, so instead he went overboard correcting me or making my job harder. After one of my shifts, I was so frustrated I cried outside when I had a moment alone. so, I quit and left for the bookstore. Not that he was too happy with that. I think he liked knowing where I was and who I spoke to all day. I couldn't help it, but this wasn't feeling like relaxing and getting away anymore. I felt like I trapped myself in a controlling marriage and I hadn't even married him yet. This evening, we planned on going out to dinner, at least it would be a nice change.

Living in a small town there wasn't a lot of choices to pick from, thankfully I liked the pub we had here. It was the weekend, so the place was pretty much taken over by the younger crowd with loud music. I could feel the vibration of the music before we even entered. My boyfriend, Reyes had hoped we would go to the restaurant across the street opting for a quieter place wanting to talk. Not that we ever really talk about anything of interest, it's always how frustrated he is with the others he works with, complaining about their lack of intelligence, how he's the only one doing any work, and the list keeps going on. I didn't have any problems when I worked there, and I got along with everyone while I finished my work. I don't think I've heard him say one positive thing since he started working there.

If he's not complaining about work, then the only other topic of conversation is usually about my family history, or at least what I knew about it. He wanted to know about my coin collection as well as my stone collections. I had left those at my aunts at the time. I was in a hurry just to get out. I took only what I needed. I hadn't owned very much at that time, most of it belonged to my aunt and uncle. I only had pictures of my parents and clothing. My aunt never seemed interested in talking about our family history, other than to ask me if my homework was finished. I didn't have anyone else to ask either. Later I found out Reyes had taken a day off from work, not that he ever shared with me where he had gone. If I had done that he would have bothered me until I told him.

Now I was busy watching the others dancing to the music, I know I could have skipped asking him even though I knew what his response was going to be.

"Want to dance? I like this music." It wasn't music you needed to know steps for, even though the beat was rather quick and upbeat.

"You know I hate dancing, but I guess if I have to, I will." His usual response

"Don't worry, you don't have to dance." Standing up, I was going to go dance without him, which is what I usually would do.

"I thought we would talk, there's always time for dancing. If you want, just play the music at home and dance to it in private. Besides, I thought you're working at a bookstore would encourage you to get to know your family history more." Always asking or speaking about the same thing was driving me crazy.

"What does my family history have to do with my working at a bookstore? I've already told you all I know about my family, besides, dancing here is different." Almost walking away Reyes had grabbed my hand pulling me back.

"Tonight's supposed to be us spending time together. I barely see you. Besides, I'm sure your bar buddies can dance without you for once. I think I would rather leave and head for home instead of dealing with this music. It's too difficult talking to you with all of this going on." I was beginning to wonder if Reyes knew what a night out together even meant.

"We spend every day together; we rarely go out and I don't have friends because I spend all of my time with you. We just got here, let's at least order food, and then after, we can leave." Sitting back down in my seat, at least he agreed to this.

All through dinner Reyes picked at his food more than he had eaten any of it. Sadly, we hadn't talked during dinner either even though I had the feeling he still just wanted to leave. After a while we did after paying the bill, the ride home always felt like a long one even though we didn't live that far out of town.

As soon as we were home, instead of talking, Reyes made his way to the bedroom. I know I've been frustrated and feeling distant from him, not that it was easy being in a relationship either. I know things change after a while; nothing was going to be like it was when we first met. He always seemed so romantic and did everything he could to catch my attention, but I started wondering if maybe I was doing something to make him distance himself from me? I know I was attracted to him before for a reason, and he was the same person just much more obsessed with my family than I was. Even though sometimes I wondered if he did that hoping to give us something to talk about together, I did like it when we talked about history, especially finding his views of it. The way he spoke it was almost as if he lived during those periods, always having a difference of opinion, on many of the facts that were recorded, either in history books or artifacts kept in museums. Anything to do with the Renaissance during the fourteenth to the sixteenth century fascinated me, its influence affected literature, philosophy, art, politics, science, religion, and so many other aspects of intellectual delving. I could talk about it for hours. He always found a way to start talking about my boring family and I would lose all interest. I can't complain too much, my family had accomplished quite a lot. We had doctors, nurses, teachers, and even an inventor in the family, which was all I had been familiar with. I could only guess I was bored because it wasn't the field I was personally interested in.

Now I started to feel bad that I didn't at least try to show some interest when Reyes tried to show his interest in my family. Before following him to the bedroom. I grabbed his favorite soft drink from the fridge bringing it up to him. Entering the room, I saw that he was flipping through pictures again. He insisted that my aunt had sent it in the mail, not that I ever saw the envelope, and he didn't have it either, he never showed it to me. Sitting

48

down on the bed next to him handing him the drink, he took it as he kept one hand on the album looking through it. As he did I realized he never did tell me about his own family.

"We always talk about my family, but I don't know anything about your family. Did you have any siblings?" Taking a sip from my cup, I was curious about what his family was like.

Maybe I was more curious about the world around me rather than my own?

"Not much to say. I was never close to my family. I had a bunch of siblings. I just never kept in touch with any of them. I wasn't exactly what the family wanted, so I left." Closing the photo album, he set it on the nightstand next to the bed.

"How long have you been on your own?" I was curious if he left when he was young.

This was one of the rare times I could ask him even though he did the same thing every time, mainly by cutting the conversation short.

"Do we need to talk about this right now?" Setting his drink on the nightstand, he turned off the light and laid down pulling the covers up without saying goodnight.

Leaning over I tried to give him a kiss goodnight.

"Does it always have to lead to sex? I would rather go to sleep." Turning over as I sat there no longer feeling stunned since I was sure this is how he would respond.

I could safely say this is one of the reasons I have distanced myself from him. I didn't know how to fix it or how we wound up this way?

"I was only kissing you goodnight. I can't get comfortable, so I'm sleeping on the couch." Getting up without Reyes even saying a word to me, I slept on the couch.

I wasn't in the mood to sleep in the same room with him right now. Not entirely sure why every night I felt more confused.

Over the next few weeks not much changed other than watching a few movies together and of course the change to the bookstore, it was being remodeled.

Then about a month ago, the bookstore had been bought out by another person, an older man who seemed great when I first met him. He liked a lot of my ideas for promoting the store, giving me more control, and being able to do more than just stock the shelves every day. He promoted me to store manager.

On one of the days, I had left my bike since it needed fixing. I had broken the rim not that I needed to leave it all day. I had to get to work and didn't want to wait around for it later, at least this way it would be ready when I needed it. Reyes insisted on driving me to work, even though I would have preferred walking, it was nice out and nothing in the forecast about rain, not that it would have been a bad thing to get wet. A lot of the things I wanted to experience were just slipping away. Being independent, to walk in the rain and get wet like a fool if I had wanted to, or even to eat outside alone on the beach sand. When he took so much time preparing food and setting it on the table, insisting we eat together. I might as well of stayed at home with my aunt having her yell at me about why I didn't go directly to college. So much for my years' dream. Not that college was a bad thing but for once I was looking forward to going.

After working all day, I hadn't wanted to head home yet. Instead, I stayed in the back room looking for the new advertisements for the new book coming out and the book of the month. Standing up on the ladder. I climbed up trying to reach for the folders overhead. When I had them in my hand, I slipped off the steps and fell very uncoordinatedly onto the floor. I wasn't sure how long I had knocked myself out but long enough. My boss Valafar found me with the folders still in my hand, when he tried waking me up slowly, I had a bit of drool embarrassingly down the side of my mouth.

"Jessica, are you alright? How do you feel? I can take you to the hospital if you need?" Lifting me slightly, my boss was checking the back of my head to make sure there hadn't been worse damage, only feeling a very sore bump forming on my head.

"I'm fine. I was going up to get the folders. I figured I wasn't going to be in tomorrow, so I would display them tonight instead, but my foot must have slipped." I tried to get up, but my head hurt worse than anything and I still felt a little dizzy.

Placing his arm around me, helping me up until I was able to stand on my own.

"I can grab the stuff that I needed and work on them at home, I can give you a ride unless you prefer calling someone?" Even as he said this, I would rather stumble home than call Reyes.

"I'll be fine. I just have to grab my bike from the shop, and I'll ride home." Walking out into the main room hadn't been fun stumbling over my own feet in the process.

"I don't think you can ride a bike, besides the bike shop is already closed. It's eleven at night and I don't think you should be walking home, especially not alone. I only came in to get a head start on the end-of-the-month papers since I couldn't sleep. Let me at least take you home?" Nodding in agreement, I knew he was right.

I waited for him to put the papers he needed into his briefcase and then we walked out front where absolutely no one was in sight. The streets were dark and not another car was in sight.

Not that I lived too far but in the driveway, I could already see Reyes standing at the end of the driveway. Letting out a deep sigh, either way. I hated coming home with such dread. I

51

even felt embarrassed with Valafar in the car. I felt as if I was going to get a lecture from a parent the moment I stepped out of the vehicle.

"Is he your husband? Maybe we should have called before leaving the store?" Valafar looked a little worried as he slowed down the vehicle not wanting to leave me any earlier than he had to.

"He's not my husband, he's a boyfriend who I never agreed to go steady with, it was just assumed when he suddenly moved in. I'll see you at work in two days, thank you for the ride." Not that I wanted to, I got out of the car, walking up towards Reyes as he hadn't looked too happy seeing me with another man.

"If you were going to be late you could have called to let me know and who is that guy? Are you cheating on me already?" We barely made it to the front door, and he was already barking at me.

Turning around to face him, I didn't know if I was angry at him, or simply didn't care. This was the sad part. I just didn't care.

"I fell at work and knocked myself out. I would have been there until morning if my boss hadn't come and brought me home. But thank you for making this into more than what it is. And if I had been cheating on you. I wouldn't have him dropping me off at home if that were the case." Turning around I left him standing there walking to my bedroom to sit down placing my hands over my face, all I wanted to do was scream.

Then a light knock on the door broke my concentration. Looking up Reyes was standing there not with store-bought flowers, but he had gone outside looking for the only flowers he could find to give to me. Coming over standing in front of me with a rather sad look on his face.

"I'm sorry I accused you. I should have known better. I just made myself worry about the worst. I should have checked on you at the store, how are you feeling, is your head any better?" No longer kneeling in front of me he sat on the bed next to me putting his arm over my shoulder as he peeked at the back of my head.

"I'm fine, but I've had a long day, so I just want to sleep." Pulling the bed sheets back as I laid down he had stripped getting under the covers with me.

I knew what was coming, he always wore something to bed so when he stripped it had become routine. Even though I had hurt myself now, feeling tired wanting to sleep, he was turned on? Not that I had to do anything.

"Reyes, I'm too tired for this tonight, maybe tomorrow? I'm just not in the mood." The second I heard myself say that, I swear, I heard my mother say that once when I was little and then I heard my aunt say it many times, even Reyes has said it to me several times.

I'm not twenty years old yet and never in the mood?

"Don't worry sweetie it will be quick." He was right.

Unless I made the mistake and letting the air come from my throat, or slightly moved he would ask any of the following questions, 'did I hurt you? Does that feel okay? I can move over if it helps. What are you doing, why are you moving, I feel like I'm having sex with a corpse.' So, at this point, I have learned to lay here, count down the minutes and know it will be over, and I can just roll over and go back to sleep. The first time he asked me what I was doing. I was trying to get into it, to get excited as I heard others had, but when he asked, it killed any romantic sexy feeling. I simply responded, 'sorry it was an involuntary twitch' and never tried to move again. At least tonight was just as quick. I rolled him over as I rolled over to sleep.

53

The next few years rolled by rather fast since I never left for college, Reyes insisted that he would take care of me, that I didn't need extra education. That I should stay at home and start planning a family. It would have been fine if that's what I wanted, which it wasn't, at least not with him. I was now running the bookstore all by myself with Valafar dropping in occasionally, he opened up other bookstores, so he was spending a lot of time traveling to keep up with them. Reyes was still working at the grocery store, and I had lost contact with my remaining family and friends. I was sleeping with my roommate who at some point just never wanted or planned on going away and I had hit thirty.

The last week had been driving me crazy. All I heard all week long had been how perfect a co-worker of Reyes had been. Even though it was nice that he was finally complimenting someone for once and not insulting them, Reyes went overboard in describing her work ethic, and home life, he pretty much described her almost as if she was some perfect goddess. I don't ever remember him describing me like that.

Then I had an opportunity of getting away for a little while. Reyes had been opposed to my leaving, which wasn't too much of a surprise, but I explained that one of Valafar's other stores was failing and he hoped that some of my plans that worked for my store and the others would help out with the failing shop. That I only planned on being gone for a month at the most. Packing my things he said he loved me, something I've yet to say back to him other than, 'make sure you feed the dog, and I'll miss you too' giving him a quick kiss on the forehead I was out of the room headed for the airport.

I never liked flying on planes. It wasn't so much the taking off part, but the landing when my ears would plug up and the unsettling feeling as the plane descended. After getting off the plane I looked forward to checking in at the hotel. I hadn't been expected at the bookstore yet until the next morning. Not that I was on the plane for very long. I wasn't sure how my hair managed to get so messed up, my makeup wearing off, and to have such oily skin. I was happy no one was waiting for me at the airport, not that anyone had seen how I looked when I had first left home, Reyes insisted it was bad luck to see me off. After the taxi ride to the hotel, I tried to check in waiting behind a crowd at the check-in desk. I was glad I had reserved a room in advance when I heard there was some event going on and no more rooms were available. When it was my turn to check in, the receptionist started looking up my information shaking her head and not looking confident.

"Sorry, we don't have you listed in the computer and our hotel is completely booked solid at the moment." I couldn't believe what she was telling me.

"I have my confirmation number if it helps. I booked a room three weeks ago and I have the papers here that say that it's paid for already." Handing her the papers she looked them over and started typing something into the computer.

"Sorry it looks like we overbooked your room, it was given to another guest who has already checked in, here's a receipt of your card being refunded the amount. Sorry, we cannot help you any further." As she looked around me to the next person in line, she announced 'next' for them to come forward.

What a great way to start my month here as I pulled out my cell phone to give Valafar a call. I thought he might know of other hotels in the area.

"Don't worry about the room. I have a guest room you can stay in. I won't be here the whole time so you can have the house to yourself when I'm not here. I'll be over to pick you up in just a few minutes, I would be there faster but the traffic in the city isn't the greatest, makes me miss small towns. See you in a few minutes." Closing my cell phone, I picked up my two bags and waited outside for him.

I could see his car from the highway, even though he had to travel down the long, private driveway before he could swing around to pick me up. When he pulled up, Valafar loaded my bags into the trunk as I settled into the passenger seat. When we arrived at his place, it felt like we were miles from the city, even though we were just a short drive off the highway. Walking from the car, I spent most of my time looking around. I had been so impressed with the way his house looked. Manicured lawn with a huge water fountain as the center attraction as the driveway wrapped around it. Even the gargoyles at the entrance of his front door let anyone looking at this house know it was not ordinary by any means. If I thought the outside was amazing my breath had been taken away the second I entered the house. Following behind Valafar, he had led me directly to the guest room.

"If you need anything just let me know, I noticed you didn't have a car, you can use the little cooper when you need it, that way you're not taking a taxi the whole time you're here. It can get expensive. I need to finish up a few things but feel free to settle in and I'll be in my office should you need me." Setting my bags down, I thanked him as he walked out of the room.

Closing the bedroom door, I couldn't believe the bedroom I was staying in. If I had my choice. I would make my regular room look like his guest room. Large canopy bed, white carpet that I felt nervous walking on thinking I'm going to leave footprints on it, huge landscape murals covering the walls, even a mural on the ceiling. Not one inch of this room had been untouched by artwork. Even the four-corner post on the wooden bed had carved artwork running up the posts. Walking over to the double French doors leading to the mini balcony looked impressive, the view was even better. Off to the far corner of the room, the walk-in closet was the same size as the bedroom. Even the bathroom was impressive, with all the usual upgrades along with a beautiful fireplace that connected between the bathroom and bedroom. The shower looked like a rock garden shower, very unusual. After settling in I left a message on Reyes's cell phone. I was surprised he hadn't answered but knowing him he was probably mad I hadn't called him the second I stepped off the plane. Walking out of my room I felt like I had been in a palace compared to the little cabin I had been staying in. It's not as if I hadn't been in a large home before but this was beyond normal, it felt like a palace.

I felt like exploring the place to see how impressive the rest of the house had been. Walking into the living room and taking five steps down, the whole area was a sunken living room; I liked the way it looked. The couch that wrapped around one entire wall with a huge screen television on the far end, an entertainment room with everything else that had been in here. As I walked to the center of the room. I heard a noise behind me, looking over my shoulder Valafar had been at the entrance looking down at me.

"I thought I would come to see if you had any dinner plans tonight. I haven't eaten and thought you might not mind joining me?" Smiling, as he walked down the steps over to me making his way to the couch.

"No, I don't have plans for tonight. If I had been at the hotel, I probably would have just watched movies." Valafar turned the television on, surfing through the channels as I sat on the couch.

"I don't watch very much television anymore, seems like I'm coming and going more often than I do to just sit around. This is kind of nice for once, let me know if you see anything you're interested in?" Flipping through the stations there hadn't been anything on, Valafar wasn't the only one who hadn't watched much television lately.

We settled on a comedy we both liked and sat back eating popcorn. We ordered pizza so we wouldn't have to cook anything. Eating in the living room, just relaxing felt nice. We talked about college, trade schools, and how he had chosen to operate bookstores which had him traveling around to so many countries. Talked about my plan for my first year off after high school and what I should have done. I hadn't planned it out very well.

"My plan of taking a year off before college didn't work out the way I thought it would have. I should have traveled like you; I probably would have enjoyed it more." I figured there would be some regrets, this one changed a lot of my life more than I knew it was going to.

"Tell you what, next time I take off for Europe. I'll take you with me. I usually go in the fall." Taking a sip of wine, leaning back as if the world was just waiting for him.

"I doubt Reyes would agree to it. I won't even be telling him I'm staying here, it's bad enough he gets so jealous. Heck, he even checks my emails and if I get spam, he wants to know why it's being sent to me, as if I know?" Setting his glass down looking at me with a rather strange questioning look on his face.

"Why do you even stay with him, you are an incredible woman and should be treated as such." Leaning back resting on his arm looking at me waiting for me to give him the answer.

Even I wondered why I still stayed around with him when he irritated me so much.

"He grows on you, there are a lot of irritating things he does and he's not romantic like he used to be. If he wasn't so moody, clingy and needy, he'd be perfect. I think I'm just having the seven-year itch late. He wants to get married, and I still don't.

58

I love having him as a friend. I just wished I had kept it that way when I first met him, but who knew it would end up like this? We never actually discussed his moving in, before I realized it, he did it. I hope you don't mind but I'm getting sleepy, so I'm thinking of turning in. Will you be at the bookstore tomorrow?" Standing up Valafar had gotten up at the same time motioning he was ready also.

"I should get some sleep also. I wouldn't be a good example if my fixer employee looks more rested than I do. I'll be at the store for a little while, just enough to show you around." Valafar sighed slightly.

When I stopped at my door, I hoped Valafar wouldn't notice, I couldn't help myself watching him.

I was slightly hesitant not that he ever gave me the feeling of doing something. I had wondered why he took the long way to his room unless it was just politeness to walk me to mine.

"I hope you don't mind. I wanted to give you a choice, to let you know that you at least had a choice, you're not stuck." Leaning into my personal space, his face hovering near my cheek I could feel the warmth of his breath and lips on my skin, he lightly placed his hand on my side. I thought he was going to whisper something in my ear, I wasn't sure I wanted to hear what was next.

Feeling around behind me trying to find the door handle I hoped I could let myself in before he let me know what choice he was giving me. I may not have been too happy with Reyes or even regretted things, but I certainly didn't want to cheat on him. At least this time if I had, he would have a right to say I did. Leaning in to kiss me after I hadn't said anything. I found the handle, opening the door falling on the floor in a thud. Standing up right away I looked at Valafar right in the face wanting to make it clear.

"First thing. I will be finding another place to stay. I may not be in the greatest relationship, but I am in one and this isn't right. I will see you at work tomorrow." Closing the door, I didn't want to find out what or how he would respond.

If I hadn't closed the door when I did. I hated to admit I would have made out with him in a second. Seriously, a handsome, intelligent man, works, and has goals, or at least tries to get them. Reyes was unhappy working part-time barely, constantly complaining, making bills, going nowhere with no future. I couldn't start an art project without him thinking there was an ulterior motive behind it. I missed painting, something I used to do a lot. I felt suffocated and for the last ten years, I've lived in limbo. I'm tired of it and I finally decided I had to do something about it.

Making sure my door was locked; it hadn't been as if I could get any sleep that night. I kept thinking about what almost happened and sadly I almost wanted it to happen. Leaving a message for Reyes. I had hoped he would have picked up. It was strange that he was avoiding his phone for this long.

I was rather happy to hear the alarm clock buzz. It had been a long night. I wanted it over as soon as possible. Getting up and leaving before I had needed to; I hoped to avoid Valafar. Taking a taxicab to work. I started right away looking around and assessing what the problem had been. Fortunately, it looked like an organizational problem more than anything. This really shouldn't take a full month to mess with. It had only taken me most of the morning to reorganize the shelves. They hadn't been too horrible, but certain areas needed to be separated, and some books were too difficult to find.

Making a central display of popular books, it started to look more like a regular bookstore. Placed ads in the windows that had collected dust in the back. It wasn't until late afternoon that I stopped for a moment. I almost think I had tried to stay this busy just so I wouldn't think about last night. I called Valafar on the phone to let him know that it would probably only take me a day or two at the most to finish up, then I would be going back home early. Only his answering machine had picked up so he must have assumed I left early. I had also let him know that I found another place to stay for now, but I still thanked him for letting me stay one night. Since I was the only one in the bookstore to close at night after the employees had left. I figured I would just sleep in the office; no one would know, they would just assume I had come in early.

I ordered pizza in, working a little later in the evening than I normally would have. At least I had the time with no one around or watching out for customers in the meantime. The store had been looking rather nice. I pulled out the Christmas decorations placing a few of them out leaving the rest for the employees to have fun with. At least all I had to do was go over the books. Most of everything had been filled out on little slips of paper rather than put into the computer. Spending several hours on this. I had lost track of the time that I only had a few hours till morning. Now I was going to be tired today.

The first person in for the morning hadn't been an employee, it had been Valafar with a hand full of flowers and a large teddy bear as large as he was. He had at least come in an hour earlier than the rest of the employees.

"I wanted to apologize. I shouldn't have treated you the way I did, it was rude, and I wanted to say I was sorry. I wasn't sure how, so I hope this is a start? I hate to lose my best employee." At least he had sounded sincere.

"This isn't a bad start; you can always feel free to give me a raise." Taking the flowers, I had left him with the large teddy bear.

As cute as it was, I didn't want to lug it through the whole airport or around here.

"Don't you want the teddy bear? He's so cute and fluffy, he might feel insulted that you don't want him?" As he pretended to make sniffling sounds for the teddy bear.

"As cute as he is he's too big, I think he prefers to be with you, much more space to roam around at your house. I'll find something to put these in, maybe leave them by the register. They should brighten the room a little. There should be a few people coming in early for interviews. I figure if the employees aren't coming in when they are supposed to, and far too often clocking in for the others that are not even here, then it's time to replace them." Stepping behind the desk I had kept up the pace I had all night.

I hadn't felt tired until around noon when I wished I could have slept, my adrenaline wasn't kicking in anymore.

At least the teddy bear hadn't been a complete waste, a mother had brought in her little one while she looked for a few books, her little girl was busy playing with it. When they checked out. Valafar asked the little girl's mother something, not anything I could hear but the little girl was rather excited when her mother repeated whatever it was, until I had seen her walk out the door struggling to carry the teddy, she had the biggest smile on her face.

I tried my hardest for the next several hours not to yawn which I was fighting back every minute of the day now. I didn't want to appear rude during the interviews since there had been a few that were rather good. Then there was one. I was shocked that she even bothered applying. She had so many conditions, not limitations that I could have understood or worked with, but actual conditions. She refused to take money from people who looked like they hadn't bathed, or refused to have friendly conversations with ugly men, she wanted a company card for personal expenses, an hour lunch break and so on, it felt like it went on forever. At least after all her demands were mentioned I figured I would let her know something.

"We are a friendly bookstore regardless of if our customers are ugly or not. We also hire people who work. The books are the only things on display, not the employees. If you want that which is a hooker's job, it's illegal. Have a nice day. I'm sure you can find the door since I'm sure by now you've had to use enough of them." Standing up I let her out of the office, she let out such a huge huff.

Sad someone like her would think I would consider hiring her.

Leaning forward I had only meant to set my head down for a moment. It hadn't taken long for me to fall asleep since Valafar had to wake me up when he was closing. I had only slept for three hours, at least the interviews were over, and a few would start training first thing in the morning.

"Sorry, I didn't mean to fall asleep. It doesn't normally happen. The hotel was rather noisy last night. I'll close tonight, there are a few things I wanted to get done before I took off. My plane is first thing in the morning I'm catching the red eye, so I won't be here for too much longer. In the interviews, two of them have worked in bookstores before so they should learn quickly, and the third that is also coming in for training is new to it, but he seems smart so he shouldn't be a problem. They should be here when the store opens, that way you have time to train them before you leave for your flight in the afternoon. I already have their schedules printed out on the desk, that way they can work with a couple of the others here." Picking up the resumes from my desk Valafar had looked them over.

63

"I trust you know what you're doing, too bad you won't be staying longer, we could use you here, but I understand needing to get back. After all, we still have a store back home to take care of. I'll be out in Los Angeles for the Christmas season so if I don't see you again before that then Merry Christmas." Pulling a small box out of his pocket he had placed it in front of me.

Wrapped in a red Christmas design with a silver ribbon and bow.

"I hope you don't mind but I'm still trying to make up for my stupidity, there was no excuse for it. I need to take off but close up whenever you want." Before I could say anything, I sat there feeling sort of dumb for not even saying thank you for the gift.

Curious about what was in it. I picked it up from the table peeling off the red wrapping paper with pictures of puppies on it. There was a little box set inside with a jeweler's name on the outside of the box. Taking it out I knew whatever it was. I wasn't going to be able to wear it without Reyes getting profusely jealous, even though for the crappy jealousy he was certainly avoiding his phone long enough.

Opening the small box there had been a white gold heart with my birth month in the center of it. The necklace itself had been a multi-tone color, it looked amazing. I felt bad I wouldn't be able to wear it. Picking up my purse. I had closed the small box placing it inside. I only needed to spend a few more hours straightening up and working on the computer. I was thankful my flight was going to be in just a few hours, that way I could sleep a little on the plane before I got home. Sad to say I was looking forward to going home.

Locking up the store, I had to wait a little longer for the taxi this evening heading off to the airport. Calling Reyes before I went in, I still hadn't been able to get a hold of him. Hopefully, nothing happened, and he was injured? This was unlike him. Just as I had predicted. I fell asleep on the airplane. It had only taken me three minutes. Usually, I never fell asleep that fast. I had problems with insomnia to begin with, but this time I couldn't help it. I was out for the entire flight, which was much better. I never did care for it when the plane landed. I never had a problem with the taking-off part, it was the landing that always made me feel ill.

Chapter Four
Second chance

I was thankful now that Reyes hadn't driven me to the airport, or I had a feeling I would be walking home right now. Getting into my car and pulling away from the airport. I only had to drive about forty-five minutes to get home, it felt strange driving my car again since I had gotten used to riding my bike everywhere. It felt strange coming home. I could barely see the house. None of the lights had been on and the dog hadn't been outside. As I drove up, I hadn't seen Reyes Moreau's truck parked in its usual spot in the driveway. Now I was starting to worry. Grabbing my overnight bag along with my purse. I walked up to the cabin rather quickly; the newspapers had been piling up on the side of the driveway with the mail not even in the mailbox. Instead, a note from the post office to come to pick up the mail or it would be sent back to sender soon. I guess it's a good thing I hadn't stayed gone any longer. Reyes hadn't been around for a while.

Unlocking the front door, I let out a gasp as I opened the door to find the cabin completely wiped out. No furniture, no curtains, nothing. Everything was gone. Heading upstairs there had been nothing in there either. Other than a note in the center of the room with my name on it in Reyes handwriting. As the note read.

"Jessica,

I have been thinking about this for a while and have decided it be best if I put my interests first for a change. I have moved out and taken my things with me. If you're going to live the life you have, you don't need my things to do it. I have also taken the dog since I am the only one around for her. You are not ready for a serious relationship and until you can apologize, I won't consider talking to you again. I may not even forgive you enough to be friends. I have chosen another person to be with, so don't try to talk me into coming back home. You're lucky I am leaving the cabin to you. I should sell it and get my money from it. 'Signed, Reyes"

At least now I can say I was no longer concerned about him; however, I was going to get my stuff back. Thankfully I had purchased things on my credit card so I could prove what they were and how much I had paid for them. Not only that but where the money had come from. So, for the next two months, I had taken Reyes to court, not that I felt like dealing with him again. I wasn't going to let him take me like this especially not after putting up with him for so long and not cheating on him the way I could have. Needless to say, at the end of it all, he wound up with nothing but his clothes, and I even got my dog back.

The sad part had been when he showed up on my steps a month later crying his eyes out about how his girlfriend dumped him before Christmas. That he didn't want to spend it alone. He was hoping to be with a friend over the holidays. Right about now you're probably thinking, I swear if she takes him in, I'll strangle her myself, don't worry. I had pictured this of myself also. I felt no sympathy for him. All I did was close the door on him. This was my fresh start, and I wasn't about to get stuck with him again, especially after what he pulled. I kept his letter to remind myself from now on never to settle and to not let another person push their way in that I didn't want. I also never realized what a narcissist he was until someone left a book on my office desk with a sticky note saying I might appreciate reading it. The title was "healing from a narcissistic relationship."

I decided not to buy a real tree this year. Instead, I bought a plastic one to use each year inside the house. I did end up buying a real tree and planted it in the front yard and decorated it with lights. The whole house had looked like a Christmas village inside and out. I had so much time on my hands after working at the bookstore and coming home to Jasper, my chocolate lab. I even decorated the bookstore even more than normal. Three weeks before Christmas I had a children's book reading day each week for the kids. It was a rather big hit since we were busier than normal. Probably our best sales yet.

On the morning of Christmas, I hadn't bothered waking up early at all. There was no point. There wouldn't be any gifts beneath the tree. I wasn't that convincing to fool myself, besides, the only one who would miss me was already sleeping, drooling over his pillow. I had let Jasper sleep on the bed with me since I got him back. No complaints from him other than myself, when he passed gas, it didn't matter how sound asleep I was. It woke me! Jasper felt like getting fed since he wouldn't stop licking my face. Getting up I put my slippers on and put my robe on. Not that I needed to be decent. After all, no one else was here to see me nude. If I wanted to walk around with no clothing on I could. Walking down into the kitchen, I scooped his bowl into one of the plastic containers filling it with food. Setting it down and filling his other bowl with water. I had taken out the last couple pieces of pizza and sat on the floor with Jasper and ate.

I didn't eat at the table anymore, not to be rebellious but because Reyes used to insist on it, or the fact that I had destroyed it with a hammer to get my frustrations out. It did feel good to do that. I just didn't care to eat at it. I felt strange eating at such a large table alone. Maybe someday I would break down and buy a small one built for one? Or who knows maybe built for one and a dog? Smiling to myself I could picture Jasper being happy eating at the table. After all, he would be closer to my food than his. Getting off the floor and crumbling the pizza box, there wasn't anything to do today. The store was closed for the holiday, and everything was done here. I could take the decorations down but hadn't felt like it, it had been depressing enough already.

I probably never would have been able to eat if I had seen what was in the living room, I was positive I would have lost my appetite. The upstairs led straight down to the back of the house, you could go to the right and end up in the kitchen or left into the den, then around the front from there was the living room with the dining room on the other front half. Pretty nice, cozy layout with plenty of privacy. No chance of neighbors being to close since I now owned at least sixteen acres. Walking into the living room I had the shock of my life, and thankfully it wasn't Reyes standing there or any person for that matter. There had been actual Christmas gifts underneath the tree. I didn't do any shopping so I couldn't have been that talented and done it while I was sleeping. Picking up one of the boxes, it had my name on it. It didn't take long to guess who they had been from. A plate of pumpkin spice cookies and a can of cola sat on a brand-new glass table small enough for two right beside the tree I had put up.

A note which was written by one I had memorized the handwriting to since I saw it so often. Especially on something very important every week. It read.

"Dear Santa,

Please make sure that Jessica still has a wonderful holiday even if her ex-boyfriend had no clue what he lost and hopefully inherits a better boss, after all, he was a dink for hitting on her. Merry Christmas Santa and Jessica.

'Signed Valafar"

Setting the letter down, every box on the floor was addressed to me. Getting up I had checked the front and back doors, even the windows had been locked. How did he get in here? I would have to say either I have a very creative stalker for a boss, or a true Santa clause on my hands. I felt like a two-year-old wanting to rip through all the packages. I was curious what he could have bought at such short notice. All I could guess had been that when I spoke to Margery at the Michigan store, she must have told him about my split from my boyfriend. Opening the first box, I wasn't sure what I was going to find. I didn't even know what kind of gifts he would give but then I had only sent him a gift certificate to a men's store.

The first box had two champagne flutes with a bottle of nineteen sixty-seven, semi-dry wine. Two different types of sausage rolls, crackers, and four types of cheeses all wrapped in a nice little gift set box. Setting it aside the second box had a pair of flannel pajamas with matching slippers and oddly enough, a cap. There was a smaller outfit so Jasper could match me. Little strange but cute. At least I can use it, the weather here does get cold and I'm always complaining about the cold. The third gift box was filled with items for jasper, chew toys, treats, and bones. Throwing a bone to jasper he was content since he gnawed on it for the rest of the night.

The largest box, which also seemed the heaviest, turned out to be a red microwave with plastic containers inside. Inside the plastic containers were two tickets to a theater play along with a dinner reservation made for two at a very expensive restaurant in Chicago. The last thing in the container had been one plane ticket round trip to Chicago. Odd at first, I thought he might have put this together before he found out about Reyes leaving but then with only one plane ticket, he must have already had an idea I would be flying alone? Who did he intend on having go with me? Him? It's not like there would be anything wrong with it now. Otherwise, was he setting me up with someone else? Several of the smaller boxes had been very expensive jewelry; at least he had my birthstone correct, sapphire blue for September.

The last box had been a long-thinner one standing upright. I couldn't begin to guess what that had in it. Opening it up quickly there was a pole and a hanger with the most beautiful dress I had ever seen. It was a dark navy-blue dress with tiny tear-drop diamond earrings hanging in a tiny little bag with a simple gold necklace. At the bottom of the necklace, it looked like a cascade of diamonds flowing over the side like a waterfall. There were ten small ones. Also inside had been at the bottom positioned as if the dress was already wearing them. Black three-inch heels with a thin black strap going over where the mid part of the foot would be and a tiny spaghetti strap to wrap around the ankle. It was a perfect-looking ensemble. It was hard to believe he picked this out not that he couldn't, after all, he did have good taste, but how would he have known my size?

Looking a little closer at the tickets they had been dated for three days from now. At least I won't have to wait for too long. I felt so spoiled I couldn't believe he spent so much. This was a bit more than extravagant for my boss to be putting out on me unless he still felt bad for hitting on me. For a split second, I did think maybe he was trying to hit on me again. Smiling I thought no, but if this is the way he keeps making up to me, it might not be bad if

71

he thinks he errors a lot. I know that would be mean, but I had to admit I loved being spoiled like this. There was a small note on a dark blue suitcase, it explicitly stated, do not open or look in. simple bring and have them handle it at the airport. Valafar promised in his note it would get there.

The next few days had gone by rather quickly, nothing exciting or unusual. I had taken the dress ensemble, leaving it in the bag and trying to roll it up, that way I could take it on board with me. I hadn't wanted to risk having it stowed underneath. I always lose my luggage when it gets stowed, that's why I no longer carry more than my purse and one carry-on. I was trying to get ready early when there was beeping out in my driveway. Grabbing my things quickly I had run out thinking it might be my taxi, instead, there had been a long black stretch limo. Since it had been a rather small town, I knew not just the driver but the owner of the limo service. I couldn't believe he got me a limo just to drive me to the airport. My co-worker picked up Jasper to take care of him while I was gone.

As I hurried through the airport, I made it to my gate with time to spare. But I had no idea if someone would be there to pick me up after my flight landed. Getting to my seat there hadn't been that many traveling right now, even though it was a rather odd time. The seat had been first-class, not that I was complaining, after all, I didn't pay for the ticket, but it wasn't quite what I expected. Once we landed and my ears popped so I could hear. I went to gather my luggage when I had seen someone already taking it off from the conveyer belt onto a cart. I hadn't wanted to pack extra other than the note saying to bring another suitcase. Sadly, I couldn't get it all on the plane, so I had to risk checking it. I had to admit I was shocked to see it. The man picking my things up was dressed very professionally as I had walked up to him, he smiled the second he saw me.

72

"This way miss, the limo waits for you out here. I have your bags." Nodding I just followed, I was getting the royal treatment.

For not knowing where I was going, at least everything seemed to be planned out for me. I think I just plain wanted to be surprised, to be swept away in all of this. That I never once bothered to wonder what was happening or where I was going. Normally I would plan everything out. I just wanted some excitement after these last few years. Sitting in the limo there had been a glass of wine already poured ready for me as I sat down. A little of a pet peeve for me, I liked to see it poured from a bottle, not that I ever had a problem, but I always felt paranoid there might be something in my glass. As we drove away from the airport far enough, I lowered my window dropping the liquid outside holding the glass firm enough so the wind wouldn't knock it out of my hand. Despite allowing myself to get swept up in the moment, I couldn't bring myself to fully let go of control. I never got drunk or did anything reckless, because I hated the feeling of being out of control. Setting the glass down. I was curious exactly where we were headed for?

Watching out the window we had gone onto the highway, there were so many cars and trucks it was difficult to get a good look of where we were, not that I would have known since I had never been here. The palm trees looked amazing as we pulled into a residential area with huge mansions. Driving much slower we pulled into a long driveway up to the most amazing mansion I had ever seen. If I wasn't curious enough before. I certainly was now! The limo driver opened my door helping me out as he escorted me to the front door. Opening the door, he simply told me to follow the rose petals. A thick layer of petals went across the marble floor leading to the back of the house as I followed, I was amazed at how the place looked with such vaulted ceilings even though the place could have used some color. It was all white and beige accents. In the front had been a staircase leading to an open upstairs even though I wound up walking past it. I was curious how far I would be going. Then it had led me to the backyard, there was a table fully decorated for dinner for two.

One main vase was full of roses, the tablecloth was red with a huge teddy bear in one chair while the other with my name on a gold pin in front of my place setting. He was still trying to give me a teddy bear. Two candles were lit. I had looked around still not seeing anyone other than I could hear light music in the background start. Looking over the porch there was a huge pool with a mini-rock waterfall next to it. The server had come out with the food placing it on the table leaving a side movable table next to it with extra on it. Motioning for me to sit down. I came back over from where I was looking and now sitting down on the chair that the waiter had pulled out. Did they seriously expect me to eat a romantic-looking dinner with a teddy bear?

Halfway through the dinner, I was beginning to wonder if I was expected to go to the theater with the teddy, if so, this was going to be a little uncomfortable. There is no way I was going to get dressed up to go to dinner with a stuffed animal no matter how cute it was. Once desert had been brought out, a different waiter was serving it. This time he left a piece in front of the bear; did he think the bear was going to eat it? Then he moved the bear to another seat pulling the chair out for whoever was finally joining me. Looking at the door I had expected to see who it was until I had two hands cover my eyes.

"Guess who, sorry I'm late. I hope the bear was good company,' removing his hands, I already knew from the voice, "I wasn't sure if you would come. I hoped you would, but you never know." Sitting down in his chair, Valafar seemed rather happy to see me.

74

At least he wasn't the only one thinking that before I had come, I kept reconsidering it thinking I was crazy for going along with it, but then I kept telling myself I needed an adventure and besides, how bad could it be? I knew the person or at least I hoped it was him. After eating dessert, we walked through the house bringing me to the room I would be staying in, there had already been clothing there for me for my stay so why did he need me to bring anything with me? My bag had been next to the bed along with the dress laid out on the bed ready to be put on.

"I thought just in case you didn't care for what I picked out, you would have something of your own with you, that you would feel more comfortable in. I'm going to get ready, so I'll give you your privacy, the play starts soon." Smiling at me, he closed the door behind him.

Glancing around, I was captivated by the sheer size and grandeur of the room. While my own bedroom was cozy and familiar, the expansive, open space here left me in awe. I quickly got changed clothing not wanting to leave him waiting for too long, so I met Valafar in the living room. We had taken the limo again. The whole night was wonderful. I loved the theater. We watched phantom of the opera; my favorite play and I had already seen so many versions of it, yet I still loved it every time. You could feel the energy in the room, the music and the large chandelier was my favorite part. I knew I would never get tired of this, but I was curious how he knew I loved this one so much. After several hours of watching the play in our skybox, we had left for home. I hated to admit it. I was rather tired. Valafar gave me a kiss goodnight as I left for my room, he already told me that we had an entire week to see each other. I still felt bad that we hadn't done more. Taking a shower hoping to relax after an exciting night. I was far too wound up to sleep even though I was tired and yawning.

There were at least four remotes on the bed stand. Picking up the one that looked like it controlled the television, it flicked on the fireplace. As nice as it was, that wasn't what I was trying for. Not wanting to mess with the others. I turned the fireplace off. Getting out of bed, the floor had been cold as I walked over to the balcony. The bedroom had been on the second floor overlooking the garden in the backyard. Leaning over the balcony looking down below. I could see the table we ate at earlier, still set with flowers only the candle was no longer lit, and the dishes had been cleared. Leaning against the balcony I hadn't realized how close I was to the next one over.

"I see I'm not the only one who couldn't sleep. Unless there's something you need?" Looking over Valafar had been wrapped in his robe.

Smiling back at him I wondered how long he had been standing there.

"I'm tired but too wound up from tonight, so I can't sleep. I was almost thinking of watching a movie. I just couldn't get the remote to work. I've never been very good with those things. I keep turning on the fireplace so I thought I would enjoy the view." I hadn't needed anything.

I wasn't sure what else to say to him, after all, he was my boss, and this was feeling weird not that I was cheating on anyone. I was single finally. It just felt strange.

"Let me help you with it." I was going to walk back into my room when I found he hadn't intended on going around, he stepped on the side of his balcony making his way over to mine rather quickly.

He moved with such grace, if it had been me, I would be moaning in pain from falling. Valafar followed me into my room, then he picked up the remotes, first, he turned on the fireplace.

76

"I can't help it. I love having it run during a good movie," then he grabbed another turning on the television.

Sitting down on the side of my bed, I hadn't wanted to just stand here feeling strange. I moved to the other side of the bed sitting down. I guess we were going to watch a movie together. As he flipped through the stations occasionally asking if I liked it. We settled on a comedy. Leaning over he grabbed the phone on the nightstand, then set it down after he had talked to someone. Within a few minutes later there was a knock at the door, not having to get up to answer it, the butler let himself in with a huge bowl of popcorn and drinks.

"Can't watch a good movie without popcorn and drinks. If you ever need anything the intercom is near the door but usually, after four pm you need to call down instead, most of the staff are gone by then other than a few." Getting rather close we both sat and watched the movie and the next one after it.

Laying back I had started to feel tired not wanting to go to sleep I tried to stay awake.

"You're tired. I should let you sleep, if you need anything the phone is here and I'm next door." He hadn't seemed tired at all; how could he have such a long day and not be tired?

I could barely keep my eyes open. The show had gone to commercial as he turned the television off for me.

"Don't leave yet. The movie isn't over, you must keep me awake. I don't want to miss the ending. Besides you need to be able to turn it off for me." I smiled at him, hoping he would stay.

He slid himself under the blankets, insisting he was cold, likely more for my benefit in case I fell asleep. Placing the popcorn bowl on the floor, he made himself comfortable next to me. Wrapping his arm around me, I felt so comfortable hugging him as I tried to watch the rest of the movie. I wanted to see the rest of it but at some point, I had fallen asleep holding onto Valafar. Not

77

bothering to move and not wanting to wake me up, he slid down a little under the covers and rested.

After sleeping. I finally felt like I was waking up stirring a little. I turned to feel something next to me, as I had looked, Valafar was still next to me sleeping. His arm was still laying over top of me. I didn't want to risk moving it. I didn't want to wake him. I couldn't help but watch him as he slept, he looked so peaceful. Moving slightly, he did start to wake up looking over at me.

"Morning, I hope I didn't wake you. I stayed here last night when you fell asleep before the movie was over, I didn't want to wake you either." Smiling back at him we had been thinking the same thing even though it would have been nice to know how the movie ended.

"I was worried about waking you up this morning, you looked so peaceful almost as if you were having a good dream. How was the movie?" Smiling I thought he had probably seen the rest of it.

"Sadly, as soon as you had fallen asleep, I turned it off and went to sleep myself. And yes, I was having a rather nice dream, almost wishing I could have kept sleeping. Are you ready for breakfast? I can have it brought to your room?" I couldn't help it. I still felt full from last night, besides usually if I slept in I didn't worry about breakfast until noon.

"I'm not hungry yet this morning. I usually sleep in unless it's the morning I'm working. It's the only thing that gets me out of bed." Leaning over kissing me on the forehead, turning the television on he had used TiVo's saving method for the movie, now I could still see the rest of it.

I couldn't believe he had saved it for me. As the last part played Valafar slipped his arm around me again pulling me closer to him, not resisting I had got comfortable as we watched the end.

78

"Not quite how I thought it would end, that was nice of you to save it for me." Turning the television off I noticed he wasn't watching the movie at all; he had been watching me the whole time.

Looking up at him as he leaned over placing his lips on mine, kissing me lightly to test if I would object, not objecting at all I moved a little closer to him propping myself up closer to kiss him more intimately. I hate to admit but this was what I had been looking forward to all night. Using his arm, he pulled me to a sitting position over him as the blankets fell backward as we continued to kiss. Unbuttoning my shirt, I let it drop to the floor, then removed my bra. Excitement had me nearly breathless as we laid back onto the bed. He'd already kicked off his boxers. Not much clothing remained from the night before - just his robe and those boxers.

His hands trailed firmly down my back, sending shivers through me. I knew what was coming and wanted it just as much. This was nothing like with Reyes, where I'd been counting down the seconds until it was over.

I wrapped my legs around him. He felt so good as he kept kissing my neck. I hadn't wanted it to end even though if my weekend had ended here, it still would have been perfect. We hadn't bothered getting out of bed all day. It wasn't until he had an important business matter to attend to later that evening that we finally got dressed. Kissing me on the forehead before he had left.

"I'll be back as soon as I can, apparently this little problem can't wait." I had waited up however as I was used to, I had fallen asleep during the movie again.

As wonderful as the day before had been it went far too fast. Taking a shower when I had woke up, I had breakfast by myself out on the veranda since Valafar still hadn't come home yet. Around noon I had gone out by the pool to sit there with my feet dipped in relaxing, the sun had felt good. Looking up I heard someone make a sound, hoping it was Valafar. It had been the butler instead with a cell phone.

"Phone call for you miss." As he handed me the cell phone already opened.

Taking it from him I figured it was probably Valafar letting me know when he would be back.

"Sorry I didn't come back last night they are swamped here. It's another project of mine, unfortunately, it's not going as well as I thought it would, I'll be home around dinner time. If you want you can use one of the cars to look around town, just don't go on the highway it's easy to get lost and if you do. Don't worry, there is a little box in the glove compartment. I rarely use it however there is a GPS device you can use, it's simple. Have you ever used one?" I know he sounded curious if I would go out or not.

But then he also sounded worried I would be bored or upset he hadn't come home.

"I'm sure I can find my way around; I probably won't go far, and I'll have my cell phone with me just in case. I haven't used one before but I'm sure I can figure it out. I'm sure I'll be home before or at the same time as you if you can't make it tonight don't worry, I understand." I wasn't sure what business he had to tend to, but I was pretty sure it was important.

"I promise if I don't make it back tonight then I'll make it up to you tomorrow, I need to get going or I won't get it done. So hopefully I'll see you tonight." After hanging up I admit I felt disappointed.

80

I didn't want him to feel bad about it. I knew I had said I would probably go out. I wasn't in the mood, besides this place was vacation enough. I had everything here plus I didn't have to worry about getting stuck in traffic. I never did like driving in the city even though the most I had been in was Chicago.

Instead, I looked through my bags looking for a swimsuit. I figured I would spend my time by the pool. Laying in the sun, the heat felt so good on my skin. I had noticed there were gardeners watching. At home usually no one was around to see. I hated being watched. Stretching out a little feeling hot enough. I jumped in the pool swimming for a while. I had noticed one of the gardeners had gone into the pool house. Not that he was gone long, he brought over a floating chair for me setting it at the side of the pool, then going back to his work. Feeling tired from just being bored I hadn't past that much time. Climbing out I wasn't in the mood to lounge around anymore, instead, I headed back in to change.

After showering and changing I figured I would try an attempt at touring the city. Coming down the steps to the front living room a young lady was standing there. She didn't seem too surprised to see me there.

Chapter Five
Unlike me

"Hello, sorry I didn't have myself announced, my name is Lorah McAllister, I'm the office secretary for Valafar's Main Corporation. I was asked to stop by to see if you wanted to go shopping, Valafar was worried you might get lost or bored. He didn't tell me much about you but then that is half the fun, getting to know someone." She seemed very friendly and extremely pretty.

She fit in with the image of people I pictured he would surround himself with. Natural blond long hair down to her waist wearing a short black leather bomber jacket, tight dark blue jean skirt, and an emerald shirt that showed off her waist, she was amazing. After seeing her I was surprised he hadn't hit on her, but then it's not like I asked if he was dating anyone else?

"If you don't mind that would be great, I was just heading out not that I had a plan of where to go? If you're driving, I'll let you pick. I'm sure you know the best places to go." Smiling she seemed rather happy with this choice.

Over the next several hours we checked out malls, strip malls, ate lunch, bought a lot, and even checked out a flea market. Lorah talked me into trying to climb a rock wall and paragliding, something I had never done before. I was worried since she wore a skirt, but it hadn't stopped her and it didn't stop anyone from looking, thankfully she was prepared. She wore tiny shorts under her skirt. Before we had gone back to the house, we stopped by the postal building and mailed a lot of the items I bought. One of the girls from the shop was babysitting my dog and collecting the mail so at least I didn't have to bring it on the airplane with me, but it would also get there on time. I was finding I liked Lorah, she grows on you after a while. Very bubbly but extremely friendly. She was the perfect person to have when shopping for clothes, it almost felt as if I had spent time with a very old friend. I was feeling tired since I wasn't used to being this active, not that I was lazy just a lot more laid back than this. Stopping at the coffee shop we sat outside for a while.

I missed having a friend to do things with, someone near my age again, not that I knew how old she was. This was something I was going to miss when I went back home. It was not only a small town, but most were much older than me and the few who were close to my age had families, it was impossible to make any friends. We sat there for a while discussing people walking by. The clothing they wore, and what we thought would look great on them. Nothing mean and no insulting anyone but enjoying talking to each other.

"If you don't mind me asking how long have you worked with Valafar? I've worked at the bookstore for close to seven years now." Taking a sip of my latte, I was curious what exactly she did as his secretary.

"That's where I first started, I was handling little odd jobs no one else wanted. Many of the jobs were much more adventurous but that was before a lot of things changed, so I started to manage his little bookstore here, usually, if he gets along with you, he moves you to another position. I think it's going on about eight years or more now; I started working for him right after his divorce from his first wife. The second one was so much better but she's never around anymore." She hadn't seemed that phased by her comment.

I never knew he was married, was he still married to his second wife? She must have realized what I was thinking since she had put her drink down right away to try to reassure me.

"Don't worry, he's not with her anymore. I don't know the arrangement they have but he's single, I'm sorry if I worried you. I know you're a friend of his, but I didn't know what he's shared with you, I guess I shouldn't have said anything about his past wives. I'm sorry about that." She looked genuinely concerned almost worried she had said something she shouldn't have.

Even though I wondered if she was upset because she told me or that Valafar might find out? She was sweet but I couldn't see her being devious. As far as I knew. I was just a friend; it's not like we ever made mention to each other about dating even though some could technically imply it.

"Don't worry. I'm not upset. I just didn't know he was married before; he never talks about it, and we haven't been friends for very long. He knew I wanted to see what Chicago looked like, so he was nice enough to let me stay with him." I wasn't sure if she would buy that excuse since I wasn't sure what to call my relationship with him either other than he was my boss.

"The strangest thing. I don't know if you have seen it yet, he has a hairless cat. I think they call it an Egyptian cat. Either way, it scared me when I house sit for him when he was away. I know it's there, but you rarely see it. I think it prefers to hide; all I know is the food disappears. Have you had a chance to swim in the pool? I have to say it's my favorite part of the whole house which is probably sad. I'm spending the night tonight with you. I'll just be one room over. Usually, when Valafar has problems with his contracting company it takes him a few days to sort out all the legal paperwork. This will be fun, almost like being kids again at a slumber party." She seemed so excited that Valafar wasn't going to be there.

Even though I missed seeing him it was nice not to have the tension of if we were going to sleep together again or not. Besides, I felt like I made a good friend today.

After spending another hour shopping my feet were killing me. As I walked slower, at least Lorah understood, and we drove home in her little red convertible. Pulling right up into the garage next to the other expensive-looking vehicles, we got out not having to bring anything else in other than the bathing suit I had just bought. I wanted to stop in my room quickly to take a breather. I still felt shocked to hear he had been married. I wondered why he hadn't told me unless it was painful for him. Maybe it's another reason he worried about me being stuck with Reyes? Lorah's room had been on permanent reserve since she watched the house quite often when he traveled. She was even given the choice to decorate it the way she liked. As she called it, her vacation home away from home.

I had been wearing my bathing suit, walking down to the pool when all she had was a towel wrapped around her. There were still a few people working in the garden setting up bamboo tiki torches. It had only been my third day being here but on the fourth, he was having a company party for his clients so there was a lot of fuss being done this evening when normally they would have been gone by now. The band had set up its instruments in the background now covering them with special sheeting to protect them. As the others had left there were only a handful of workers who stayed to finish putting up decorations and setting out the moveable wood dance floor.

Lorah had gotten into the pool leaving the towel on the side as she swam from one end to the other. I could see how the others were watching her now more than they were working. Sort of like they had earlier with me, except this time they had more to see, she was skinny dipping. I had only put my feet in the nice cool water. It had felt so good after walking for so long, a swim was the right idea. Swimming over to me she rested her arms on the side of the pool.

"Come skinny dip with me, it's the best way to experience the pool. The waters warm enough, don't worry about the guys watching, it'll give them something to dream about." Giving me a wink, she had pulled herself out of the water now sitting next to me.

"I've never gone skinny dipping before in front of anyone other than at the lake, but then it's my beach frontage by my cabin so no one would see me there." Not only that, but I also wasn't sure if I was comfortable getting nude in front of so many since I had never done it before.

Reaching behind me she had already untied the top letting it fall into the water. Slipping in I figured I might as well drop in since my top already made it into the pool. Not much of a choice. I could see her getting me into trouble if we had grown up together, we could have been partners in crime, it was easy to follow along with her. She was right, it had felt good feeling free even if they could see us, occasionally for the most part we had been covered in the water.

"Want to make their day?" As she was watching then she smiled even more, "kiss me," she wasn't joking she had wanted to.

"I don't kiss girls, and I don't think Valafar would appreciate it either, I don't want to upset him." Now I was feeling nervous.

"I don't go around kissing just any girl either, but trust me, this will be fun to watch their reaction. I love messing with their heads." As she leaned over, she leaned in and kissed me.

I had never kissed another woman before. I felt comfortable enough with Lorah, but I kept picturing Valafar, I didn't want to hurt him by doing this. Even though I had to admit, I was curious. I tended to get lost in my thoughts and Lorah took my silence as being ready. I felt her lips brush across mine. She lightly pulled at my lower lip with her teeth, slightly grazing my lip as she kissed me more passionately each time. I was even more aware that I was nude in the pool than before. I kept thinking of Valafar, would he be upset if he caught me doing this even though Lorah was trying to get a rise out of the others for watching us so much. She figured if they were going to watch our every move, why not give them something to watch and talk about.

It seemed strange thinking this, but her lips felt soft but firm at the same time. I was more aware of her perfume; how did it not get rinsed off with the cholerine in the pool. I felt her body pressed up against mine. We were at the shallow end of the pool as she half laid over me, I was lost in the moment that I hadn't paid attention to the steps behind me. Lorah kissed me longer than I thought she would, feeling her lips gently glide down my neck kissing it, I had a hold around her waist keeping her close to me. Her left leg kept rubbing up against mine, I didn't know it could feel this intoxicating.

She made a huge production out of it, not that it was difficult to fake, it felt incredibly real. Even for areas, they couldn't see, I felt her hand slide down my leg. As she kissed my neck, I gently brushed my lips on her shoulder, giving her small kisses as she moved.

I was guessing this wasn't her first time being with another woman, she had given a few hints she was lesbian, but I was positive now she was, it felt too intense for it to not be real. Moving down a little she started kissing me again. Then standing upright, she had taken a quick peek.

"They won't be forgetting that for a while, but I have to admit neither will I." I was so absorbed into what we were doing I didn't notice we were out of the pool and on the grass.

Standing up, she reached for my hand helping me up, I had grass pressed into my back. They weren't the only ones who wouldn't be forgetting. Everyone had stopped to watch what we were doing. Trying to act as natural as I could even though I felt embarrassed now that everyone was watching us, we walked into the house. She had gone into her room to shower as I had gone into my bedroom to shower. I couldn't believe what I had just done. I never would have been attracted to a woman or done something like that if I had thought about it, but I couldn't stop thinking about it, it had been amazing. I almost liked it more than I had with Valafar, but I think it was because of the rush of excitement. The whole adrenaline feeling and the fact it was all new to me. It was exactly like having sex for the first time again.

I couldn't even stand in the shower. I sat on the floor as the water poured over me, it had felt good just to lean against the side shower wall relaxing. I had been in here for a while when I heard the shower door open. Looking up I had almost expected to see Valafar except Lorah had been looking down at me.

"I swear you should be lesbian, you're a natural, it was pretty good." Sitting down across from me she was getting wet again.

The shower had two shower heads, one on either side and a large one overhead. We were getting doused. We had both just sat there letting the water soak us until we had both felt waterlogged. We both put on a matching white terry cloth robe as we both went and sat on the bed and watched the late-night shows. Halfway through one of them the phone had rung, since Lorah was closer she had answered.

"Yes, I'm still here. we were watching a few shows. She's right here if you want to talk to her." He talked to her for a while and then she handed the phone over to me.

"So, did you have fun shopping today? I take it you're both getting along pretty good if she's still with you?" He seemed rather curious.

I wondered if he knew what she was like or that this would even happen? Maybe one of the workers had told him what we did?

"Lorah is great, she's like the friend I always wanted." This was true without having to tell him too much.

I didn't want to explain what we did. But then I started to think, would I be able to look at him now that I have done this? We weren't exclusive but I was feeling strange again.

"I'm not sure if I will be able to leave right away or if I'll be there in the morning. I'm waiting for a phone call. I wanted to check in and find out if everything was working out. Or if you need anything?" I still had the impression he was fishing for something, so unless he came right out and said it, I wasn't going to offer anything and neither had Lorah.

After I had hung up with Valafar we finished watching our show. I hadn't even bothered to cover up. I was so warm that we both fell asleep. It was nice having such a huge bed, eventually when I did leave for home, I was going to replace my full size with a California king-size bed.

Early in the morning when I woke up, all I had heard was, 'I got it from here' as I felt Lorah stir awake and move from the bed. Opening my eyes, I had seen her wave to me goodbye. Smiling I waved to her. I hoped I would see her again before I had left for home in a few days. We had both picked out outfits to wear to the company dinner. They were slightly different as one had been the classic strapless black dress with silver accents, as mine had spaghetti straps on my black dress with little silver accents. She had chosen silver shoes while I went for the more traditional black strappy shoe. Both had three-inch heels. I felt like I was dressing like my sister. So at least I knew later tonight I would see her.

"I see you had a girl's night. I'm glad you had fun. Lorah is a very sweet girl. Hope you didn't miss me too much? Looks like Lorah did a good job at keeping you company." Sliding back sitting next to me as I sat up now.

I hadn't even thought of the fact he might find me in bed with her, would he think anything of it?

"She kept me busy; we went shopping for most of the day, then came back and relaxed by the pool. A fun girl's night. You missed out on the fun; we stopped at her favorite coffee shop which I must admit is now my favorite. Are you ready for tonight's party? Lorah and I picked out dresses for it." Smiling I had felt embarrassed telling him this, I wished we could move on and talk about something else.

"Yes, I am ready for this evening and after the party, I have no plans," he gave me a huge smile now pulling the blanket off the foot of the bed placing one leg on either side of me moving my robe aside to show my naked body laying here.

"I didn't miss out, one of the gardeners sent me a streaming video of the two of you making out by the pool. Everyone that works for me reports back to me. I know Lorah rather well and she likes to shock people, it is my fault for not telling anyone about you, especially her. I admit I was nervous when I saw the video; she is an amazing woman, it's okay that you enjoyed it, I certainly enjoyed you myself. I only hope you look at me anywhere near how you looked at her. There are a lot of things I've kept from you, and I don't know how to define us, but I truly hope you want me. Valafar looked nervous as he watched me for any expression."

"It's not something I ever set out to do, I'm still shocked by it myself, but I want you."

I felt embarrassed that he caught me in the act not only doing it but watching the whole thing. Looking down I hadn't wanted to look at him. Placing his hand under my chin lifting it so that I had to look him in the face, he started to kiss me.

This week was one I would never forget. It was almost as if I was living the life of another person. Things were going to seem slow when I did get home even though I wondered where Valafar would be when I returned home? He had a place out in California, Texas, Florida, Illinois, and Michigan. I wasn't sure what to expect, would he want me to visit more often? Even by now, I was curious how the bookstore had been doing while I was gone. I was starting to miss my dog. We hadn't spent too much more time together since he had guests that were coming early, I hurried to get dressed just to stand around. Not that I needed to be entertained all the time, but I couldn't help but feel incredibly bored. I did perk up when I had seen Lorah, even though now I was wondering who else had seen us as she made her way over to me.

"Didn't I tell you that you would be great in that outfit! More than I thought showed up for this, it must be his biggest party yet." As we looked around, I couldn't even see where Valafar was, he blended in with the others.

I was thankful not to be here alone. For most of the night, Lorah and I stuck close together other than when we stood near the dance floor listening to the music, a gentleman had asked her to dance with him leaving me to the side. That was fine, I liked dancing, but it was also fun watching the others, there were plenty of songs that didn't require a partner. It had been fun dressing up, normally I wouldn't have a reason to dress up this much. I had finally spotted Valafar. He was busy talking to someone, so I hadn't talked to him all night. Around that time, I started feeling bored since I didn't know anyone, and the freshness of the party started wearing off. Lorah had made her way back over to me.

"Let's take off for a while, no one will notice we're gone." We had slipped out to the front and into her car, it felt good to leave.

I had nothing in common with anyone and when they asked what I did for the company, it was all the same expression as if I was the same level of trash they threw out or as one put 'oh, you're just an employee' and walked away. Not a place I wanted to be anymore. At least we stopped to eat. I hadn't touched anything on the table, it was all pretty much sushi. I'm sure there were ones who loved it, but I will never gag down fish eggs, eat squid or whatever the brown glob was! I would prefer fast food where I had a clue what I was eating or at least nothing but simple mashed potatoes. Not sure where we were heading, it looked more like a factory than anything else. It also looked abandoned with broken windows, vines growing along the sides of the building and grass growing between the cement sidewalk and parking lot, even parts of the parking lot was bumpy. If it hadn't been for the cars all lined up on one side of it hidden from view until you were right there, I would have assumed no one ever came here. Parking the car, I had just followed her assuming she knew where we were going. It had been rather quiet outside but once in the building, the music was blaring so loud I couldn't hear Lorah speak to me.

Taking my hand, she led me through the crowd of partiers as we made it to the far side, we were close to the dance floor even though people were dancing everywhere. It was one of those famous "warehouse parties" that I heard about. Everyone was dressed so differently from each other that we blended right in. Here I was having a lot of fun dancing with whoever wanted to dance, there was no picking and choosing, you just danced or danced with whoever was closest to you. No one cared who you were or what you did, they were there to have fun.

I danced with so many different ones I lost track of how many and what time it was until I noticed the place getting a bit brighter. That was the only difference here, all the decorations were extremely dark with very little lighting until the sun started to come out. The crowd dwindled as Lorah had finally found me. I lost her hours ago hoping she was still here. With her purse and my jacket, we had left on the table she took my hand guiding me past the last remaining ones as we headed out to her car. That had been a fun night, don't get me wrong, the elegance wasn't lost on me at Valafar's party, but if you're doing a real party, this was it, the only part I had a problem with had been just how crowded it was. We had made an extra stop dropping off one of Lorah's friends who happened to be at the party. After leaving her at her home, Lorah had taken me home.

"Hope you didn't mind leaving Valafar's party last night, as nice as they are they get to be extremely boring if you're not there for business, even then I think it would still be boring." The entire time I had been getting to know Lorah I have yet to see her not smile.

She must be the happiest bubbly person I know and if she isn't, then she's an amazing actor. Dropping me off at the front steps, Lorah had to get going so I walked into the huge house alone. Well, at least as alone as you can be with people working at the house still. The decorations and everything had been pretty much cleaned up along with the band and catering services. Now

93

only the maids were cleaning up after a long night. Not seeing Valafar, I had been exhausted so when I heard he had a meeting this morning, I was relieved. I wanted to get some sleep before I saw him. Heading off to bed I kept wondering if Valafar had looked for me after the party. I hoped he didn't think it was rude that I left. At least he left me a note that he was going to be out for most of the morning. I was curious exactly when he left.

Not even bothering to get in the shower. I kicked my shoes off on my way to the bed letting my dress drop to the floor, pulling the blanket back. I barely got into bed before I was asleep. Normally it took me forever to fall asleep, but not this time, my body and mind were out of it. I had slept for most of the day even as the sun started to go down, I hadn't started to move around, let alone get out of bed until then.

I woke at night with a note on my dresser next to me from Valafar. If he had seen me like this then he had to of known just how tired I was, not wanting to bother me. Stretching as I had reached for the note as it read.

"Jessica,

You looked so tired when I finally did get home this evening, I didn't want to wake you I can only assume you had fun with Lorah. Sorry about not being able to spend time with you during the party but I can see that Lorah more than made up for that. I'll see you when you wake."

Being up so late I wasn't sure when he thought he would see me, since I slept in so long unless he had planned on being up late also? Not wanting to bother the staff since I knew they would answer the phone. I got up and walked to the kitchen. This had been one of the rooms I rarely went into. By now the staff had memorized what I liked for breakfast, lunch, and dinner. Even if I were to come in for a drink it was usually being poured by another person, it was kind of nice being down here on my own.

Opening the fridge, I found there wasn't that much in there, so I had made a sandwich along with a glass of milk. There had been a huge group of metal thermos bottles in the lettuce crisper and a few of the other bins had been filled with the same thing. They looked just like the metal thermos containers that Valafar would bring to work with him for his lunch. Odd they would prepare his drinks this soon? Curious what was in them. I had taken one out unscrewing it. I tipped it a little to see what was inside.

Whatever it was it had been a dark thick red, I wasn't sure what that could be unless he mixed liqueur in it? There wasn't much of a scent to it other than smelling like iron, but it was difficult to explain. Not wanting to look at it anymore I had replaced the cap and set it back in the fridge. Going back to eating my sandwich and then I had washed the plate and glass putting them back in the cupboard. Not feeling like watching television. I had gone back to my room to change into my swimsuit. At least it was still warm outside. Laying the towel across the patio chair I had sat down on the edge of the pool dangling my feet in. I couldn't help it but every time I sat here, I was going to think about what Lorah, and I had done. Slipping into the water I had decided to swim a few laps until I heard a strange sound. It had almost sounded like hissing. Looking around trying to find where the sound was coming from, there was a light on now in the kitchen. The sound seemed to be coming from inside even though it was loud for being heard way out here. Who would be cooking if it was coming from there? As I watched the window, no one walked in front of it, then the light went off, and no more sounds.

I didn't have to wait long before Valafar had come out from the patio walking over towards me, he hadn't looked as happy as he normally would have. He almost had a look of deep concern or frustration. I waited until he got closer before I said anything. I didn't like trying to speak loudly where anyone else could have heard us.

"Is there anything wrong? You don't look too happy." I couldn't help but feel concerned as he had come over to me.

Not speaking right away Valafar sat down taking his shoes and socks off to put his feet in the pool. Still, dressed in a suit. I wondered if he had gone somewhere or if I had missed something I was expected at?

"I didn't have the best day today, but things are fine now that's over and I can relax. Did you go in the kitchen earlier?" He tried to say this with a relaxed voice, but it still sounded a bit strained.

Not wanting to worry him I thought I would leave out checking the thermoses.

"Yes, I was in there just before I came out here. I made a sandwich. I know I could have had the staff do it, but I didn't want to bother them, it was rather quick. I washed the dishes I used and came out here." As I told him he looked at me with a bit of a shocked expression on his face almost as if he wasn't sure how to respond.

"I have a lot of unusual items in there. I just hoped they hadn't upset you." As he said this he never once took his eyes off me.

Trying not to look too concerned even though the red liquid was a bit strange looking. I wasn't sure I wanted to find out what it was.

"There wasn't anything strange that I could see but then I didn't look around for anything. I grabbed the sandwich stuff from the main shelf. The milk was in the jug so no problems there. I'm sure everyone has something strange about their diet, not that you need one." I was hoping he might think I only thought he had a strange diet, but then if it had to do with that red stuff I didn't want to know.

Maybe when I saw Lorah later I would ask her what it was. I never felt uncomfortable until now. I guess even if it was easier to get something myself. I will bother the staff from now on. I was thankful I only had one more full day here, then I would be taking off for home rather early. I would miss Lorah but for once I couldn't wait to get home and back to my old schedule. I would have to make sure Lorah has my address. I hoped we would be able to keep in touch.

"Where did Lorah take you last night that kept you sleeping all day?" Now Valafar started to sound more like himself.

He must have felt better thinking I hadn't gone through the fridge. I couldn't help but notice a bit of a jealous tone in his voice.

"We went to a late party; I liked the one here at the house except I didn't know anyone, so it was uncomfortable standing around, Lorah showed me around on the way there. I was hoping you wouldn't feel insulted that we left but this was more of a business party, and I didn't have anything to say to anyone, most stopped talking to me once they found out I was only an employee." I was hoping that excuse would work.

I hadn't wanted to talk to him about the party we had gone to or the simple fact that I enjoyed myself more than I did at his.

"Don't worry too much. I hadn't expected you to stay for the whole thing. I knew Lorah had another party to go to that night, she usually doesn't stick around for too long at my functions. I was glad you had fun. I'm heading up to get changed so I'll be right back." Leaning over to kiss me on the forehead Valafar almost slipped into the pool.

Getting up, Valafar left me swimming in the pool while I waited for him. Not that I had to wait very long. I swear he could change faster than any man or woman for that matter. He was down rather quickly. I was curious if he kept clothes on the lower level since his room is on the second floor set far in the back like mine was.

Coming out of the house with two drinks in his hand, sitting down at the edge of the pool. I swam over to the edge near him. As he handed me a wine glass, I wasn't sure what was in it. I couldn't place the scent, but it smelled different from wine. At least it was a glass of white wine. I hoped I could ditch it when he wasn't looking. I didn't know why I was suddenly feeling this way, but I couldn't help but feel nervous still from the way he had reacted about the kitchen and suddenly acted as if nothing was wrong. Now I was curious why he was so worried.

"Do you know if Lorah will be coming by later today?" I was hoping she would be since I wanted to talk to her even more now than I wanted to before.

"I believe she will be. She's coming over to handle some paperwork that I need straightening out. All the faxing that comes from the different stores, she organizes them for my taxes and makes it so much easier for me." I could tell he was curious why I wanted to know not that I asked before, but I stayed relaxed hoping he wouldn't pick up on anything.

Slipping into the pool turning for a second, I had thrown out the wine towards the grass away from the pool. I placed the glass near my lips pretending the second he had turned around as if I had drunk it quick. Setting it down on the small cement piece surrounding the pool. Holding up my hands I could see my skin had wrinkled from being in the pool for so long. Reaching out for my hand, Valafar had taken a good look at my hand.

"I think you've already been in the water long enough, maybe I should let you change. Let me help you out." No longer reaching for my hands he reached in looping his arm around my waist getting his arm wet in the pool as he pulled me straight up and out of the pool with ease.

Standing on my feet I couldn't shake the uncomfortable feeling.

"I think putting on some dry clothes would be a good idea." Even though I was more thinking of trying to be alone right now so I could think without worrying what Valafar was thinking.

Walking alongside him heading into the house now. I tried not to act unusual even though I planned on calling Lorah as soon as I got inside. Walking me up to my room Valafar seemed a bit distant.

"I'll be in the living room after I change my clothes if you want to join me." Kissing me on the cheek he hadn't waited for me to walk into my room or close the door since he started walking away right away.

Now I was curious what he was thinking, not that I wanted to come out and ask. As soon as I had closed my door, I went straight to my bags pulling out my cell phone instead of using the house phone. I dialed Lorah's number hoping she would pick up right away. Sadly, all it had done was ring. She wasn't answering so I left her a message on her phone hoping she would call me back, not that I wanted Valafar to know that I called her or why she would be calling me or returning a call.

Changing my outfit quickly. I wasn't sure if I should join Valafar, but then if I didn't, he might wonder what I was doing. Not that I had to worry about too much while staying here since I was planning on leaving rather early in the morning. I could at least spend more time with him. Not wanting to take too much time I hurried down the stairs, on my way to the living room when I heard a strange sound. Stopping for a second, I wasn't sure what it was. I wanted to check it out. After all, my aunt was always telling me that curiosity killed the cat, and it would most likely kill me. Instead of heading toward the living room. I stopped at the room just before that where I started to hear Valafar talking to the strange-sounding voice, it hadn't sounded awful but more like a ringing bell and rather high pitch. Either way, Valafar didn't seem so happy when he spoke to the person, it was difficult to tell from the tone of the other persons' voice, but I could tell from Valafar's side, they were arguing with each other. He hadn't been in the living room waiting after all. Then I heard him say the strangest thing when I realized what was going on, the person was in the room with him.

"Why do you insist on having that human here? It was difficult enough to find another place to conduct the business; she better be gone by this weekend. How do you think she will react with several vampires in the room?" I wasn't sure if I heard him right or not.

Did he say, vampires? Or was I finally losing my hearing.

"She would never know the difference; besides, she still hasn't picked up on me yet. She leaves tomorrow, there won't be any problems." The two voices had quieted down.

I was worried they would hear me or find out that I was eavesdropping. Carefully walking backward away from the door, I was worried about the typical creek or noise that might give me away. Thankfully it never happened as I made my way to the living room. I waited for Valafar to eventually join me. Not that I had to wait for too long. I hadn't been paying attention to the channel that I left the television on; I didn't know what I was watching. I wanted it to look as if I had been in here watching the

100

television the entire time while I was waiting and not listening to them talk.

"I'm sorry I kept you waiting. I had an important phone call to take. I hope I didn't leave you waiting for too long?" As he said this, he looked at the television in slight wonder.

At least he believed I had been here the whole time. Sitting down next to me, still looking at the television he seemed surprised at what I had on, but then as I noticed I was surprised also. It was a documentary about earth worms and different bugs, not my kind of show. I should have paid closer attention to the channel I had on.

"There wasn't anything on, so I picked this channel, for a while there it was interesting. You can change it any time you like." Not that I had tried to find anything, I hoped he accepted this explanation.

"Interesting show to settle on when nothing else is on, how about a walk? Since this is your last night here. Maybe I could take you some place nice?" I knew he was trying to make up for not being around a lot but then if what I heard was true, at least I could understand why he wasn't traveling by day and his business kept him out late at night.

Even at the bookstore, he stayed in during the day never leaving the shop until it was later in the evening. At the party, he hadn't shown up himself until the sun started to go down. Then it hit me, he was a vampire? Did they exist? His skin was colder than normal, not that he was pale as I would have expected, he had a rather nice healthy glow to his skin, not what I would expect from a vampire. He showed all the typical signs but did the writers of the books on vampires ever know one, or did they, and that's why they're accurate? I swear I must be losing my mind!

Chapter Six
The Truth

I must have paused too long since he had a bit of worry come across his face. I would have hated trying to come up with an excuse to explain what I was thinking about, it would probably be such a lame one that there was no way he would buy it. But then I also didn't want to come right out and ask him a silly question like, 'are you a vampire?' After all, how did I expect him to react to it let alone answer it, and was I ready to hear it if it was the truth?

"A walk would be nice. I've been rather hot all day and the sun is going down, so a stroll in the moonlight would be great." As soon as I mentioned the sun, I felt so stupid.

Would I have said that before if I hadn't heard them? Not wanting to raise suspicion. I stood up right away to show that I was eager to go for the walk. I had even turned off the television. Taking him by the hand we worked our way outside. Trying not to pull him too quickly. I hadn't wanted him to wonder even though he seemed curious about what I was thinking since he wouldn't take his eyes off me.

"I wanted to thank you for a great vacation, this has been wonderful staying here, I miss home, and I'll be happy finally to be back but it's going to feel strange not having you around." As soon as I said it the thought had occurred, the simple fact he hadn't been around here very much either.

Looking down at the ground as we walked, we didn't need to go anywhere, his backyard was huge for being almost in the city. Either that or the way he had it decorated was rather deceptive looking. There were a lot of shrubs, self-made waterfalls, and even a second pool in the farthest part of the property which I hadn't known was there, not that I walked the grounds since I've been here.

"Your too kind, even though I've been absent for most of it. I was hoping to make this a dream vacation for you. I guess I rather failed at that. I'm sure you would be missing your home. I miss being at my home when I've been gone for a while. Sorry to say I won't be able to drop you off when you leave, I will still be gone on a business meeting from later tonight. Sadly, I have another late run, so I'll be there by morning." Now that I was hearing him give me his excuse, I could hear him hesitate as he was saying it.

If I hadn't overheard their conversation, I never would have noticed it. He was right. I wasn't very observant, and I hadn't figured it out, or at least not until now.

"Don't worry. It's been very relaxing here; the staff is always willing to get whatever I need. I loved meeting Lorah, she's been an amazing friend to me, I wish she could have been around more. Not that I wouldn't have liked having you around more, it's just nice to spend time with another girl. It's been a much-needed rest from my regular life. Who knows, maybe next time I'm here in the city or your back where I'm at, we can spend more time then?" Slightly gripping my hand, a little tighter I knew he felt bad he hadn't been around very much.

I felt perfectly fine around him until today with the issue of the kitchen and hearing the conversation he had with someone.

Was I overreacting? I wished Lorah would call me, but then I hadn't thought about it until now, she could have called me while I was eavesdropping, and I would have been caught. Thank goodness it wasn't then, or I would hate to explain why I was listening. We had stopped walking for a bit as we stood near the little pool house by the far end. It was much more jungle-style décor on this end while the rest of the yard had been so open. From the gaps between the trees, the highway appeared startlingly close, as if I could reach out and touch it. At least this way it had blocked that view.

The gardener left a few of the tools out probably planning on picking up where he left off. Looking at the shovel for longer than I planned to, I wondered what it was that he was digging, there was a lot of dirt on the shovel and no places that looked freshly dug. The flower bed hadn't been touched, not that a large shovel-like that would have been needed. Come to think of it, as often as I had seen the workers outdoors working, nothing ever looked different. After all, how often does a bush need to be trimmed? The only real change had been the lawn when it had been mowed twice. I only remembered it because it affected my allergies. But then I also seemed to be the only one affected by it.

Leaning against the pool house wall. I looked up at the full moon. If I had been at home, I would have sat outside for hours with my dog staring at it, especially this one, it seemed even more breathtaking than it normally had.

"Fascinated by the moon?" Valafar seemed to be amused with my interest.

"Fascinated would be an understatement, I'm more obsessed with it than anything. It's sort of why I love working during the day, that way I can watch the moon at night. I just feel drawn to it. The moon and thunderstorms." Usually, when I told anyone this, they would think it was unusual, or I needed a hobby.

Valafar didn't seem to be bothered by it at all. While we stood there one of the kitchen staff was walking out towards us with a cell phone in his hand. Not handing the phone to Valafar which I expected since he said he would be heading out tonight.

"Lorah called for you." Had been all he said when he handed the cell phone to me.

Placing it by my ear I was nervous, not that I wanted to talk to her about what I heard in front of Valafar since he was the one, I wanted to ask her questions about.

"Are you going to be home later tonight? I wanted to talk to you before I left in the morning but right now, I'm busy with Valafar." I didn't want to sound rude, but I hoped this would sound like a good enough excuse and hopefully, I would find out if she was home later, or at least this way she would be ready for a phone call from me.

"Yes, I'll be home all night. You sounded rather urgent is everything okay? Your voice was rather off and rushed when you left the message. I tried calling you, but I kept getting your voice mail instead." Reaching into my pocket I felt so stupid.

When I pulled it out my cell phone was turned off, no wonder she hadn't been able to get a hold of me earlier.

"Sad to say I had my cell phone turned off. After our walk, I'll call you back." Before I could even say another word Valafar leaned in kissing me on the cheek telling me he would be right back as he turned and walked towards the house.

I guess I could try and talk to her now while he was gone.

"Actually. He's going in, so I'll talk fast. Is there anything about Valafar that I should know?" Waiting for her answer she hesitated but then it wasn't a direct question, and she could have been trying to think of something.

"I guess I don't understand. He's pretty straightforward, what do you expect to know?" She seemed relaxed enough when she asked me, so I blurted it out.

What happened when I went into the kitchen and had worked my way down to the living room later, and the odd conversation that I overheard. I let her know normally I would be fine; it was just the way he reacted that made me very nervous.

"I'm sure he's just self-conscious about his diet. He might worry about what you think of the things he eats. Besides, he was rather riled up from his last business trip. He's probably still upset by it and his reaction was more based on that than anything else. I'm in the car and I'm almost there, just a few blocks away. I needed to come in to talk to Valafar, but maybe you and I can hang out at the club for one more night, that is if I can sneak you away from him?" Lorah always seemed upbeat and positive, her cheery personality was rather infectious even if you were not in the mood to be happy or smiling, it was difficult not to when you spoke to her.

I almost jumped out of my skin when I felt a light touch on my shoulder. I spun around to see who it was as the chef had been standing behind me to take the cell phone. Shaking his head almost in disproval he had taken the phone walking into the house. Was he going to tell Valafar that I told Lorah what I heard, heck forget that, was he going to tell him I eavesdropped in the first place? Now I really couldn't wait for Lorah to get here. I could almost feel myself shake. I didn't know if Valafar was going to be upset that I listened, or how he was going to react when he heard. Not that I had ever seen him get angry or felt he even had a mean bone in his body, which is why when I heard how upset he was getting with the person he spoke to earlier, it surprised me so much. Looking at the house, I could see Valafar making his way back to me. I was trying to figure out what he was thinking, he

106

was obviously told since he did have a look of concern on his face. I hated to admit that my first response had been the feeling to run but then if he had been a vampire, it would have been pointless if the whole speed thing existed.

"Did you get a chance to talk to Lorah?" He seemed to be thinking rather hard, but I almost wondered if he was choosing his words first.

"Yes, I did, and she was already on her way over. She said she had to talk to you about something dealing with one of your companies. She thought we might be able to hang out tonight at the club before I leave for tomorrow. It would be more fun if you came with me." I didn't want him to feel left out or that I would rather spend more time with Lorah.

After all, he spent a lot of money to fly me out here to spend time with him, but then as he said himself, he wasn't able to be around very much.

"You would want me at the dance club? I think you and Lorah would enjoy yourselves on your own." Smiling at me, at least he was in a good mood even though he was still staring at me without taking his eyes off me.

So, what if he turned out to be a vampire, that didn't change the fact how I felt about him. I don't think he was expecting my reaction when I stepped towards him wrapping my arms around his waist leaning against his chest hugging him. I don't think I was feeling fearful of him since I still felt so comfortable and safe with him. I loved it when he wrapped his arms around me holding me close. It was the best place to be.

"You're not afraid?" His voice was so soft that he almost whispered it to me.

"There's nothing to be afraid of, it's still you." Not that I knew how else to respond, do I admit that I knew what he was, or do I let him say it when he feels comfortable?

Holding me close as he could squeezing me tightly, I hoped I could stay here for a long time. I would hope for an eternity, but I knew I was leaving the next day, not that I wanted to, but reality has to hit at some point.

"Do you need to leave tonight?" I was hoping he didn't have to take off.

I wanted him to stay here with me. I would have even skipped going to the club to stay here with him.

"This is more family business than anything tonight. I asked Lorah to distract you tonight, which she didn't seem to mind at all. I felt guilty taking off on you again, but I knew you would have fun with her. I haven't been any better than your other boyfriends, have I?" Leaning back to see what my expression had been.

"I understand you can't be with me all the time, but you've been there for me whenever you're able. Trust me, you're nothing like my last boyfriend and I didn't date in high school, it wasn't something I thought to do. I just wish you had more time." Which was true, the hours seemed to be going by so fast now that it was my last day.

As much as I loved spending time with Lorah. I wanted to be with Valafar.

"This is nice and all, I told you that you never should have had that human here. She knows about us. Are you going to take care of it, or do I have to?" The same chiming voice had come from behind me.

Not that I had ever seen him coming.

"Nothing is happening to her, she only spoke to Lorah, and I don't believe she will do anything. There's no danger, she's fine." Valafar was getting rather protective of me as he moved me to the side to stand between myself and the other gentleman.

From the looks of him, he was a much older rather distinguished gentleman.

"Then I guess I'm going to have to take care of her. I can't let humans know what I'm doing. Or are you going soft? The great and powerful Valafar falling for a mortal? How typical. I knew you were interested in her, sadly most humans would have died when they hit their head from falling. I knew I should have hit her once she had fallen off the steps." Feeling a bit of shock as I thought back to when I had fallen in the bookstore.

I knew I had the step ladder positioned safely. I couldn't figure out how it slid so far back to fall. I thought it was an accident, but this guy was trying to kill me then. Why keep me from Valafar? What secret could they need to keep that was worth killing another person for?

If it was just the secret of being a vampire, I guess I did break that trust. I spoke to Lorah about it, but how did she not know about it? She worked for him for so long. If this guy didn't like humans being around and he relied on Lorah so much, was she a vampire also? Then I had thought back to when I had shaken her hand when I met her, and when she kissed me by the pool. How could I have missed it? Now, this guy was going to possibly kill me. The strangest sound was coming from Valafar as he pushed me aside and the other guy came lunging forward. Leaning against the pool house. Their movements were a blur, too rapid for my eyes to follow. I caught only the briefest flashes. A subtle shift, a sudden lunge before they vanished in a frenetic exchange of blows. Yet even as they struck at each other with blinding speed, I could discern the occasional spatter of blood, the only sign that their clash was real and not some optical illusion. Reaching the side of the pool house I grabbed the shovel, not that I knew what I was going to do with it, but I didn't want to risk running, in case it made it easier for the other person to come after me.

Holding the shovel to the side. I finally had the use for it as he had turned to make a lunge at me, hoping I wouldn't hit Valafar, I swung the shovel as hard as I could. I don't think he realized I would risk trying to hit him with it. The metal part of the shovel had broken off, but I was lucky enough to hit him right to knock him over. He just laid there as Valafar stood still looking at me. I couldn't tell if he was happy, surprised, or just upset.

"Did I kill him?" Dropping the pole that was once attached to the rest of the shovel, it hit the ground as I covered my mouth with my hand.

"Don't worry you can't kill what's already dead, you just got lucky and knocked him out." I couldn't help it, but that comment seemed strange.

How could I knock out a vampire?

"I didn't know a vampire could be knocked out. If they don't sleep, then what happens when they get knocked out?" As I had looked him over, I was curious about it.

"I don't know, it's difficult to tell what happens to you when you're knocked out, the person doesn't have a memory of it, sadly I should know. I've been knocked out a few times. But then some of us don't need sleep while others do. Some of us enjoy resting and it's more of a mental or old habit than anything. The venom affects everyone differently." As he spoke, I could see a figure coming toward us out of the corner of my eye.

As I looked up, I felt relieved to see Lorah even though she looked shocked when she saw the man laying down on the ground with both of us looking at him.

"Wow, what happened here? I take it she figured it out?" Lorah was looking him over giving a rather odd expression when she saw exactly where the shovel hit him on the side of the face.

110

"Yes, Jessica figured it out and took out Kristopher Vondrak, think his wife will notice the mark?" It almost seemed like Valafar was cracking a joke, not that he seemed to be worried about it now that the guy was out for a while.

But now getting serious when Lorah pushed him aside with her foot.

"He's going to be waking up soon and I highly doubt he has a sense of humor himself, so I better get Jessica out of here before he does. What are you going to do with him?" Lorah looked him over with curiosity.

Running his hands through his hair thinking over his choices, Valafar smiled.

"Don't worry about that, I'm good at coming up with excuses but your right, she will be safer at the club than here, we have more friends there just in case he doesn't let it go." The staff must have been watching as Lorah, and I made our way up to the house.

I felt like everyone was watching me. Some approvingly while others hadn't hidden how they felt. I knew some hadn't wanted me there and I wouldn't miss being spied on all the time. My bags were packed and put in the trunk so that I wouldn't be coming back here. Giving me a firm hug, I sat in the car as Lorah drove us away. I watched Valafar stand there at the front door until I could no longer see him. I wished he could have come with us, but he had to stay behind to take care of the situation when the man came to. I just hoped he would be safe.

Most of the places we passed hadn't looked familiar at all, I would never be able to find this place if I tried, but then once we came to the area where no people were walking around outside, and we started driving past a few abandoned-looking factories. I finally recognized the place. The only thing that made this place stand out so that I would remember it, was the odd-shaped door

111

with the peculiar lights around the frame. This time we hadn't parked right next to the building like we had last time, we parked in a parking lot further away from the building. We walked across at the same time as another couple was making their way into the party. It almost seemed like Lorah knew everyone by name that was here as we made our way in, she was saying hello to everyone we past working our way over to the same table she used every time she came here. Even with the loud music and watching everyone dance. I couldn't get Valafar off my mind. I wondered if he was okay. When will I see him next?

There were a couple of people I recognized from before, even a woman who had spoken to me last time when I watched Lorah dance with a friend of hers. The woman was here again only she looked like something was bothering her. She hadn't approached me this time. She did smile and nod in my direction but never once tried working her way over. This time she had sat at a different booth with another woman who seemed equally interested in those around them as they spoke to each other. I had gotten up and danced with a few people but for the most part, just joined the large group on the dance floor that was rather packed, this time even more so than last time.

We had already been here for a few hours listening to the music when I heard a familiar voice off to the side as I looked over, I was so excited I tried not to run anyone over as I made my way back to our table. Valafar made it after all. I could see that he was in deep conversation that didn't seem to have him too happy when he was speaking with Lorah. As soon as I was close, he stopped probably not wanting me to know what he was talking about. I was wondering if it had to do with that other guy and if it hadn't gone well, especially if he still wanted me dead? Not giving me a chance to sit down, he took my hand leading me back out onto the dance floor. I was surprised at how great he was at dancing. I barely had to do anything; he led me into every step I needed to take as we danced in between everyone making our way around. I couldn't help but notice the others who watched either in curiosity, or appreciation of him. After all the fast dancing and moving nonstop with him for about four songs straight in a row my legs were getting tired, I was happy for a slow song.

My favorite part, leaning against his chest as we swayed to the slow music, it felt wonderful. Sadly, they hadn't played too many slow dances, and they had a rather fast upbeat dance after this one, so our slow dance wasn't very long. A few times I had noticed that while we were dancing, Lorah kept looking over to the corner of the room. The one girl I met had been sitting over there but now they were gone, and a man was sitting there. A person I never expected to see here was Reyes. Did Lorah know who he was? Had that been the reason Lorah kept looking over there? Working our way back to the table, Lorah tried smiling, acting as if nothing was wrong as we both sat down at the booth. Looking at her, I couldn't help but say something.

"Do you know Reyes? I used to date that guy, but I don't know what he would be doing here, it's not even his kind of place. I was shocked when I saw him." As soon as I had said that, both Lorah and Valafar looked at me in disbelief.

"That's the man who was waiting for you in the driveway when I dropped you off that first time?" Valafar almost seemed to be holding onto me tighter than he was before.

I almost felt as if he was ready to take off with me as fast as he could if needed.

"Yes, that was my old boyfriend, but he never would have come to a place like this in a million years. Two women were sitting there earlier but I don't see them now. He's sitting in their spot. They were there the last time we came here. I just can't figure

113

out what he's doing here? It's just not his personality." As I kept saying this, I noticed that Lorah and Valafar were looking at each other.

Then I had looked over in Reyes direction and he was watching us the entire time never once trying to look away, he made it rather clear he was watching us. The only thing that worried me about it had been that he looked so different.

"Jessica, he's a vampire and has been as long as I have. I understand what he wants with a human, he kills humans, and he doesn't make friends with them unless there's something he wants, but they rarely live for very long afterward. What is it that he wants with you?" As he said this, I looked over at him as he smiled but not the way he used to, almost as if he had a sinister intent behind it, which sent a shiver up my spine.

The idea that he has been a vampire this entire time started to turn my stomach.

"Are you sure you can't think of any reason he would be with you? Is this the guy who just moved in and then suddenly left?" Lorah asked as I could tell they were racking their brains trying to figure it out.

Even I had no idea what a vampire would want with me, especially since he didn't seem to be too happy with me in the first place. He was extremely possessive. I just thought he found something better unless he had not found what he wanted. Or maybe it was all a game to him?

"I think until we can figure this out, we need to get Jessica out of here. I don't think sending her home is a safe idea." Valafar seemed to be plotting out our next move as he started talking to one of his friends.

"I must go home. I need to get my dog; the store is waiting for me. I have a lot of stuff at home I need to take care of. I doubt he expected to see me here, not that he seems to be hiding it now.

114

Do you think he would follow me home?" Now that I was finding out the truth about him but then my entire world didn't seem like it had before.

"I can go home with her. She should be fine, but he might follow her now that he's seen her with us. Maybe it's why he was so possessive or hadn't done anything. Maybe he was surprised to see her working for you, even though that was just a coincidence, but then who knows maybe it's not. Maybe she's who the rumor is about, after all, he is searching for that person hoping to prevent it. He and Luther have been at war with each other for centuries." We started to get rather crowded on our side of the dance floor as we made our way out of our booth along the row of friends, separating us as we went towards the door to head out.

"Either way, we need to get her out of here and safe." We almost made it to the other side when I felt a bump at my side separating me from Valafar and Lorah, with two people standing between us as I felt myself getting pulled out onto the dance floor.

As soon as I could see who had a hold of me, it was Reyes pulling me onto the dance floor as he pulled me closer to him starting to dance. I wasn't sure what to do, not that I wanted to dance with him, but then I also didn't want to start a fight with him either. How could I have not noticed; I was beginning to realize I wasn't the most observant person that I once thought I was.

"If I knew you were into vampires, I would have had fun with you. Is Luther a friend of yours also?" As he spoke to me, I looked over at Valafar who looked helpless as he watched.

Reyes had a few friends with him keeping Valafar and Lorah from me. All I could do was dance with him and wait to find out what he wanted.

"I don't even know Luther and I just found out that you were a vampire. Heck, I just found out Lorah and Valafar are vampires earlier today. I always wondered why you moved in with me. I thought we had a relationship at the start and then you were so different. What did you want from me?" I was curious about what he wanted.

"Maybe they haven't talked to you yet. I knew what I was doing, but you played such a fool card. I highly doubt you didn't know what he was when you worked for him." He seemed rather sure of himself.

"I don't know what you think I was aware of, but I am a simple human who has had a pretty sucky life, fell in love with a person when we first met and then he changed into something that didn't even want to be there, and at least I know you were there for an alternative reason and no, I had no idea about Valafar. I just thought his parents made a poor choice in names to name him after a demon. That's the most that I knew. There is nothing special about me or my family, so how the heck was I supposed to know that vampires existed? Now I'm wondering what else is real and not just imaginary." I was serious as I spoke to him, and I think he was picking up on the fact that I didn't know.

I was hoping he wasn't going to get too angry, not that I thought he would risk pulling anything in here. As he danced with me, I noticed more people watching and I could tell which side just from watching the others who they had sided with.

"You should come with me; I can teach you; I can even change you. I can show you a life that you never knew even existed. I can give you such great power you can control anything around you. All you must do is come with me. We don't have to turn this into a war in here. Besides, if we do start fighting in here, I can promise you that the first to die will be you." He started holding me tighter so that my arm was starting to throb in pain.

116

I tried not to show it. I didn't want to worry Valafar since he was already panicked-looking. I didn't know what to do. I didn't trust Reyes but then I didn't want to risk anything happening to Valafar or Lorah. As I looked over his shoulder, I could see the two women again as the one woman moved her lips, I wasn't sure what she was saying. Lorah said she never saw who I was talking about, but I hoped this woman I could trust.

"If I'm going to take off with you, then I want to move further away from Valafar, so he won't try anything." I wasn't sure if he would fall for this or not, but I hoped the woman who I had personally not known very well would be protective of Lorah and Valafar, even if it meant that, I died I hoped they would be safe.

As we had started to dance further back away from the others, I could see that both Valafar and Lorah were both panicked. The looks on their faces had been as if I had driven a stake through their hearts.

"If you're wondering, they can hear us. They heard our entire conversation. Maybe he won't bother with you after this or maybe he will want revenge for you." As we turned so that I was facing to look over his shoulder to see them, but then I had also heard the woman's voice behind me as we worked our way even closer to her.

"They can also hear me when I say I told her to work her way over to me; there is always another way out." Before I knew what was going on, I felt a hand on my shoulder while she spoke and had seen the look on Reyes face when he was trying to figure out why she was saying this.

Then it hit him exactly who she was as the three of us vanished, leaving everyone staring in surprise as we disappeared. They weren't the only ones in shock. I had no idea what had just happened or what was going to happen, but after this, I know I was going to be questioning the possibility of everything now. I wondered what danger I had gotten myself into now. The ones we had left behind were not the only ones in shock. My first instinct had been to run but then where we were standing just the three of us, I had no idea where to run to. I wished that Valafar or Lorah was here with me.

Chapter Seven
Life turned upside down

I hoped something would happen. I had no idea what to expect, but the moment the full reality of what had just happened hit me, I nearly jumped out of my skin. As soon as I felt my feet back on solid ground, I instinctively jumped back, unsure of what might come next. The only other two that were near me had been the two women. I could only hope I could trust them. They both had a look of concern on their faces even though I felt more concerned for Lorah and Valafar than I did for myself now. I knew my going back wouldn't help them, not that I could do anything they couldn't accomplish themselves. Besides, I would be more in the way than helpful.

"You needn't worry about your friends. They are well protected by others, besides, the object to fight over is no longer in Reyes mist. He will be searching for you, we only have so much time to teach and test you." I was curious about what they had meant to teach me, but I don't think I was going to look forward to the testing whatever it had been.

What did Reyes want with me? He could have done whatever he planned when we first met unless he was searching for something? Whatever made me worth something to them, he had also wanted to teach me something, would it be the same? If it is, should I trust them?

"Where are we? Can I at least call my friend Lorah and let her know I'm okay?" At least if they answered me, I would find out if they ever intended on letting me leave.

As the one glanced at the other their expressions hadn't changed.

"Right now, that would be a bad idea. They would be expecting you to get in contact with either of them, I know you're eager to get back home, but I hate to say that's not possible. We need to make sure you're well-guarded for now, until we know you will be safe." I didn't like the sound of it, I started feeling tightness in my chest.

I didn't know if they would ever let me see Lorah or Valafar. I was beginning to regret my choice of trusting them, but then if I had not, I would probably either be dead or stuck somewhere with Reyes. But then who knows what he would be doing with me right now or I could have underestimated Valafar? I might have been fine, not that I wanted to risk his life or Lorah's.

"Are you familiar with others like us?" I had the feeling they were trying to find out just how much I already knew.

Not that I was sure what they were, otherwise, if it had been that easy Valafar would have poofed me out if he was able to.

"I don't even know who you are? I only found out that Lorah and Valafar were let alone, Reyes. I had dated Reyes, but he was a jerk when I knew him. I thought he was human until today. I usually eat my dinner sitting on the floor with my dog. That sums up my life. There's nothing special about it. I don't know what anyone could need me for, I'm just a bookkeeper. I work at a bookstore and that's it." I wasn't sure if it had been the answer they were looking for but either way, they seemed rather calm still even with their tone of voice.

At least I didn't feel threatened yet. There were a couple of chairs they chose to sit down at neither telling me to sit but leaving it to me to choose if I wanted. I couldn't help it but standing felt better now not that I could take off. I had no clue where I was. The room we were in had been dark as the nightclub.

Not feeling like I could go anywhere I gave up and sat on the chair in the corner slightly away from the other two. Not that I was trying to avoid them, but then I hadn't felt like sitting right next to them as if we had been close friends. The one girl who sadly I couldn't remember the name of, I had spoken to at the dance club, even though it had been rather brief she seemed friendly enough. As she turned on the light, I could see a lot better versus just the little light that had made its way through the small window with rather heavy curtains. This had been the first time I had been able to get a good look at both women. They looked familiar almost like two ladies who tried to talk to me before. After work one night I had been invited to join them at the local restaurant back at home. At first, I thought they wanted to talk to me about an author signing at Valafar's bookstore, and I had set up several of those. However, they started talking to me about mystical magic and how I was connected. They said they knew my mother before she died. The one-woman had been best friends with her growing up. That somehow this great power followed down being protected by great guardians, not that it had been the original plan, the stone had been neutral always following the family line going from one human to another. Somehow my father's distant family connected us.

They explained how the stone had been absorbed by her except she wanted to split its power, so that in case she was ever corrupted she could be stopped, otherwise, it would be difficult for any creature to stop her without dying. She tried to explain how powerful of a gift this would be. She hadn't even known if

121

she would be able to successfully transfer it, but she also wanted to make sure she could preserve the power in case she was to die. The power would still be around to protect. That I had been the one she was drawn to. Somehow there was something magical about me already that could handle the power. When they first told me all of this. I hadn't sat there because I believed what they were telling me. I thought what institution was searching for two missing people. But then now after what I had been learning. I would have taken them much more seriously, but then it was still hard to believe that myself. That there was nothing special, no talent, exceeded at nothing other than being good at organizing. I didn't have much going for me. Even though I liked the idea of being special, it was still hard to believe any of this was happening let alone to take it seriously. I could think of so many others who would be better prepared for something like this than myself.

"What are you going to do with me exactly?" Not that I wanted to know.

I felt it was inevitable now that I was with them and who knows maybe I'll be able to eventually defend myself, Valafar, and Lorah. I just wished I could see them.

"First, we must find out if it will work. So far it hasn't lasted very long, we hope to find a way that will make it permanent. There is another way we just don't know if we can capture and transfer it with the simple fact that it could kill me while trying it along with the person assisting me." Sitting back down in her seat, next to the other woman who seemed to be observing my reactions, still not speaking yet.

"What happens to me after this is done? Am I expected to do something? Is it something that will eventually kill me also? When do I get to see Valafar?" Judging from their expressions, I would have to admit even they didn't have to tell me the answer to my last question.

It hadn't looked possible that I would see him again. I couldn't help it but at that moment my heart sank into my stomach.

"Normally the transfer would have been done, and you could have gone back to your everyday life. Sadly, Reyes knows that you are the link and that I was going to do this. I can only guess that my one-time trusted friend filled him in. She had known this is what I wanted to do at some point. He probably thought if he took you out or found out if you knew anything he could either control the power. Or take you out so that you would not interfere with Alana's plans." The other woman had stood now getting something from the inside of a drawer.

She looked like she had taken tea leaves out. Going into another room, she left us talking before she came back with a serving tray, it had a tea kettle, and three tiny teacups already poured. Sugar and cream on the side to choose from, she set it on the little table and sat down helping herself to one of the cups, the other woman who had been speaking with me, also picked up a cup. I had to admit I was rather thirsty myself, but I felt strange taking the cup. I almost wished I could have had it tested first. After taking the cup and drinking it down rather quickly. I felt nervous, and I tend to do things without thinking. The tea didn't exactly taste like tea. It had a strange aftertaste to it.

I didn't know what had been in the tea itself, but I started feeling extremely ill almost as if I could vomit. They must have expected this since the one who picked me up moved me to another room and laid me down on a bed. Oddly enough even up to this point. I hadn't known what their names had been. I know they introduced themselves at the restaurant, but I couldn't for the life of me remember what they had been. My muscles were in so much pain. I could feel parts of my body I wouldn't normally. I felt like I had been electrified by a jolt of lightning. It was starting

123

to feel excruciating to the point I wondered if they had infected my drink with vampire blood. I wasn't sure what to expect since I had only watched movies, besides, based on those I wasn't sure what had been accurate and what had not been. Either way, the look on both of their faces hadn't been too positive as I started throwing up. Not until about an hour later had I started to feel better. I just hope I wasn't going to be subjected to this repeatedly. Regardless, I decided there was no way I would accept any more drinks from them no matter how thirsty I was!

After several hours of waiting for me to regain my strength and start talking again, they figured out I wasn't going to accept any more drinks from them, when they started to hand me bottled water. I checked to make sure the protective seal was still on the cap which it had been. It had been the only time I would drink anything; it had to be in a bottle with a seal intact.

"That didn't go as we hoped. I'm not sure why you responded that way to it. We will have to try another method, but we would like to try to train you first with a few things. How familiar are you with meditation?" This had been an interesting question my aunt used to ask me.

We would leave for retreats that would last for a few weeks. I wasn't allowed to stay home, so I would be stuck meditating with the rest of them. For the entire vacation, we did not speak once. Meditating and relaxing had been the primary goal, not that I minded it. Rather than endure my aunt's endless lectures about how I was a disappointment to her and whatever other grievances she felt compelled to air, I much preferred escaping into my own imaginative inner world.

"I've very familiar with it." Not that I felt like explaining all of it to them.

I figured straight to the point was enough.

"Good, then this shouldn't take as long. There are other things we need to work on as well. Especially your endurance, this power will give you a lot, but you can still tire out. The better you are now the better off you will be later." Not sure why but I suddenly felt like I was stuck in boot camp from hell.

Over the next several weeks, at least I had not been that ill again. However, I was kept very active. Teaching me different fighting techniques, even though she had taken it easy on me. I still had a hard time keeping up. I eventually heard her name when the other woman called her over asking her a question. Sydney had not used her powers to teach me, however, she had shown me several of the things she could do along with how she performed them. She had also given me a history lesson from the point she learned as well as from the standpoint of her teacher, who happened to be the other woman with us, which had been Sophie.

Over the next week, I met several other guardians while learning from them as both Sydney and Sophie had. Not that all the guardians agreed with the arrangement since there had no longer been a physical stone to prepare me to use. However, they had agreed with separating the power, not that any of them knew if it would work. While they talked about all of this, I had felt like I won the position of being a guinea pig for them to test on. After a while, I was given a tour of the entire place we had been at. The Augustus family that had been believed to be dead had come back to power, thanks to Luther bringing them back. Instead of eliminating the new power, they had simply taken in the new individuals using their strengths to empower the already strong family. The only reason they approved of what was going on with me had been their believing I would join them. Sadly, it didn't seem I was being given any choice in the matter.

As I found they rarely would get involved unless they were questioned, or someone broke one of the natural laws. Their existence meant everything to them, and it was not to be shared. The things that I witnessed while being here had been the most horrific thing I had ever seen. I watched as they killed off three people for breaking their laws. There had been no justice for them or waging a lighter penalty, it had simply been death. Instead of Sydney controlling things, they had gotten much more ruthless, but then after watching her. She started blending in with the others as if she had been with them her whole life. As I had heard she used to be such a different person, yet being here brought out the cruelest person she could be even though at times she still had her way when there was the rare acceptance of a person being allowed to be free. She no longer showed any expression as neither did the others had when there was an execution. There were now fourteen members that had to agree on a punishment depending on the crime. Not that it ever seemed like they were ever in disagreement. This wasn't anything that I wanted.

As I found they drank blood but only human blood without having to struggle or fight for it. They felt it was beneath them to search after a helpless animal who had no way of defending itself. Or killing off a human which would only make other humans question how they had been drained of their blood, bringing attention to themselves. There had been loyal human servants who worked for them donating their blood. It almost felt like they kept more of a human farm rather than followers. This is the last time I tell myself to go for it, what could possibly go wrong? A romantic week that is paid for by my very sweet normal boss, and then I go home to reality. This is not what I was expecting. I had promised myself that if I could find a way out of this, I would.

One of the few times I didn't have someone following me around I had explored the place on my own. This place had been amazing. If I hadn't seen the other horrible things, I would have loved living here. I felt like I was living inside of a palace only underground. The former family had very expensive taste and still preferred the old Elizabethan style. As I walked by, I looked into a room not aware it had been a personal bedroom. I could see Sophie sitting at her chair next to a very old desk as she ran her hand over a large crystal ball. Not that I could tell what she was seeing in it. I had been too far away however she seemed caught up watching whatever it was to notice my being there. At least I thought she wasn't aware. She hadn't been like any of the others, which is probably why I felt safer around her. Throughout this whole situation, she hadn't said much.

"It's rather rude to stand at a door and watch, feel free to come in." She still hadn't taken her eyes off the crystal as I opened the door to let myself in.

"Sorry. I didn't mean to spy on you. I was curious about what you were so interested in with the crystal. I was looking around since I didn't have anything else to do." Pulling up a chair next to Sophie I was hoping she didn't mind me interrupting her.

"Originally, this isn't how I saw all this happening. So much has changed but then that's what you get with free will, the choices of so many other factors that can change things. As much as I respect the family here, I miss my own family as I can only imagine you miss your life. This is certainly not what I had planned for you, and neither had Sydney, until we had found Reyes coming for you. You're simply stuck here as Sydney is for the safety of the group."

"Where is your family? I thought this was your home also?" I felt confused not that they had ever clarified to me what was expected, all the rules, or who were permanent here.

127

Taking her attention momentarily from the crystal looking at me with concern.

"I had at one time simply been a mortal who believed there couldn't possibly be more to my world than what I had already found. Then the way I get obsessed with people and places. I fell in love with an old home and everyone in it. From that moment on. I discovered an entirely different world not that it's been quite how I would have wanted and neither had my love planned on our lives this way, but then nothing ever is, even in death. It can surprise us. My life has been changed forever as yours is about to. I am sorry if this isn't what you want, I'm sure we can find some way out. Not that Reyes would ever believe someone would turn down the chance at being powerful, he may always come after you. I think at some point he had the wrong human, which is why he wanted to separate from you, he almost felt sorry for you which is why you did not end up dead from him. That and he was fascinated once he found out you were working for Valafar." Moving the crystal on its stand in front of me she nodded towards it.

I knew to put my hand over it and watch as it slowly filled with a cloud of white smoke. Looking into the smoke I could see a face not that it was too clear until I had stared at it a while. The image became much clearer as I could see that it was Valafar, eventually, it started showing the full image of him and not just his face, as I could see him pacing back and forth, as Lorah seemed to be trying to calm him down. Even to this point. I wondered what was upsetting him unless they were trying to find me, and he was frustrated. After all, I was told they would have no clue where we were hidden.

"What's supposed to happen to me if Sydney can share part of her power with me? What am I expected to do? I won't kill anyone like I've seen the others do. I just want to go home and take care of my dog." I know I sounded pathetic, but I also felt that way.

"For safety, you would live here and assist when you're needed, your main purpose had been in case Sydney was to be corrupted you would balance out the odds so that she could be controlled still. But as I see it things are already changing. I don't know if her plans are the same anymore since the rest of the group likes the idea of added power. Sadly, I am as stuck with this as you are. She was at one time very different, but this old group has made her into another person. A part of her that had been dormant has become her new personality." As Sophie said those last words, she had let out a rather heavy sigh, not bothering to mask her disappointment.

What I had been expecting, which Sophie never once asked had been if I saw anything in the smoke.

"She can keep coming for us when she wants us. Does she want all of this?" I couldn't help but be curious. At moments she seemed so concerned, but then when she was with the others she seemed as ruthless as they were.

"Yes, if she feels she needs us she can call us to her at any time. My job was to protect the life stone from being used in the wrong way. I never saw what would eventually happen to the last guardian, but then I never thought it would be absorbed into someone. Otherwise, I am sure the stone would have left or at least I keep hoping it would have. There are times we see something and it's not exactly what we think we are seeing, it's times like those we need to remember what it was before." Her last comment had me so confused as she tapped the crystal.

Even though she wasn't exactly asking me what I had seen she was either hinting at what I had seen or what she was staring at when I first came in. Either way, I had to admit I was confused but then this whole situation was confusing since it hadn't felt like it was about to end any time soon. Thinking about it ending scared me realizing the end may be the fact I die if there is an ending.

"This is depressing, nothing remotely like what I had planned. Do I ever get to leave this place even if it's just to go outside?" I was hoping that if it was inevitable at least I might still be able to see the sky and breathe fresh air occasionally.

"When they feel they can trust you. That you will not take off. I am sure going outside will be fine; however, you have to make sure you are available and come at once when you are called. I know what you planned. I've seen it in the crystal." Smiling, Sophie stood, walking away from her desk with an envelope in her hand.

There was a light knock at the door as she opened it only wide enough a small hand reached in; she handed over the letter closing the door behind as soon as it was gone.

"I know what Reyes is considered and Valafar and Lorah are the same, then does that mean both you and Sydney are the same? Am I going to be changed into a vampire?" I liked the idea of immortality, but then in the same line of reasoning I hadn't.

There were many positives and negatives that I could think of besides the fact that I had no clue what it was like to be one.

"Not all are vampires. Only myself, Seth, Sakarabru, Luther, Adhene, and Lilitu. Luther happens to be Valafar's brother. The second line of family here are Angelita Voss, Ruby and Kristopher Vondrak, Lucius Delgado, Pollux Moretti, Regulus Delarosa and Damar. Reyes Moreau used to be a close family consultant, until he left and joined Alana. Sydney along with Nikolai, Philip, Phoebe, and Jaron are the only shades. Nikolai will be leaving at the same time as myself, we prefer to stay neutral." Not leaving the door, Sophie motioned for me to follow her.

"I wish I could use that excuse and leave. For some reason, I don't see that happening. If Valafar is related, does he live here also?" Letting out a sigh myself, at least I felt I could be honest in front of Sophie.

I wasn't sure how Sydney would take it if I had told her. Not that I felt threatened by her. She had been fine around me however when you see someone executed it changes how you think and feel around the person.

"No, he does not. He chose to be independent of his family, more nomadic even though he seems to stay in the same place long enough. He split when the family decided to vanish for a while. We should be going, today Sydney is testing another idea however we are hoping this will be the last time. I hate putting you through all of this." Opening the door again it had looked as if she wanted to make sure the hallway was clear before we emerged from her room.

No one had been down any of the hallways as I followed Sophie closely, not that she walked that fast. We walked down the hallway heading to a familiar room they used as the meeting room. I could hear their voices as we approached; I hadn't been paying attention as I should have, when I bumped into Sophie. Stopping for a moment before we had gone in, she pulled this long black bag out of her pocket. She slightly unzipped part of it to reveal eight vials inside, then closed it up handing it to me. Putting her finger over her mouth to a motion not to speak, she pointed at my pocket. Putting it away. I could only guess it was something she did not want the others to know about.

I was hoping we would have privacy during this test, sadly that wasn't going to happen. As we entered the room. I looked around and it looked as if everyone was there. Apparently, the others were curious if it was going to work this time. They had all been interested in watching the transformation, if there had been one. In essence. I was the guinea pig they were all going to watch suffer. If it didn't go well, which I know they hadn't said there would be any negative reactions, not that I had to be told. I could guess. I never felt this nervous before but then I never had this many people staring at me either. What caught my attention had been a few people I had not even known were in the room until they walked away from the shadow along the far wall. They blended in with it. As I looked, Sophie leaned over to explain that they were not regular shades. They were a rather rare form of shade unlike others that were inherited from birth, these few could infect others with the gift, problem with that was it would either give the gift or take your life. They had a rather unusual glow.

There was a chair obviously for me to sit in with straps to hold me down to make sure I didn't run. They were extremely worried I would take off but then if the power did kick in, wouldn't I still be able to take off? Or would I take off just strapped to the chair? Either way, I didn't like the looks of it. Sophie stayed next to me for the majority of all this while everyone had watched, even Sydney stood next to me holding my hand in support.

One of the people who had hidden in the dark now came over as Sophie walked away from me standing next to Nikolai. I had hoped she would stay with me during this, at least Sydney had. Then I saw something I hadn't expected, Reyes walked in with Luther, standing almost in front of me. Trapped in a room surrounded by strange creatures, I sat strapped helplessly in a chair, bracing myself for the experiments about to begin. I started to wonder if I could count this as hitting extreme rock bottom, I didn't drink, or smoke and had never done drugs, so I always figured I would never have to use that phrase, but I guess for being a human in the situation I was in now. I think I can safely use it, after all, how much worse can this get? At that moment I didn't exactly want to find out.

I wasn't the only one with a strange expression, we had all been surprised to see Reyes in here. A few of the others stood closer in case their brother Luther crossed them by joining Reyes. It would have been the worst way to do it with so many around that could kill both. Angelita stormed over to Luther, her anger palpable, but he remained unfazed.

"What is he doing here? He has no purpose with this family anymore other than death." Angelita looked as if she was ready to take him out herself.

"I was under the assumption the next test wasn't going to happen until tomorrow. No one notified me it had been changed. Why the hurry? Besides, all of you knew I was bringing him here, he said Alana has found a way of taking the power and infusing it back into a similar stone, the original had come from. If she can do that then who knows how many times it can be split, why keep risking experiments, especially on such a weak human?" Luther seemed rather sure of himself.

I wondered if I was the only one noticing the look on Sydney's face, as she was more watching Reyes than anything else. Was she about to trust him? How could Luther possibly trust this person with someone he supposedly loves, unless relationships with vampires aren't anything like I have read about? Wouldn't be the first time I've been wrong.

"We decided it was best not to wait. Sydney had no problems with it unless you had plans for tomorrow, we are not familiar with?" Angelita looked at Luther accusingly not that she was the only one thinking it.

"Only one thing which I doubt any of you will deny me. After we get the power out of Sydney then the two of us are leaving. She will be nothing more than a human with regular shade powers. We both discussed this possibility and have planned on leaving the new stone with all of you to decide what to do with it; we don't want anything to do with it anymore. We hoped to fill you in before this test." Luther said, it seemed like a legitimate reason.

Besides, the family had known Luther never liked being cooped up. He would rather be out heading off wherever he wanted. At least he had wanted what Jessica had at one time. While the others listened, they had kept their eyes on Reyes.

"If that's true. I have no problem disposing of this human having one of our choosing?" Angelita seemed happier with the result even though a few of the others had slight problems with it.

"This one has already been trained and knows full well. Besides, she might be a better asset. We have no problem with you leaving, Valafar had also done so for the same reasons. Before we make any choices, we need to make sure this works first, which is why we will still go ahead and use the girl." When Pollux spoke, no one argued with him or suggested any different.

He seemed to be the leader of the group since all treated him with the highest authority next to Damar. Both Luther and Reyes stood closer. Reyes held a large black stone in his hands. During this whole time, neither Sophie or Nikolai moved from their spot or said a word. If I could have died from being nervous, I'm positive I would have died a few minutes ago.

Sydney was still holding my hand when I was approached from the side. This person stopped right in front of Sydney first, they had withdrawn blood from her directly into a needle. Usually seeing blood drawn would make me feel

134

squeamish but I think the fact her blood looked rather strange. It wasn't the dark red I was used to seeing, it was black. I was more shocked by seeing it than realizing they had just drawn blood. Or at least I hadn't been thinking about it until they came over to me, I felt the poke of the needle. It burned as soon as they stuck it in. Closing my eyes, I wanted more than anything to be somewhere else. I had been concentrating on Valafar that it almost looked like he was looking directly back at me. My concentration had been broken as soon as I felt a whoosh of wind shoot past me, I opened my eyes, only to see that Reyes decided to go against everyone else, and risk being killed on the off chance he would get the power. Why go after it if it was meant for a human? Even Sophie told me this.

What I couldn't believe had been how relaxed Sophie and Nikolai were being. Being bitten, the power had separated itself from Sydney knocking her to the floor and shoving the chair I was sitting on into the wall. She only lay a few inches from me as the bright flash of light shot out. Most had been protected by the shades while I could see Reyes ripping to shreds from the light. I had seen them go in the light before, why would this kill them? Unless there was something powerful or magical in the light? I know Valafar had problems seeing in the light and he seemed to drink a lot more. I was beginning to wonder if the whole light thing was an issue or not. If I ever had the chance to ask, I wanted to find out. But for now, I wasn't going to. I couldn't help but think about what Sophie said to me. Almost on instinct as I saw Sophie tap her nose. I tried to grip Sydney with my feet since my legs had no longer been restrained to the chair, only my hands. I closed my eyes and concentrated on Valafar, not sure what to expect other than the fact I could feel my entire body feel as if it were igniting on fire. I was in so much pain that the idea of Valafar almost lightened it. Without fully being aware of it both Sydney and I

135

had vanished while the others could only watch, not being able to stop us.

I didn't have to guess what they would do with Reyes if he was still alive. Most likely they would be assuming Sydney would be dead, but then so had I since I wasn't sure what was happening or where we were, let alone what I would do with Sydney if she was dead. I didn't know if I could take her to a doctor or not? I was completely lost and confused. When I could start breathing without feeling panicked it took me a while to know where we wound up. I felt so dizzy I wasn't sure if I had a bad nightmare and dreamed the whole thing or if it happened? I hadn't eaten anything in a while, but I didn't think that had anything to do with it even though it felt like wherever we landed. I was on fire. Looking around the place hadn't looked any better than I had felt. The place looked like a bomb went off at first, I was worried we hadn't gone anywhere. There were a few things that looked familiar as I started to piece it all together. It was my old house. It had looked like a war went on in here. At least we were not back there with all the others.

Looking down I could have sworn that Sydney had died laying on the floor, when she started to move to get up, she had a look of concern on her face as she watched me closely. Everything around me was blurry almost that disconnected feeling from my own body. I started to think perhaps I was the one dying, maybe from her blood that had been injected into me or maybe Reyes had bitten both of us and I never realized it? The last thing I noticed was Sydney standing over me whispering something to me that I couldn't hear. She could have been yelling, and I doubted I would have heard a thing. I knew I was going to pass out from all this pain. I was welcoming the possibility of not feeling anything as I did finally go unconscious.

136

I wasn't sure how long I had been out or aware of anything around my body. I think from the pain I hadn't wanted to be too aware. It wasn't like any pain I felt before, not just the burning feeling. It felt like something was trying to get out of me, almost tearing my skin. I felt as if I had fallen into a nightmare and wished I would wake up. For now, I was imagining that I was back at Valafar's home before everything had gone wrong. Long before I found out any of this existed. I found myself standing next to the pool in his backyard. It felt good to be standing here as I looked back at the house, I could see two people standing near the window not that I could tell who they were. I hoped it was Valafar and Lorah. The door to the kitchen opened. Before I knew it, they were standing right next to me. Still feeling extremely lightheaded. I wondered if it was possible to pass out in a dream. As Valafar stood near me he looked almost too worried if he would touch me, I might break but then who knows after what I've been through I just might.

"How did you get here?" It seemed like a legitimate enough question for him to ask.

"What do you mean how did I get here? There is no way any of this is real, it has to be a dream. I'm at home. I should be able to go anywhere I want to." Not that I was sure if that had been true but for now, it's what I understood.

"What home are you at Jessica? Where have you been? Did they drug you?" Lorah asked me with a curious look on her face.

She looked like she was ready to brace me in case I did fall.

"I'm back at my old home but it's been trashed. I'm sure I can dream it back to normal. Sydney had me injected with her blood, I feel incredibly dizzy. Sophie told me to think of what I saw in the crystal instead of ending up here. I wound up at home."

137

I wasn't sure how long I was going to be aware of my thoughts, my head felt so cloudy.

"If she's the same one, I think she's talking about Sophie my sister-in-law. She's phasing out, so she is projecting herself, that's something I'm sure she learned from Sophie. We should go to her house before anyone else does." I know they kept talking as they watched me.

Sadly, I could no longer hear them as I saw nothing but clouds surrounding me, unless it had been smoke or simply my eyes worsened. Either way, I know I was no longer there speaking with Valafar. I was now rudely awakening to strong shots of pain. Not that Sydney had been feeling any better than I was, her own body was reacting to Reyes biting her. Apparently, we were both dealing with something foreign attacking us. We had to wait and hope for the best, hoping it wouldn't end our lives.

Chapter Eight
New plans

I still didn't have much physical feeling back except I could feel the ground moving from underneath me. Something lifted me off the ground, but I couldn't see what had a hold of me. I wished I could have seen what was holding me. I felt too limp to respond in either fear or any other emotion for that matter. I simply felt like a rag doll and whoever was holding me could have done anything they wanted. Not sure how much time was passing by. I was only aware occasionally that I was being moved either by someone holding me, or it felt like I was laying on something soft. At times either there would be hints the sun was out and other times I couldn't tell if I had been indoors. Whoever had me didn't seem to be interested in killing me or they would have done it by now unless they wanted something from me? Then I wondered if Sydney was still with me or if whoever had me left her behind? After a while, my eyes started to clear. I wasn't sure what caused them to blur so bad, unless it had been the same reason I felt as if I was on fire. When I was able to see well enough, I looked at my skin for any signs that I had been set on fire earlier. My skin was perfectly fine. I couldn't find anything wrong with me. No one was near me now as I sat up to look around to see where I was at. I wasn't at home anymore.

Looking around, I didn't see Sydney except the room had looked familiar. I was back at Valafar's place. Pushing the blankets off me. I moved off the bed making my way close to the balcony not that I wanted to be seen. I hoped I might see someone standing outside. There wasn't anyone there. Heading back to the bedroom door that led to the hallway. I opened it up. I could hear Lorah and Valafar talking except it sounded like they were talking right outside. Stepping out I couldn't see them, so I followed their voices. It almost felt as if I was still imagining this, but then I wasn't sure if I had a vivid dream earlier of them or if it happened.

Then I heard a rather strange sound. I was having a hard time deciding if I should follow the strange sound or if I should keep following Valafar's voice? Instead, I turned around following the strange sound I heard. Down the hallway, in the opposite direction, I heard it again. Walking a little faster than I was used to catching me off guard. Had their experiment worked? I could hear the sound getting louder as I was getting closer. Soon standing outside of the very door it was coming from. Only a short distance down from the bedroom I was left in. Opening the door, I could see Sydney laying on a bed struggling with pain. At least they had taken her with however she was not looking as though she was doing well at all. Closing the door behind me careful not to make a sound. I worked my way over to Sydney. Looked down at her. The look in her eyes was of confusion.

"Can you hear me okay?" I wasn't sure what else to ask her, but I wanted to know if my speaking to her would help at all.

"Yes, I can barely hear you, but I can hear." She had a hard time talking as she moved her mouth.

Picking up the glass of water on the table next to her I helped her take a drink.

"Was Reyes supposed to bite you? Luther seemed surprised when it happened, and that bright flash. Where did that come from?" I hoped to ask a lot more questions, but I wasn't sure how long she was going to live just from the looks of her.

She used to look so young but from the last time I saw her, she looked as if she aged twenty years in such a short time.

"That wasn't part of the plan. He was only supposed to perform a ritual to take the power out, I can only guess he acted that way because he didn't want to wait to find out if this last attempt would work or not. I'm sure by now the family has put him to death if the flash hadn't already. I wasn't giving him the full-strength power, it was only going to be temporary and make him believe the power was no longer existent. This isn't a safe place for us to be, they know you're connected to Valafar and will search here to find you. I don't know if I have any of the power in me anymore after being bitten, however, I don't feel well. We need to leave." She was concentrating so hard trying to figure out our next move.

I couldn't help but feel bad for her, this hadn't worked out not that I exactly liked being experimented on.

"Any ideas where we should go? I must be honest. I don't want to go back to the tunnels even if my sharing powers with you is supposed to be a good thing. Is there somewhere safe we can go that there might be someone that could help you?" I wasn't sure if she had seen herself and how she looked, not that I wanted to be the one to point it out to her.

"There's nothing that can be done. I must wait to see what happens with my body as the venom takes over. I was surprised it didn't kill me which is what Sophie, and I believed it would do, if I were ever bitten. It was a mistake trusting Reyes, but Luther didn't think he would try anything with everyone there. I guess he was more desperate to get at the power than either of us thought." Sydney couldn't think of any safe places.

141

I used to go to my parent's cabin when I wanted to get away from anything but then once it became my home there was no more escape. I hoped she knew where she wanted to go even though I still felt safer here with Valafar and Lorah.

"Do you think they've figured it out that it worked? When will I find out if it doesn't stick?" Not that I knew another way of asking her.

I hoped I didn't have the power, and they would all leave me alone.

"I'm sure they have figured out it was you, who transported us out, however, I have a plan on making sure no one abuses it again. It's going to involve you keeping a rather big secret to yourself and not letting anyone else know. I can make it seem like it didn't stick, that the power was lost. But we need to start moving or they will know at least one of us has power. I know I still have it except when I use it, I seem to be aging so it's fighting against the new venom in my blood. I have to be very sparing with it otherwise I don't know how long I will be around." Oddly enough she didn't seem too upset by that prospect.

"If we stayed here, I'm sure Valafar would protect us. We should be safe here." Not that I wanted to risk him getting hurt either.

"He can't stand against his own family. They know his strengths and weaknesses. Besides he doesn't have enough friends to stand behind him. You're going to have to trust me with this one. For now, think of the farthest place you can think of and transport us there. I will explain the rest when we are somewhere safe." I hated to admit it, but she was right except I needed to do something first.

"We can take off in just a second. I want to grab something quick from my room. I'll be right back." Before she could answer I was out of the room down the hallway and back into the bedroom that I had been staying in.

All my things were in my bags left on the bed. Not that I was worried about my old stuff. I mainly wanted to get into the safe that Valafar had shown me. He wanted to make sure I had spending money if I ever needed it, not that I wanted to use his money before, but I was sure he would understand for this reason.

In the personal bathroom, I opened the medicine cabinet. There was a large prescription bottle on the top shelf. Taking it out and opening it up there was cash inside of it. Taking it out I placed it in my pocket while I emptied another one. Valafar liked to hide money in different places like this. Being careful not to take too much more time, in case either Lorah or Valafar wanted to check up on me. I wrote a quick note leaving it on the bed. I hoped they hadn't let anyone else know that we were here, otherwise, I wouldn't have risked leaving the note. I wanted to let Valafar and Lorah know that we were alright and that as soon as it was safe, I would contact him but for now, I didn't want to risk him getting harmed or must contend against his family. That it was best not to let anyone know they had seen us or know what condition we were in. That I loved him and hoped he would understand why we had to leave.

Making my way back to Sydney, at least no one saw me. Now standing near her I held her hand trying to think of a place we could go that would be far enough away. I thought about a pen pal I wrote to quite often, not that I wanted to suddenly show up there. And try to explain why I was there with such a sick person. She used to tell me about her grandparent's home and how no one lived in it. They tried to preserve it for personal family history. Firmly choosing this place to go, at least we could hide there until we figured out what we were going to do and the last time I had written her, I was living with my aunt. I hadn't kept

143

any of the letters so there should be no ties to us being there. I tried to remember as much detail as I could from the photo she'd sent, I felt a strange, almost physical sensation wash over me. A tide of salt-tinged wind seemed to buffet me from all sides, as if I were being drawn into the scene itself. The air pressure shifted, and the room's lighting suddenly intensified. In the span of a heartbeat, I found myself transported to the very place I had been visualizing. We were there within seconds of my thinking of the place.

"It looks like you're mastering the power much faster than I had. I panicked much more which never helped, but I used to be horrible at thinking quickly, I don't think I truly knew what I wanted. I highly doubt it should take very long to teach you. Do you remember how to speak with the other guardians?" Sydney looked rather hopeful.

"Yes, I do, did you want me to contact them? Sophie might be wondering what happened to us even though I'm curious. I hope she's okay. I was wondering how Nikolai and Lorah made it out so quickly." I wasn't sure if they would physically keep Sophie, thinking she would know where or how to find us.

"You still have training especially if you wish to keep this quiet." Sitting down on one of the chairs she seemed to slip into her thoughts for a while.

I hoped I remembered the place accurately enough as I walked over to the window to check. From the loud sound, I heard it was raining heavily outside. I doubted anyone would be wandering around this old house. Stepping away from the window I could see that Sydney sat down on one of the few chairs that were left in the house. It was a basic home, however, very old. The only room down here had been the kitchen that was closed off. There was a rather large living room but as my friend said, it was built for a rather large family. The stairs were on left side of the room going upstairs. As Sydney waited for me downstairs, I went to explore the upstairs to make sure we were alone. The hallway had gone along the far wall with only four doors off from it, after checking them I could see these used to be bedrooms. Two of the rooms still had extremely dusty beds, and cobweb-filled sheets, not that I would want to sleep on them, but the metal iron frame was still in good condition.

The stairs leading up went to yet another floor above. Not quite an entire area, however, it looked more like a lookout with windows all around as the room was a large circle. There were two iron beds up here also. There were old pictures of family members up here lining the walls. I could see where my friend inherited her looks. If we stayed up here, we could see anyone walking up to the house. I had cash on me so I could buy some sheets for the beds, not that I was sure how much a mattress would cost. There was a broom in the far corner of the room, it wouldn't take long to sweep in here. I missed the way the older homes looked with the wood floors and all the odd-shaped rooms that gave them their personal character. I thought this place looked amazing from the pictures, however, in person it looked even better. The pictures didn't do enough justice to it.

I was hoping the rain would let up except it kept raining so strong I could barely see a few inches from the window. My friend told me that when it rained here it tended to last for quite a while. At least they hadn't emptied the entire house. Not that I would normally snoop but with nothing else to do. I looked through a few of the dressers. There were pieces of clothing, sadly most of it had been attacked by moths or my other guess, mice. A few dresses were hanging in the closet that were in plastic bags, other than the odd musty smell from being hung for so long they were in good condition. Even in a few of the dressers, there was weathered paper not that any of the pencils were sharpened, but that wouldn't be too difficult to get something so I could use them. Whichever relative lived here last, left a lot of their belongings.

While I was busy exploring, Sydney hadn't wanted to bother me since there wasn't much to do, she simply sat on the chair trying to figure out our next move. Sitting there silently for most of the time, I did worry about how she was doing. Before she looked as if she was in her twenties and now looking at her, she looked late fifties. She was aging rather rapidly. I started wondering how much more time she was going to have before I had to worry about her dying. I wished Sophie could have been here. She would have known what to do. I would have felt much safer with her around.

I didn't want to sit, so instead, I stood by the window giving Sydney some peace as I watched the rain fall outside. It was such a steady rhythm on the old roof that it almost lulled me to sleep. I wondered what Valafar and Lorah were doing, also if Valafar found I took the money from the medicine cabinet yet? My life had been so simple and boring. Now, I wasn't sure what to expect. I didn't know if the others would keep coming after me or not, or what Sydney was going to plan and be able to handle. Feeling a bit chilled. I moved away from the window. One of the drawbacks to older homes had been the cold air that came in around the windowsill. Grabbing one of the extra chairs I sat down next to Sydney joining her.

"I have a plan but you're going to have to trust me for most of it. I know we don't exactly have that relationship yet, but for now, we need to stick to each other and trust each other, even if we might question some things. It might come up, but we need to cover for each other and stick closely if it's going to work. It's best if I don't share everything right away. How long do you think we can stay here before the owner of this place checks it out?" Not that Sydney looked at me while she spoke, it had looked like she was still concentrating.

"No one comes down to this end of their property anymore. Most of the younger ones live in town instead of out here in the country. As long as we avoid drawing any unwanted notice, we should be able to remain here for as long as necessary. How long do you think we need to be here?" I was hoping it wasn't going to be for too long.

"We won't be here for long. How badly did you want to go back to your old life?" This time Sydney looked directly at me not looking away.

I wasn't sure how to respond to it.

"I just want my dog. I never had anything to go back to other than Valafar, but if I went there than the others would find me too easily anyway, so I doubt that choice is open." I hated the fact that option was closed, or at least it had felt like it.

"For now, until we get things moving. If anyone does ask, I'm simply your mother, at least I look the part now. Sadly, I almost look more like your grandmother. Once the rain stops you need to pick up a few basic supplies since we will be here, if you need money I know where we can get more. I'm going to go into one of the other rooms and try to meditate. I know Sophie will be expecting me." Standing up, I watched as she slowly made her way up the stairs to the second floor.

Hearing the door close I knew it would be safe; I would get wet but at least the rain had slowed down a little. I was anxious to get something to sleep on, even if it was a clean towel from nearby so I could put it on the floor.

I watched to make sure no one was looking or at least within distance. I started walking rather briskly to the dirt road. At least the house wasn't too far from it, but it would have been more beneficial if I had a car, otherwise, the road didn't help

147

much. I didn't know the area well enough to make myself reappear near the store, my luck I would pop in next to someone and how was I supposed to explain that? My feet were still getting wet and now muddy. There was a road on either end of their property, so I knew which direction I had to go. From the stories, she told me about how her brother, and she used to play at the old house when they were little and would go into town. It didn't take too long to get there, but I hoped when I bought the few things we needed, hopefully those things wouldn't get wet. They would be in a plastic bag so that should help. I hoped I wouldn't draw too much attention to myself when I went into the store dripping wet. It wasn't too late in the evening even though it was dark out because of the rainstorm. I could hear a strange sound coming up from behind me so I stepped over off the road and looked back as I could see headlights coming towards me. I expected them to keep going except the person pulled right up next to me.

"Need a lift?" The older gentleman was nice sounding.

"Yes, my car broke down. I just need to get to town." As he pushed the door open, I didn't hesitate for a second to get in.

Normally I would never ride with a stranger, but this offer I wasn't going to refuse. I felt bad I was getting his car seat wet.

"Do you have a ride back once you're done?" He seemed genuine enough not that I wanted to risk getting a ride back from him.

"Yes, I'll have a ride back; I appreciate you giving me a lift in." At least this way he might not wait around for me while I did my shopping.

I'll have to be careful when I take off, at least it's getting darker naturally from it getting later. I should be able to blend well enough that I was wearing dark-colored clothing. He was truly a gentleman; he drove me right up to the shopping center doors.

"Thank you so much." Getting out I closed the car door behind myself.

"Any time sweetie, always good to be a kind neighbor." I Stepped back under the awning out of the rain as he slowly drove off.

At least it didn't look like he was going to be sticking around to see me when I left. It wasn't a large shopping center, more like a huge store in the far back and two smaller ones on either side with a large roof over all of them. Either way, I was just happy to be out of the rain. As I walked around the larger store with a cart picking up a few things I needed I knew I was being watched, not that they were thinking I was stealing, but probably more wondering why I was so wet. I picked out two outfits for myself, mainly sweatpants and a sweatshirt. I wasn't worried about impressing anyone but if we were going to stay in that old place, I wanted to be warm. I also picked out the same for Sydney only in a different color. Not that I was sure what she liked. I picked out the blue for her and purple for myself. I was girly but not pink girly. A hairbrush, shampoo, and conditioner, at least we could wash our hair. The water worked just fine in the place. I was surprised to see there was electricity, they added a few modern conveniences. So, I also picked up a hair dryer as well. I also picked up a few things we could eat that didn't need to be cooked. I figured I would worry about more food later.

One person was making me nervous as I walked around. I stopped picking up things trying to figure out why this person was following me all over the store. Finally, I had gotten ahead of him just enough that I could hide down another aisle and hide my cart behind a row of clothing. As I saw him looking around trying to find me, he pulled out a cell phone. My heart felt like it stopped.

149

I was worried if he had been a friend of the vampire family Augustus and was reporting to them. Trying to stay as quiet as I could without anyone else seeing me, I hid closer to the clothing hoping not to draw attention to myself as I listened to him make his phone call. In a low voice, he started speaking to the person he called.

"Are we expecting company?" There was a pause on his end.

I wished I could have heard what the other person was saying to him.

"Grandpa said he gave a young woman a ride into town. Apparently, her car broke down somewhere. She was sopping wet when he picked her up, but I swear it looked like Jessica. I was following her, but I just wasn't sure, but I lost her." His voice trailed off a little as he started to walk away.

I could still hear him talking to the person on the phone.

"Yes, it was a stupid thing to follow a stranger around, especially a woman. I probably scared her off." If he only knew how right he was.

I was worried about who he was and then it hit me. If he knew my name it had to be Zack, but do I risk telling him? I hadn't talked to him or his sister in a long time. How would I explain what has been happening without making them think I was crazy? Let alone not expose the other world. There were rules to this after all. I was with the biggest supporter of keeping their world a secret. I had only gotten the short end of the stick in all of this because of my family lineage. I've heard about people complaining about not being able to let go of the past, but this gives new meaning to, 'the past will haunt you,' at least in my case it did. I was still debating whether I would say something when I felt a poke at my back. Turning around a woman was standing there.

150

"Can I help you?" She was looking at me rather strangely.

I had to act quickly hoping he wouldn't see her speaking to me not that I wanted any problems with this woman either.

"I found what I dropped, clumsy me." Flashing my ring on my finger.

I stood up facing my back to him. Stepping aside from the cart. I stood up and started pushing it away. At least one update they had to the house, probably the last one had been the plumbing. I was worried I would have to use an old outhouse but at least the bathroom worked. Getting the toilette paper and large duffle bag to carry it all in. Thankfully they had two blow up mattresses. I headed up to the front cashier. Looking around I hadn't seen him around waiting. I hoped he had either left already or was still at the back of the store. Either way, I didn't want to stick around for too long.

As soon as I bought everything there were only a couple of plastic sacks, taking those and leaving the cart. I shoved the bags inside of the duffle bag, at least this way it would be easier to carry. As I was walking outside of the store now standing under the awning, I looked around to make sure the older gentleman hadn't been there. At least I didn't recognize any of the cars to be his. As I was about to take off, I felt another tap on my shoulder so turning around I almost jumped making him jump back a little.

"Sorry I didn't mean to startle you, but I think I know you." I wasn't sure if he was happy to see me or satisfying curiosity.

"You wouldn't know me. I'm not from here, I'm just visiting family." I hoped he wouldn't ask any more questions except I was wrong.

"The person I know doesn't live here either, but you look like a friend of my sister. We were very close at one time. Her name is Jessica, is that your name?" I was trying to think fast, I didn't want to involve either of them, but I also didn't want to lie to him either.

"What would you say if I said it wasn't?" At least this way I wasn't saying it was but then I didn't exactly answer his question.

"Why don't you want me to know who you are?" Sadly, now I piqued his curiosity more.

"I can't tell you because if I told you, I would have to explain why I'm telling you and I can't exactly tell you, not without sounding like I have completely lost my mental functions and if you knew what I knew, then you would know why I couldn't tell you. Unfortunately, you don't know that." I tried sounding as complicated as I could without telling him anything.

Lowering his one eye lid for a second as if in deep thought he then shook his head, letting go of whatever thought process he had.

"Try me. I pick up on things well and don't worry. I won't start thinking you've gone crazy. I'm already thinking that." At least he was being honest with me.

"I need to get going. I hope you won't push it. I can't tell you. I wish I could but there are strong reasons I can't." I tried to walk away from him except his hand landed on my shoulder holding me back from leaving.

Turning to face him he now had more of a concerned look on his face.

"If you need a ride, I'll drive you anywhere you need to go. I won't ask any more questions." I wished I could accept his offer, but I couldn't risk it.

"I can't let you see where I'm going." I wasn't sure just how long I was going to be stuck here now talking to him.

I had hoped to get back before Sydney was done with her meditating. At least we would be able to sleep on the portable air-filled beds. There was a lot I needed to get done at the house and this was taking time I didn't feel I had. I picked up two round foams that I planned on taking two long pieces of wood I had found at the house putting them across the springs and laying the foams across to soften the top.

I couldn't lead him to the house if he insisted on following me. I could pop out of here, but then I would be leaving a possible trail for those who want to find us or for others to talk and gossip about if they see me and the way news travels, we will have the Augustus family here in no time looking for us. I had far too many possible scenarios going through my thoughts.

"Is there any way I can convince you to let me help you?" He was exactly as I had remembered him, at least he hadn't changed.

Always kind. At least now I know firsthand who he had taken after, his grandpa. His sister was very much like him also. I could use his help, but I didn't want to risk Sydney knowing let alone put him in danger.

"If I tell you, will you promise not to get involved?" I wasn't sure what other choice I had other than I hoped he would let it go.

"I can't promise that. I have to hear it first before I can make a genuine promise. But I can promise whatever you tell me I'll keep it between you and me." He stated firmly.

At least that I could work with. Heading out into what was now a drizzle. I followed him to his car. Turning on the heat it felt good since I was still wet only colder now from the air that was blowing around in the store.

"Can we go away from the store first before I start telling you? I don't want to risk running into anyone else right now." Without asking why he started up the car and drove away.

At least it had been in the same direction of the house following down the dirt road not that I wanted him to know I was staying on his family's property. I was going to have to figure out a way around that one if he wasn't too favorable to what I was about to tell him, but then if I had heard it, I would have thought I was crazy and not taken it very well. Parking on the side of the dirt road, he shut off the car and lights and then turned his attention to me now.

"I know a lot of this is going to sound insane, but I will back it up, but you're going to have to trust me when I do. To start with, you're correct, I am Jessica." Before I could get another word out, he reached across and hugged me.

"I knew it was you. I still have your picture by my computer at home." At least now I knew he was excited to see me.

"I've had a lot of strange things happening to me since I last spoke to you. I met a guy and started dating and before I knew it, he moved in with me. I hadn't asked him, and I thought things were normal but later I found out he was only dating me because he thought I had something he wanted. He was even more convinced I had it because of who I worked for. I worked in a bookstore doing my everyday job and I found out that my boss wasn't exactly as he seemed." I was trying to think of the best way of explaining it without coming out and saying exactly the word.

I felt strange telling another person my boss and the one I'm with right now are vampires, that they exist.

"Is he a drug dealer?" I could tell he was trying to figure it out and he was way off.

"Zack. I don't know how to tell you this. And I will apologize for not asking for permission first because I didn't have very much time to figure out where to go or where to hide. So, I'm staying at your family's old house on the far side of the property. I know you said no one ever uses it anymore and it was the furthest place I could think to get to that would be safe." I stopped for a moment as he nodded his head in agreement.

"That's okay. You can stay there for as long as you need to especially now that my parents are traveling. They won't be back for another six months. Part of their retirement plan. Is it a guy or a girl that's with you?" Thankfully he wasn't bothered by my staying there even though I could sense a bit of jealousy about who might be with me.

"Not to worry, she's an older woman. She's pretending to be my mother. I'm not sure how to tell you other than showing you something, then trying to explain something when all it would do is clarify that I'm crazy, I know it will be easier to believe. It's not raining right now. Will your car be safe here on the side of the road?" Opening the car door, I stood outside as Zack followed me.

I only walked partially into the field. I could have tried inside the car, but I didn't want to risk ending up landing on something if the car came along, I wasn't sure how powerful this magic was yet.

"Stand in front of me and hold my hands and whatever happens, do not let go and don't speak yet." Closing my eyes, I tried concentrating on a place I knew would be closed right now so we could pop in without anyone seeing us.

I was concentrating on an image of a zoo that my family brought me to on one of our vacations. Just like before, the bright flash of light hit, and we were gone, reappearing at the zoo at the exact spot I remembered standing holding my dad's hand when I was very little. Looking at Zack. I could tell he was shocked by what he was seeing as he looked around trying to comprehend how it happened. Nodding at me I knew he was eager to speak.

"Yes, you can talk, it's safe now. I had to make sure my concentration wasn't distracted, or we could have wound up in

155

the middle of the ocean or a garbage dump, or worse in the lions den." I highly doubted I could have regained my concentration if we wound up in the ocean or trapped by a lion.

"How long have you been able to do this? This is absolutely amazing!" At least he wasn't scared off by it but then he always was adventurous.

"Roughly about two days with the actual power, but the last two months I've been getting trained and still have more training. I don't know how you're going to take this, but my boss is a vampire and so is my friend who also works for him. The woman with me is a shade but she was recently bitten by a vampire, however, because of the power she had which is what I now have. I don't exactly know how I got it. She's waiting for me and probably wondering if I ran off on her, and I don't want her to risk using any more power because the more she does, it ages her. The power is fighting against the venom in her system. She's trying to help me right now or at least I think she is." Waiting for his response, I wasn't sure how he would react when I told him the bad news.

At least I had an easy way of jumping into it now.

"So far it sounds cool. What were you so worried about?" At least if I can tell him the rest, I can certainly tell him this part, especially since he will need to know, that way he doesn't show up at the house.

"Sydney is a very powerful shade, and she knows other kinds of magic and has another type of magic right now. She along with a very long surviving family of vampires called the Augustus family strongly upholds not sharing the secret of other creatures. Mainly to avoid old witch hunt situations. Anyone exposing their secret they destroy and rarely allow exceptions. Right now, that's who we are hiding from, so I might be on their hit list. They would harm you if they found out I told you. That's why I can't have you show up at the house and I don't know if Sydney will harm you or not. She doesn't have a lot of strength. She's getting older and weaker every time, but I don't want to risk anything. I still need to let Valafar know how I'm doing without him knowing where I am at. This is still new to me." There was so much I wanted to tell him but so difficult when I hardly knew very much myself. I hoped that with the smallest information, he might be able to understand better.

"Let me get this straight. They would kill me if they knew you told me?" With a bit of a questioning look on his face.

"You were the one that wouldn't let it go. Now that you know. I'll bring you back but promise me you won't speak to anyone. There are some exceptions, others do know but we keep it private. Some work for vampires or other creatures, and this is allowed if it doesn't make a scene. I need to be getting back because Sydney worries easily. I took off while she was meditating, and I don't want her coming looking for me, thinking something happened." As I said that before he could say another word, I grabbed him by the hand and transported him back to the car.

At least this part of the gift I could get used to myself, maybe Sydney was right. I had the hang of this after all.

"I don't know about you, but I feel dizzy after all that. Can I at least see you? Maybe we can meet somewhere, this Sydney person doesn't have to know. I could help you out while you're here or at least get things for you or meet you places. How long do you think you'll be staying?" Standing rather closely Zack hadn't let go of my hand yet, but then again, I almost think he was doing it to balance himself.

"I don't know how long we will be here. It sounds like at least a few days but she's hoping not for too long." I wasn't sure what to tell him since neither of us knew or at least I guessed Sydney didn't know either.

Reaching into his pocket Zack pulled out a small shiny little thing.

"In case you need anything or need help. If there's anything I can figure out, I'll help you no matter what it is. I'm good at figuring out problems. They may be creatures but as humans, we can still outsmart them. I'm here for you. This is my cell phone. I have another one, it's connected to the same service so you can use this any time you need even if it's just to talk, you can call me also. Just push pound and five, it will ring me." Getting the duffle bag out of his car I stood back watching him drive away.

I knew he hesitated quite a bit not wanting to leave me there but at least he felt safer knowing I had his phone. I had to admit it was nice having a normal regular friend who knew what was happening with me.

Instead of walking back to the house. I planned on running, except this part I hadn't gotten used to yet, just the wind blowing against me it felt as if my feet swooshed right out from underneath me as I fell backward. At first, I thought maybe I slipped but the speed caught me off guard. I was thankful that Zack hadn't been here to see it. By the time I made it to the door, I looked like I had been dragged through the mud. Opening the door Sydney had been sitting there in the chair again waiting for me. As soon as she had seen me caked with mud she started to laugh.

"Did you try running?" She could barely control her laughter.

At least she had a sense of humor.

"I thought I had the hang of this but unfortunately when it comes to running, I don't. I would have left you a note letting you know how far town was so you wouldn't worry. I couldn't find anything to sharpen the pencils." Closing the door behind me I opened the duffle bag pulling out the stuff from inside of it.

"Don't worry. I would have done the same, besides there's nothing to do right now. First thing after we sleep, we have the training to do, Sophie and Nikolai are ready with others to finish teaching you control and other aspects of your power. Right now, you're the first in a long time to have the power you do. Most that could infect others with the power have long since died off and if there are any survivors of them left, they are very well hidden. The majority of shades only inherit from birth now." At least she seemed understandable not that I was looking forward to more training, but I guess it was necessary.

Putting everything away in places so the mice wouldn't get at it, Sydney had been cleaning after I left, so she must not have meditated as long as I hoped she might. Making the makeshift beds on the third floor both Sydney and I were exhausted and ready for sleep. Laying down, I was so tired it barely took me any time at all to fall asleep, except all I could dream about had been Valafar.

Chapter Nine
Fitting In

For the first time in quite a while I slept even though when I turned over, I felt incredibly sore. I had found two flat boards placing one each on top of the iron frames that were upstairs. Placing the long yellow foam covers over the board protected the air mattresses from getting scratched or popping, then covering with sheets helped however it was still a hard surface. At least it was better than sleeping on the floor. The old mattresses I didn't bother trying to lug them down the stairs. Instead, I threw them out the window to the ground below. They had been so chewed through and wet from some of the water that leaked through the roof onto them. Sydney slept up here for most of the night. I could only guess she had woken before me as I looked over at her bed, it was empty and already made looking rather nice. Either that or she never joined me like I thought she did. The sun was filling the room so at least it was rather nice out. Stretching and getting out of bed and looking out the window, immediately to my right it felt good not to see the wind blowing or the rain coming down after yesterday.

Walking down the hallway I could see the first door opened on the second floor. Sydney sort of claimed that room to meditate in. I left her on her own and walked downstairs to the fridge to grab a bagel. While Sydney was meditating, I guess I could try practicing what I knew even though I felt confident I would end up where I focused on, as long as I wasn't interrupted. I know I couldn't avoid it, and it would be best to learn now. I just wish we had more of a plan. I hate not knowing what's happening or feeling like we are going to get caught and stuck hiding for the rest of my life.

Sitting down for a while feeling relaxed. I liked the window seat. At least I could feel the warm sun shining on me. Feeling lost in my thoughts I hadn't exactly been that great at meditating. I could never fully clear my mind. I kept drifting off to thoughts about Valafar. I still hadn't asked him if I saw him that one day or not even though I still feel somehow, I was able to show myself to him. Being careful not to concentrate on him too hard, after all, Sydney told me if I do, I will automatically flash there if I'm not careful. I've been so worried about what thoughts I've had that I've been trying hard not to think about anything. What if I started to think of a beautiful whale in the middle of the ocean and flashed there and wound up crushed to death from pressure in the ocean or because I was too far underwater and couldn't breathe, that was what I feared the most. My thoughts were even more intrusive when I tried to sleep, almost as if my brain was trying to stay awake by desperately remembering every tiny thing that happened, went wrong, mistakes, accomplishments, memories or things I wished I had done differently. Even conversations that I had ten years also would creep into my thoughts.

At least I knew most of the lessons I was about to be taught involved control. I needed to control my thoughts and how deeply I concentrated on them, so I could separate simple personal wishes to intentional thoughts, so that I would only move myself physically when I meant to. It had only been a day even though it felt like longer. I pictured Valafar. I wished I could

161

tell the difference between thinking of him and when I shadowed myself to him. At least that had been what Sydney explained to me before, to those who are not sleeping I can shadow myself so that they see an image of me, not that I've ever seen it and then there was projecting myself into others' dreams. Not everyone was susceptible to this, it depended on how open they were. At least when I flashed, I knew when it was happening. I could feel the wind pick up and almost a tight pressure surrounding me, not that it hurt but it does take you by surprise when you're not expecting it.

In a few minutes I was standing there in my old room, I wasn't sure why I chose this spot to pop in except it had been easier. The cabin would never be my sanctuary again. I checked on my dog; I noticed all his things were gone. He was at the girl's house playing with her kids excited, at least he was being well cared for. I still felt guilty for abandoning him. The second place I let myself into was Valafar's home. I know this wasn't the smartest idea and probably not something Sydney would have liked, but my heart would not stop thinking or aching for him. The room I stayed in had been left exactly the way I left it. The note I left for him was gone. At least I know he read it. Reaching for the door and opening it I was rather surprised I was able to do it, except it left this strange tingly feeling in my fingers. Making my way to Valafar's study. I thought he would be in here even though it was silent. I could see Valafar sitting at his desk leaning forward with his face nestled in his hands. Walking over closer to him, he didn't have anything on his desk. I hope he wasn't upset that I had taken the money out of the medicine cabinet.

"How long have you been sitting here alone like this?" I was worried he was depressed and sad.

Unfortunately, I couldn't do anything right now to change things. I just hoped he was alright.

"How long have you been standing there watching not saying anything?" Standing up slowly turning to look at me a small smile came across his face.

"Just for a few minutes, I didn't want to bother you yet if you were working on something." I wasn't sure what else to say and what I wanted to tell him I couldn't.

"Are you at least safe?" Very simple and to the point, he was so careful when he reached out towards me almost as if he thought he might hurt me.

"So how do I look? I've never actually seen myself in this form?" As I looked at Valafar he was still trying to figure out how to touch me.

Lifting out my hand to take his, my whole hand felt that tingling rush, if I hadn't known what caused it, I would have thought it was Valafar doing it to me. Once he had my hand, he pulled me to him hugging me still being careful not to crush me.

"You look rather faded out. I can't figure it out but there's something different about you. My family has already been here looking for you. They want to know if Sydney died or if you inherited her power or not? I told them I hadn't seen you, so I wasn't sure. Lorah said the same thing. I found your note you left me; I destroyed it so no one would find it." After glancing at me for a moment he started hugging me again.

It felt good. I wished it had been the real me and not the projected or shadow of myself.

"You haven't answered my question if you're safe? I will go anywhere you need me. Where are you two hiding right now? I didn't know my family wanted you until today. I can help but you need to let me." I know he meant well but until Sydney established a plan, I couldn't say much.

For now, it appears that no one is aware of Sophie and Nikolai's involvement. I didn't want to take the risk and jeopardize their being involved still with Sophie and me.

"I'm safe and getting used to a few things, I can't tell you much. I don't want to risk your life, but I also can't say much because Sydney has told me not to. I'm already breaking one of the rules by seeing you. I couldn't help it. I wanted to see you, I needed to." I didn't want to leave him, but I could start to hear Sophie talking to me.

"You know that I would keep you safe, you need to trust me. I would never put you in danger." Valafar pleaded with me.

I could see the guilty look on his face. I know he felt bad for what happened at the club. If it hadn't been for that. I would probably still be with him and not have gone through all the testing and training that I had, not that he knew all of that. I still wanted to ease his mind.

"I do trust you; I trust you with my life and without question, but for now you need to trust me. I need to go; Sydney's ready for me. I'll be back when I can." As soon as I said that I snapped back to my physical body.

Looking up I felt a bit dizzy trying to focus on Sydney who was standing in front of me.

"How is Valafar? I hope he's coping alright. I don't blame you. I would have done the same thing. We need to finish your training; however, I need you to do something more important, it might not make sense right now, but it will later. I need you to find a way of volunteering at the retirement home nearby.

"How did you know that I was visiting him?" Now I was curious, was she able to see us somehow?

"I don't need magic to let me know you were visiting him right now. I can guess the heart would draw you to what mattered more to you. Besides, you were smiling more than normal.

Something I haven't seen you do since I've known you." Her comment was very sad but true.

I wish I knew how I looked when I wasn't here in my physical body, when I get a chance, I plan on videotaping myself to see.

"Are you coming with or staying here?" I was curious if I was the only one volunteering and if there was a reason she couldn't go.

"If I went, I'm pretty sure they wouldn't let me leave. Besides, going out in the sun is becoming a problem for me. Light is fine but my eyes are very sensitive suddenly and my skin feels like it's pinching. So, for now, I need to avoid going out during the day or at least when the sun is out." Her explanation made sense.

I was wondering why she wasn't going out even though she planned on spending some time outside this evening.

Not that I was being told the entire plan but for now there was some sort of start. I wasn't sure if they would let me get a job there but at least for volunteering, it should be rather easy especially when they see they don't have to pay me. I felt bad for not picking up an outfit that I should wear around others. My main need had been just to stay warm. I'll have to pick up something later. I hope they don't think I'm lazy wearing sweats, at least they were not baggy. Not wasting any time, I had left the house, leaving Sydney waiting for me to find out if I was able to get into the nursing home. Not sure where the nursing home around here was, I pulled the cell phone out of my pocket and dialed the number that Zack had shown me. I didn't expect him to answer his phone as fast as he had. I almost wondered if he was waiting for my call, then he confirmed that he had.

"Took you long enough. I wish I could have told sis you were here, but I kept my word. I didn't say anything. Where are you at?" At least he seemed eager to help and hopefully, Sydney wouldn't find out, but then she expected me to be around people for a while, at least I would have an excuse for having him around now.

"I need to find the nursing home. I'm supposed to find out if they need volunteers, I know it sounds strange but so far, it's what I'm working on. I'm almost to the dirt road right now." Not that I had expected him to be there.

I was walking along watching the ground since the same cricket kept hopping right directly in front of my path, I was oddly enough preoccupied with it. As I looked up there was Zack's car sitting there already waiting for me.

"I was hoping to have an excuse to run into you, so I've been sitting here for the last few hours. I woke up rather early to get here. I'll drive you to the nursing home. We only have one here in town and I'm sure they would accept you as a volunteer. You're not sure why Sydney is having you volunteer there?" He seemed surprised but then so had I when she first told me.

"I'm guessing there's something you can get from a nursing home or who knows maybe it's easier to get into rather than a hospital? I don't know, either way, I guess I have to wait to find out what it is she's after." I was happy not to have to walk around searching for the nursing home.

I would have had to search for the store last night except I had a ride for that also. I wasn't familiar with the town other than memories from what Zack and his sister told me. Sitting in the car, not sure what to talk about, at least the nursing home wasn't that far away. Before I could get out of the car, Zack had come around to my side opening my door. The only other person who had done this was Valafar.

"I know one of the managers here. I'll talk to her and help you get a volunteer job. She's known my family for a long time.

Her name is Avani Isha; she's Native American and extremely sweet." Nodding I figured I would just agree since I hadn't met her yet.

I could probably use all the help I could get. At least Sydney couldn't complain about the logic in this, besides, she can assume he was helping me not probing for secrets. I had never been in a nursing home before other than when my elementary class had gone to sing a song for the seniors. We were all paired up with a senior we were supposed to get to know or play a game with. Mine had signed up for bingo except she made it very clear she didn't want me to bother her, so I wound up sharing my best friend's senior. Since I had never stepped foot in one again, I figured once I was old. I would spend enough time in one.

Stepping up to the counter Zack asked the girl who was typing something into her computer if Avani was in. She nodded and agreed to let her know he was waiting to speak with her. We didn't have to wait for very long. The woman had come out from her office in the back with a huge smile on her face. She was happy to see Zack. She wasn't as old as I had pictured her. I was thinking she would be an older woman instead she was our age. Avani had gone to school with both Zach and Melanie. She didn't have too much time to speak with us; it was their special events time when they would take a few of the residents to the theater house for a play this morning; she was not only arranging it but also the main one for taking them.

After I was introduced to her, Avani agreed to let me volunteer. I would be able to start first thing the next day. Giving us both a hug we watched as she had taken off to take care of things. One thing I noticed that I wasn't used to had been that she was a very affectionate touchy-feely person. Oddly enough I wasn't uncomfortable with it, she was naturally friendly, and it fit her personality as I saw her walking down the hallway almost about to pass a resident of the nursing home, she stopped for a moment to say hello and hug the person before she went on her way.

It hadn't taken as much time as I expected it to. I didn't feel like heading to our temporary home right away even though I was sure Sydney was curious if I was able to get a spot there or not. We had sat in his car for a while outside of the nursing home before he asked me.

"Anywhere else you need to go. I don't work today so I have all day free." The hopeful sound in his voice was nice to hear, I knew I was needed back at home for now.

"I appreciate your help. I should be getting back not that I feel like it, but Sydney is expecting me." Zack hadn't started the car almost as if he was thinking about something first.

"If you don't have to be cooped up all night, we could hang out. I know sis would love to see you. She doesn't have to know how long or where you are staying. Or just you and I could spend time together?" I knew this was the time to tell him I only hoped he hadn't wanted more than just friendship.

I couldn't say that Valafar and I were dating but if there were a chance of something more, I wanted it with him.

"I need to be upfront about something with you. I am involved with another person; I love being your friend and I do like spending time with you, but I wanted to make sure you understood it wasn't going to be any more than that." Judging from his reaction I could tell he wasn't too happy with it, but he covered it rather well.

"Can I at least still occupy you or is he the jealous type?" Smiling at him I couldn't help but laugh a bit.

"Actually. I'm not sure but he is the vampire type, so I wouldn't want to risk it. I can't promise anything but maybe we can get together tonight. I'll give you a call. And thank you for letting me use your cell phone." The ride home hadn't taken very long, not that I wanted to get out.

I knew whatever Sydney was planning that if we could just get it over with, I might be able to live a normal life again.

Getting out of the car I knew he was watching me as I walked away. I even walked slower deliberately not wanting to be in a rush to get back, but it also felt good knowing Zack was not too far away now. Either way, I knew it was inevitable. Sydney would be waiting for me at the door. It was hard to tell how she was feeling, there was no change in her expression but then as she seemed to age more, it was much more tiring for her to show expression. At least it hadn't surprised me by the first question she asked, and I was ready with a response.

At least I practiced one in my mind in case the situation were to come up.

"Who drove you home? Do they know the owners? Do we need to move? Did you get the volunteer job?" I knew she was eager to find out asking so many questions right away.

"We can stay here as long as we need to. I did get the volunteer job at the nursing home, and I never would have been able to get it without the help of the one who drove me home. He knew the manager there personally and he helped me get the job. I didn't have to interview or anything, they do need a driver's license to verify who I am, but other than that, it's all I need. Zack was being nice enough to drive me home. I did get invited out tonight except I said I had to make sure we didn't have plans for tonight, that I would call Zack to let him know." I was hoping she wouldn't ask too many questions about him, that way I could avoid the fact that I knew him.

"Is this a date with the young man? I was hoping to test your sense of control because as soon as I can figure out whether you can fake your way through testing, we might not be ready yet. Tomorrow night if you wish you could head out but be careful not to draw attention to yourself, we don't need anyone finding out we are here. We need as much time as possible to get you ready. This isn't going to be easy." As much as I would have liked being away from all of this for a while, I knew I had to be patient, not something I was ever good with.

"No, it's not a date and I made it very clear so there wouldn't be any misunderstandings, that I was already seriously involved with someone else. I don't know if I will ever be able to be part of that anymore, but I can still hope. It would be a group of volunteers going to watch a movie together and maybe listen to music later, but not much after that." Taking the cell phone out of my pocket I hit the two buttons to automatically dial him.

I knew Sydney was no doubt curious about how I got the phone probably worried that it was my phone. She did have a concerned expression on her face. I didn't have to wait long; it barely rang when Zack picked up.

"Hi, this evening isn't going to work but tomorrow night will, I won't be able to stay out late. we have a lot to work on, but I'll let you know more tomorrow." I knew he would be disappointed.

I didn't want to say very much with Sydney listening and I couldn't say much even if I had wanted to, so I hoped he accepted this.

"Not a problem Jess. It will give me enough time to get ready for tomorrow. I'm guessing you can't tell me what you're working on. I'll see you at the nursing home. I decided during my two-week vacation I would volunteer with you, after all, I don't know when I will get the chance to see you again." At least he was being positive not that I wanted him wasting his vacation.

At least it would sound more convincing to Sydney this way.

170

"I'll see you at the nursing home tomorrow." Closing the phone, I placed it back in my pocket so I wouldn't lose it.

I felt disappointed but I needed to hide it as well as I could.

"Where did you get the cell phone? If it's your old one, we could be traced by it. We will need to get rid of it and take off right away. We can't risk getting caught this soon." I knew it was a concern from the look on her voice.

"It's not my old cell phone. I left that at Valafar's home. This belongs to Zack, I told him we didn't have time to get a phone put in yet, so he loaned me his extra for now.

"Random strangers are just not that friendly without a reason. Once you hand his phone back, I think it would be safer to keep a distance from him when you can, even if you are working with him." Sydney still sounded worried.

I was hoping not to have to admit to this, but I didn't see any other way around it right now. I had to explain the full truth to her. It couldn't be avoided. I hoped she would accept it.

"He's not exactly a random stranger. His family owns this house, and he recognized me when I was at the store buying a few things we needed. I tried not to tell him but it's hard keeping a secret from a close friend. He won't say anything to anyone, he hasn't even said anything to his sister yet, and I was the closest to her. He helped me get the volunteering job at the nursing home and he's been helping me get around town. It's been helpful, otherwise, he has a large family around here and it's been the best way of not being noticed." Sydney watched me the entire time I explained this, still not showing very much expression.

Something I started to wonder if she learned from being in power for so long. The odd thing had been that I didn't want to disappoint her, but I also didn't want her to say we had to leave either.

171

Sydney hadn't said anything for a while almost as if she was contemplating something. During that time, I could feel my stomach feeling sick. I was positive we were going to leave again, not that I knew where else we would end up going.

"Did you keep that information about your friend from me on purpose?" Sydney looked right at me.

Not breaking eye contact I knew I needed to be honest with her.

"I knew how important it was to keep secretive about our being here and I trusted him, so I chose not to say anything. I am sorry I didn't, but I hoped we wouldn't have to keep traveling around finding a new place." I didn't have to wait long for a response.

"Anything else, make sure you at least tell me. We can work out problems better that way but if I didn't know you had known him, then if we had a problem occur, we wouldn't have been ready for it. It's not always smart to trust mortals. They may have been great as we knew them before but when they learn what kind of power you have, it sadly changes them even the great ones."

"Do I still need to avoid him? Or are we leaving?" I was hoping we could stay.

"We can stay, for now, eventually you will be leaving but that will come in time. Now we need to work on more important matters and then you need to sleep so you can function for tomorrow. I need to get something." Sydney walked out of the room without further explanation heading up the steps to her room she usually retreated to when she wanted privacy.

I knew I had been standing in the same place when Sydney left the room. I hadn't been concentrating on anything now and yet the whole room turned entirely dark. I couldn't see anything, not even my hand out in front of my face. Had the power gone out? Even if it had there still should have been some natural sunlight coming in from the window from outside. I tried to make my way over to where the window was in case the shade had come down, not that I seemed to be getting anywhere. I walked far enough. I should have walked into the wall by now.

"What are you looking for?" The voice startled me as I jumped, turning in the direction I heard the sound.

There was shading around the person not that I needed to see who it was. I knew by the sound of the voice exactly who it was.

"I was checking the shade to see if it went down on the window, I wasn't sure why the lights went out." I tried to keep my voice calm.

I hadn't wanted him to get angry by anything I said, not that I was sure how he was going to react finding us here. How did he find us already?

"Where is Sydney?" Not asking too many questions other than to get to the point.

I wasn't sure if I should tell Pollux.

"I'm not sure, she left for a while, and I decided to stay here." I was hoping this would give her enough time.

If he was asking me where she was then apparently, he didn't know she had gone upstairs.

"Where did she go?" Again, short to the point.

"I don't know where she went, she didn't tell me." I knew it was a lie but I was trying to stall as long as I possibly could so I could think of something.

"Does she have her powers anymore? And are you still able to perform powers?" As soon as he had said that I raised my hand to block the fire bolt he shot out at me.

At that second, he disappeared as the lights came back on, I was still standing in the same place as I had been before all of this started. Did I hallucinate? Or was I still hallucinating?

"That was your first mistake, instead of reflecting the shot you should have simply dived out of the way. Even if it means temporary pain, it is far better than a lifetime of it. If he had wanted to, he could kill you with no problem. You still have not been in an actual fighting situation yet. It is best to take you off guard then when you are ready for it. When they do come, we will not know it and you need to react exactly the way expected of someone who has no powers. You also need to say the right things as well." Sophie was standing directly in front of me instead of Sydney.

I hadn't expected to see her here.

"I don't know what I'm expected to say. I don't know if Sydney wants the others to know if she has powers or not. I have no clue what we are doing other than hiding ourselves here." I wished someone would fill me in.

At least if Sophie was going to be involved now, I knew I would find out what was expected or going on.

"We are going to convince the others that neither of you has powers. I have talked to Sydney, and she let me know that you still wish to see Valafar, I'm not sure that is a good idea. I hate to see you be separated from him, however, sometimes it has to happen to protect those we love." I understood what she meant, even in this situation it made it even harder because it was his family that we had to convince and hide from.

"How do you know they won't kill us when they find out we don't have the powers? Won't they wonder where they went?" I know I would be wondering where they had gone if no one owned them and if I had wanted them.

"They might still try to kill you to cover up, so no one knows they don't have the powers any longer in the family, they are not worried what mortals would think." As soon as she said that I knew I wasn't going to like this.

There had to be something else we could do. Maybe if I could talk with Valafar and let him know what was going on he might be able to come up with an idea?

"Valafar knows his family better than we do. Maybe we can talk with him, and he could help us figure something out? At least he might be able to know if they would still kill us." Not a part I was looking forward to.

"They killed Reyes for betraying them. They may feel you're flashing out is a form of betrayal unless we can find a way of covering it. I'm not sure how we can do that. Besides, for both of you to disappear and be hiding it's not going to be easy." As horrible as Reyes had been especially for what he did to Sydney, oddly enough I still felt sad about his death.

"I think I have an idea, but I will need Valafar's help. I don't know what Sydney is planning on with the nursing home?" The rest of it made sense to me except for that part unless there was something she intended on using.

I don't know if Zack would stand back while I tried to sneak whatever it was out of the nursing home.

"I know what she is planning with that, but for now that is for Sydney to share with you if she chooses to." For the next several hours we rehearsed every possible question I might be asked and how to answer it.

I felt strange doing this. she let me go to my bedroom so that I could relax and try to meditate so I could hopefully find Valafar without anyone else knowing. I was there to see him. I could have done this in front of her, but I wanted some privacy while I talked to him which is why I was surprised that she went along with it. At least I was sure he would be home, he only left so often when I was there because of those he worked with. I chose to enter my old room again since I knew no one would be in there. I didn't want to pop into his office in case he wasn't alone. I was glad that I hadn't, he had a business meeting with a few people. I didn't recognize the voices other than one, and sadly it was one I wanted to avoid. It was Angelita, she scared me the most out of the group. She seemed to be the only one lacking empathy. It was a good thing that the final decision was never hers to make, or there would never be survivors even those she simply did not like. Other than her looks there was nothing angelic about her. She was purely an evil demon, and she let everyone know it. I almost think her own family was nervous around her.

I wasn't sure if she could detect whether I was there. I didn't want to risk it, so I popped back into my own body. I figured I would try again later. Going back down the stairs Sophie had looked up at me as she kept talking to Sydney who had now joined her downstairs.

"I couldn't risk talking to him, he had a business meeting going on so I thought I would try again later." I was hoping they wouldn't mind, but I knew they wouldn't want me to risk being seen by anyone else.

"We've been talking, and we both agree that Valafar could help us out a lot if he agrees to it. His family is extremely loyal as long as they don't feel the family is crossing them so hopefully, he will be loyal enough to you not to call them in. If it works, this is the best way for you to get out. Don't worry about trying to contact him anymore tonight, you can try that again tomorrow but for now, you will need your sleep. We will continue to discuss the issue of the supposed lost power." Not that I felt like sticking around, it was nice to be let out of something for once.

176

I still wanted to talk to Valafar anyway. I also wanted to know what they were talking about downstairs except I had to admit I was tired. Meditating usually made it far easier for me to fall asleep. I had been told before by Sophie to keep one place for private meditating and not to do it in bed, but I wanted to try to contact Valafar one more time before I went to bed for the night. In case I went to sleep right after coming back. I set my alarm clock.

I couldn't help but wonder what Sydney wanted me to get from the nursing home? It seemed like whatever reason I was there for she would want me to know, what would be the purpose otherwise?

Wearing my pajamas, I laid back in bed thinking about Valafar as I slipped back into his familiar home. I was getting much better at this already even without the sharp headache when I would come out of it. Standing in his bedroom this time. I walked around. He had his robe hanging from the back of the door. Standing next to it. I could smell the cologne he used. It felt good to smell a familiar enjoyable scent. Feeling lost in my thoughts for a moment. I was quickly brought back to reality when I heard someone rustling around in his closet. Stepping into the bathroom quickly, I wanted to see who it was in case it wasn't Valafar. I didn't want to risk being seen even by the household staff, even though I was sure they would be more loyal to Valafar than his family. Waiting for the person to come out of the closet, she came out with her hands full of plastic dry-cleaning bags. I didn't want to scare her, but I was so excited when I saw who it was. As I ran out of the bathroom to her. I hoped she wouldn't yell in surprise.

"Lorah!" I kept heading over to her as she dropped the bags to see who was calling her.

She looked rather shocked to see me. I kept my voice low enough now that I knew how well the others could hear, but I wanted to let her know I was here. I knew she could fight quite well if she had to. Rushing over to me she hugged me tighter than I would have cared for, but I was as happy to see her.

"What are you doing here? Angelita is in the other room. She is not one you want to have finding out that you're here. Not that I'm not happy to see you but right now, this isn't a safe place for you." I thought she might not be gone yet but I had to try.

"Can you meet me somewhere without anyone following you? Or somewhere safe I could find you or Valafar?" I thought I might not get a chance to see either of them today, but I was hoping to at least get a chance to find when I could safely talk to either of them, even if I had Lorah pass on the message to Valafar which might be safer.

"Are you still safe? I know Valafar will feel upset he missed you. There won't be anyone here tomorrow, but I can always drop back here to pick up something to make it look like I have a reason to." At least she seemed to be picking up on the urgency in my voice.

I didn't want to risk worrying her because I know if she's worried, Valafar will be also when he finds out I was here.

"I'm safe for now but we have a plan of what we are doing. I need help from Valafar or at least to see what he thinks of it. I'm hoping it works and at least I can fill him in on what's been going on." I've felt bad excluding him for so long.

Not knowing what was going on had to be driving him just as crazy as it had been for me.

"I'll be in here tomorrow at the same time. That way we can plan this well. Is there anything I can do for you now? Where are you right now?" I knew she wanted to know but it would have to wait until tomorrow.

"I'll have to wait to tell you tomorrow. I think someone is coming and I don't want to risk getting caught by Angelita! I'll see you tomorrow." As soon as I said that I allowed myself to slip back into my physical body.

The one thing that I had not been able to control about projecting myself had been a rather large part of it. Feeling exhausted from it. At least now I could go to sleep, and I knew I would sleep well.

Chapter Ten
The nursing home

I felt incredibly tired. I wished I could have slept in a little longer. Dragging myself out of bed. I knew I couldn't indulge myself in extra sleep yet. I promised myself that when all of this calmed down, I would spend a week in bed doing absolutely nothing. Getting dressed; I rushed out of the house. I almost expected to see either Sophie or Sydney, except I hadn't seen either as I left. Once out of the house I ran towards the road, I was thankful I wasn't going to have to run to the nursing home even though I kind of knew Zack would be waiting here for me. Not wasting any time, I got into his car as we headed off to the nursing home. I had to admit not exactly where I wanted to spend my time but there had to be a reason that Sydney asked for me to be here. Not that I had any expectations, however, none of them would have included working with other mortal humans, especially when you're trying to keep your secret and with my being new to magic, I might do something by accident and be seen. Unless Sydney wanted me to learn how to hide them around humans. Ones with Alzheimer's would be the best to make mistakes in front of, after all, they would be the ones who would most likely forget. I was positive they were wonderful people, and I hated the way I was thinking, but honestly not spending time around the elderly I had no clue what to expect. My grandparents died before I was born. Most of my relatives were either deceased or had nothing to do with me.

The idea of being inside a nursing home always seemed depressing. The idea of being cooped up in a building when you're old and not able to take care of yourself any longer. Your life became those four walls around you but then I guess I wasn't that far off from living like that. Losing your freedom and independence sounds horrible to me. We came rather early in the morning, not many other visitors were here other than the staff that was working. I was curious about what we would be doing as volunteers. I felt like I was standing inside of a hospital, it wasn't one of the more relaxed villa or home style nursing homes. Making our way to the main desk, there had been a list of things for us to do. Nothing major just minor things to help the place keep up, making sure different ones had things they needed.

We hosted a bingo game for some of the residents even though Zack had to announce the numbers. I couldn't get my voice to carry loud enough for them to hear me. The medical facility was an average size with at least one hundred beds even though only sixty of them had been filled. I felt depressed knowing most of them would not remember me the next day that I came in. We spent time talking to a few of the residents and playing games with them. At least this part I liked. I was learning from one of the ladies how she used to be a nurse herself. She didn't have any family left but she had a large box full of pictures we had looked through. She even had pictures her daughter made for her when she was little. She didn't want to talk about her daughter since remembering she passed away depressed her more. I learned she was in a car accident when she died. Many were here because they had no one to care for them, and for others, the reasons were unlimited. Except for this particular woman who suffered from a traumatic brain injury from the car accident causing her to be here, since she couldn't take care of herself. Many of the people I got to know felt more like family. I found myself loving my job here, helping. I can't say everyone was ecstatic to humor my visit but for the most part, they were happy to have a visitor.

It felt like a long day, and I still wasn't sure why I was supposed to be here. Even if it was to volunteer or even to get me out of the house, I wondered if what I did today even helped? I didn't feel like I made a difference at all. Zack kept reminding me that while we were there many of the residents didn't have family or anyone else for that matter to visit them. That spending time made a difference. I guess if I had been in the same circumstances, I would be happy with anyone that wanted to visit. I planned on being out for the rest of the night hanging out with Zack and his friends, even Avani Isha was going to join us as soon as she was finished with her shift. First, I wanted to make a stop at the store to pick up a few things. Not telling Zack what I was getting I told him he would figure it out tomorrow. I ran into the store while he had parked. Not taking too long I brought everything out leaving it in the car as we joined the rest of the group at the pub.

Despite the small-town setting, the pub was surprisingly crowded. As I stepped inside, an energetic, bouncy person suddenly embraced me from behind before I could get a glimpse of their face, though I already knew it could only be Melanie. Across the room, I caught Zack's eye as he tried to slip through the crowd, a guilty smile on his face. I didn't need an announcement to know he had tipped Melanie off about my arrival.

"I can't believe you're here!" At least she didn't know I had already been here for a while as she introduced me to her friends; she told them that I had just got into town and Zack picked me up from the airport.

Zack later backed up this story by telling a few people that came in late that he was late himself because he had to stop at the airport to get me. At least no one asked where I was staying however for the time, I wasn't sure if Melanie knew either? After a few hours of listening to the regular music, they started karaoke. It didn't seem to matter if you sang well or not as long as they had fun, and several of them were enjoying themselves, when they would break out laughing when they were up on stage singing. I was surprised by what a good singing voice Zack had. I almost think others were intimidated to go up after him. After a few hours of this, the bar closed the karaoke and switched back to the music again. It was nice to have a change. Even though I liked the party music they played when I went out with Lorah, this place had more variety. Almost like the weather if you didn't like the music playing now just wait and it will change to something else.

I think I had just as much fun watching everyone else doing things then I did when I joined in. Melanie and Zack's friends were friendly and willing to act goofy with anyone. If I had wanted to sit on the side, I never would have been allowed to, at least someone was always grabbing my hand and pulling me out onto the dance floor to dance either with the group or individually. I was hoping Sydney didn't have too much planned for tomorrow, after volunteering at the nursing home for a second day and after tonight. I was going to be sore but tired as well. There was only one time I panicked when I saw a stranger standing over by the door that seemed like he was watching us. He hadn't stayed around even though I knew Sydney would want to know about it in case he was someone she knew. It was much harder for her to hide anywhere than it would be for me.

Even though I loved listening to music. I never used to stay for very long. This had to be the longest I ever stuck around. I swore I was going to be deaf from the loud music by morning. Quite a few started to leave. I hinted to Zack that I was ready to leave also. I know Melanie was dying to know where I was staying, she invited me to stay at her apartment. I had to tell her I was staying with another friend while I was here, but I promised I would see her again. Hugging her goodbye, we headed out for the car. The stranger who had been hanging around was facing the opposite way, either talking on a cell phone or doing a convincing job talking on it. As we drove away, I tried to cover my face hoping the person hadn't seen what car we had arrived in. I kept an eye on him as we passed, not that he looked at us once. I was hoping I was being paranoid but either way, I still had to be careful. Even Zack noticed my odd behavior.

"Who are you hiding from?" Curious, Zack looked out my window trying to figure out who I would hide from.

"I don't know if he is anyone, but a stranger was watching our group. I must be very careful not to get caught. Before we go home stop by the store real quick, I want to go in and get one more item." At least we were still in town and not far from the store.

I should have gotten a prepaid phone earlier, so I could easily prove that I called Valafar, instead of attempting to communicate with him through supernatural means. I could show I had done a very normal mortal action outside of the magic. Not only for that reason but in case they tried to trace the phone. I knew Zack would be safe. They wouldn't end up at his home. Finding the cheapest phone, I could and put the minimum amount of money allowed on it. I slipped it into my pocket so Zack wouldn't see it and ask questions. As I had come out of the store the stranger was still nearby instead of being over by the club, he made his way over to the store. He definitely wasn't human for moving this fast. I didn't recognize him, but I knew I couldn't lead him to Sydney, not that I knew if she was safe or not, he might have been there first. Getting back in the car, Zack looked at me rather strangely.

"Didn't they have what you wanted or is this another thing that I'll find out about tomorrow?" Trying not to let the person following us know that I was aware of them following us.

"Not exactly, but when you drive away drive slowly and don't take me back to the house yet. Is there somewhere other than your apartment we can drive to?" I was hoping I might be able to contact Sydney.

I could try and do it here in the car, but if we were being watched the person would pick up on what I was doing.

"We can go to my grandparents' house. I dropped them off at the airport this morning to join my parents on the last two weeks of their vacation. What's going on that you can't or don't want to go back to the house?" I figured he would be asking me this, after all, I would be curious too.

"I'll explain soon but I'm positive that I'm being followed and I'm not ready to lead them to Sydney. They might have already found her, or they might not have but on the off chance, they haven't. I don't want to lead them right to her. She's not exactly in the best of shape right now to defend herself." I was hoping she was still safe.

I was tired from such a long day; all I wanted to do was go home and curl up under my warm blanket.

At least we were heading out in the opposite direction. I hoped the person wasn't going to surprise us inside the house but if he was a vampire, at least I would find out if he had to be invited or not to get in. I could use the gift I was given. There was no way

185

I was going to risk Zack's life for mine. Even though I was sure it would mess up whatever plans Sydney was making for us.

"In case I end up telling you anything, just trust me; I'll explain later but I might not always have time at the moment, just in case we get ambushed while we are at the house." Taking a glance at him I didn't want to scare him, but I needed to know he would listen.

"You won't have a problem with me." Still concentrating on the road and going slow as I had asked him.

I noticed every so often there was a fast movement alongside but not close enough to easily see. I wanted Zack to drive slowly so it would appear we were not noticing anyone following and to remain low-key as humans would be. We drove much further than I would have preferred but at least it was secluded, so hopefully, this will work. Pulling up to the house the garage door opened as we pulled the door close behind us. Getting out carefully almost worried the person would have already come in without us seeing him. I followed Zack into the house as he locked the door behind me.

"What do we do now?" Not that I had too much of a plan right now.

"First, I need to find out if that guy is going to do anything other than watching us, but I need to make sure you're safe before I try to project myself, I need to make sure he doesn't see me do this and isn't inside when I do it, because I won't be aware of what is going on here. I want to make sure you're safe also." While I spoke to him, we worked on closing all the drapes in the living room making sure no one could look in.

"You're going to be safe also, won't you?" I knew he was concerned but I didn't have an answer.

I had no idea how this was going to turn out. I knew the main family was searching for both of us and regardless wanted the power or at least to control me if they knew I had it.

"I can't say either way, but in case we are being overheard we need to watch what we talk about out loud." I never tried to meditate with any distractions before other than feeling rushed by my old instructors.

I turned on the television to a game show hoping it might cover up any other sounds since I still hadn't perfected controlling my outer self, not that I think I showed too much. Sitting down in front of the couch, Zack sat down next to me.

Visualizing Sydney. I hoped to show up at the house which I did. It took me longer than what I was used to. Sydney had been patiently waiting for me downstairs by the door. I surprised her by showing up behind her. Trying not to scare her I called out to her.

"Sydney. I'm behind you. I couldn't come home. I was being followed but I don't know who he is? But he seems rather interested in sticking to me. I'm in a safe spot for now that no one can see me. I didn't want to risk bringing him to you in case they hadn't found you yet." Her once youthful features had rapidly deteriorated since our morning encounter, the signs of aging now etched deeper into her face as she slowly turned to face me.

"That is a wise decision not to come back here yet. Have you used your magic at all? If not, do your best to blend in with the mortals. I have found that no one knows you were dating Valafar, so they may believe him even more if he is willing to help us. We don't have as much time as I hoped if their messenger has already found you." It felt strange hearing the television in the background still being aware of my body and hearing Sydney and walking around in the house at the same time.

"I haven't used any magic. That way if I'm seen, they can only report that I haven't done anything, hopefully, they will assume I don't have any. I don't know if it will be safe for me to come back tonight since I don't know how long this person will be following me, but I can stay at the place I'm at. The people are not here for two weeks. I'm sure Lorah is waiting for me. We arranged to meet tonight, it's supposed to be safe, but I will be projecting there, so no worries of being followed." I was hoping that if we were running out of time, Sydney would tell me what she still needed me to do before time ran out completely.

"Stay there tonight as long as you're safe and then go to the nursing home as usual tomorrow, I'll take care of my part, but project to me to let me know what Valafar is willing to do for you. If he's loyal to you then you can tell him where to find you." For some reason, I didn't like the sound of that.

I hoped whatever she was planning, Sydney was going to be safe also. I had to admit to myself that as much as I wanted to get away from her when we were stuck with the others, I didn't hold anything against her. She did what she needed to in that environment.

"What if they follow him here, are you sure I should tell him where we are? I trust him but if they can find me then I'm sure they would follow Valafar if he traveled here." Why would she want us to share our location now?

"They are already tracking you. If they follow him then it's fine. There's a reason for it and you are to trust me. Now go find him and talk with him." I hated to admit it, but the pieces were slowly coming together not that I liked the idea of it.

As I allowed myself to slowly drift back to my body, I didn't completely come out of it. I wanted to keep the same state of mind so it would be easier to block out the sounds from the room. I was physically in and moved to the place I needed to be.

Focusing on Valafar's room as we had agreed on. It would look legitimate if Lorah had gone there to collect something that was forgotten by Valafar rather than be seen by accident going into my room. I was surprised by what I had seen, not that I had been betrayed by Lorah, but after she spoke to Valafar he must have decided not to be anywhere else but here. I was very happy to see him right now.

"I was beginning to wonder if you were still going to show up tonight. I was able to change my meeting so I could be here. Lorah told me that she was going to be meeting with you tonight. No one else knows, but she said you needed my help. Anything you need, consider it yours. I'll help any way that I can, just tell me what you need or want me to do." Lorah was in the room also eager to hear what I had to say.

"I'm being followed at the moment, so I must be careful how I contact anyone right now. Oddly enough I am allowed to tell you where I am. I'm not back at the cabin since it's destroyed; besides, I assumed they would have looked for me there already. I don't know how you will do this, but we thought if your family heard neither of us had the magic power, they might leave us alone. I'm sure I know how Sydney is going to prove she's mortal without any powers again, but I'm still not sure how I'm supposed to prove that I don't have them, unless you can come up with something?" I was hoping he would be able to come up with something since he knew his family much better than we did.

"I'm sure I can convince my family that you no longer have any powers. I could have you work for me as you did before and offer this as my watching over you to make sure there isn't anything, I'll work it out more once I've had time to think about it. The only problem I can think of is how to explain your long life. How is Sydney going to prove it for herself?" I hadn't thought

189

about the long life span myself, it wasn't as if I could have Valafar change me, otherwise most likely I would end up like Sydney.

I might not be eternally mortal, after all, shades do die and with the power, we were associated with shades from the way our lives are affected.

"I don't know how to explain that either, but for now hopefully this will delay things until we can find a longer solution. As for Sydney, I think she will be at the nursing home tomorrow also." I wasn't entirely sure how her plan was going to work. I guess I would have to wait like the others.

"You still haven't told us where the nursing home is? How am I supposed to find you?" With all the explaining I guess I had forgotten an important part.

"Do you remember asking me about my friends. I said I lost touch with all of them. The only ones I could think of at the time had been Zack and Melanie, my pen-pals, distance was never a problem since we always wrote. There's only one nursing home in town. It should be easy to find the address of the old house Melanie and Zack grew up in. It should be in my address book, and I know Lorah has that. I had it with me when I first came here, and I know it was on top of my things when I last saw it." At least I hoped she still had it.

"I remember looking through it, which might be why they decided to check out the town there. I'm sure I wasn't the only one who saw it. I know where the location is at least. Go ahead and go, we will try to figure something out. Don't worry, we'll do everything we can to keep you safe." At least now something was going to happen, that all of this was either going to end, or something I would rather not give too much thought to right now, I did wonder what else could possibly happen.

"Before you leave, make sure you call my cell phone number. That way it will explain how I found you, I'm sure their spy already knows I haven't been there yet, and I don't want them thinking I knew this whole time without saying anything. Saving you time from earlier I told them I hadn't heard from you at all." At least it sounded like a reasonable solution.

Reaching into my pocket it was empty. Then it hit me.

"I guess I haven't mastered the projecting with things yet, I'll have to work on it if I ever get a chance to. I'll call you as soon as I get back into my physical body." Leaning forward I hugged Valafar even though I wished I could have done more than that.

I didn't want a make-out session in front of Lorah.

"Zack is just a friend? You don't have to answer. I'm just curious?" It was cute that as long as Valafar has existed he could possibly feel jealous.

"Yes, Zack is only a friend, and I've made it very clear to him about my relationship with you and he doesn't have a problem with it, he's very much like a brother." I didn't want to tell him right now that Zack was the one I was hiding out with at the moment.

I didn't want to make Valafar worry. Trusting Valafar and Lorah could come up with a plan. I slowly let myself drift back to my body. As I opened my eyes Zack was still staring at me wondering what I was doing. I could only guess he was curious if anything happened since it's hard to tell from his side of things. Making sure I wouldn't forget. I reached into my pocket and pulled out the prepaid phone dialing Valafar's phone number letting it ring. He had even been faster than Zack was when answering the phone.

"I was worried something happened. I thought you would have called quicker." I couldn't help but laugh.

"I couldn't have moved any faster if I tried. Besides, I already called you faster than I needed to, your just overly anxious. I promise I'm safe." Putting my hand over Zack's mouth I didn't want him to speak while I was on the phone.

I knew he wanted to ask who I was speaking to and why I hadn't used his phone. As I told Valafar I loved him, that I would see him tomorrow, part of his question had been answered.

"So that was Valafar then?" Leaning away from me against the couch now.

I could tell he wasn't looking forward to tomorrow.

"Yes, that was Valafar and he's coming tomorrow with my friend Lorah. They probably won't get here until at the end of our shift tomorrow, you're still planning on staying longer tomorrow hopefully?" I was hoping because Valafar was coming that Zack wouldn't cut short his time there, even though I would understand if he did.

I loved him as a friend just sadly I didn't feel the same as he did. I should have been more careful and not let him insist on helping. I hated hurting him, but I made sure to be careful how close I got to him and acted around him which sucked. It's never easy when one person has feelings when the other doesn't. And who knows, if I didn't know Valafar. I might have given him a shot. He was genuinely kind and certainly didn't hurt that he was a handsome man.

"I don't think I'll be able to stay. I was going to help for the morning and then take off unless you need a ride?" I felt bad having him feel I only needed him for things.

"I couldn't have asked for a better friend. I know that's not what you want to hear but you have made this horrible experience bearable. I do wish we could have had more time." It didn't exactly sound good to me either.

"You don't have to try to make me feel better. I know you were never available. It's just hard to convince myself of the truth. We can sleep out here in the living room if you want. You can

192

have the couch. I'll grab the sleeping bag from the hallway closet."
Standing up I watched Zack leave the room.

I could feel my heart ache. I didn't want to make him feel any more uncomfortable than he was already feeling. Sadly, I didn't know what else to say. I felt bad trapping him like this. I shouldn't feel like this, but he is a good friend, and regardless of the reason, I hated hurting him. Taking a blanket and pillow from him as I watched him set up where he was sleeping on the floor. Not tired yet I laid down on the couch pulling my blanket up over my shoulders as I could only see Zack's backside as he faced the fireplace.

I wasn't the only one that didn't seem tired even though Zack didn't move very much probably pretending to be sleeping to keep from talking to me. I needed to get up and walk around so I used the excuse of using the bathroom. Closing the door behind I hate to admit. I snooped around mainly out of boredom. I used to have a bottle of perfume, a razor, and floss in my medicine cabinet. I never did keep a lot in there; this one was filled on all four rows of medications and crèmes. Not wanting to stay in here too long. I opened the door to a very light snore coming from the living room. At least he finally fell asleep, sad to say but I almost think he needed me to be out of the room. Laying down on the couch it hadn't taken me very long to fall asleep either.

At least I knew I slept soundly enough when I was startled awake by the phone ringing. Jumping up off the couch and pulling it out of my pocket, I answered it. I assumed it would be Valafar or Lorah since they were the only ones I had given the number to. When I had gone to answer it, Zack was already awake excusing himself to the restroom. I wished I had caller identification on this thing. Not that I had a chance to say hello, but Valafar started talking right away.

"I need you to do exactly as I say. Your volunteering at the nursing home is a way for you to find a safe place for Sydney to be cared for during the remaining part of her life. You had not contacted us until yesterday because you were fearful of how the others would react when they found out you lost the power. The last thing you remember is a very bright light shooting through the air almost like a shooting star going away from the two of you. When you see me, you are to treat me the same way you would the others. They do not know we were personal at all; it helped a little with the display that Lorah put on for the others at the pool with you. They are assuming the boy you're with right now is your boyfriend." He cleared his throat before finishing.

I knew he hadn't liked calling Zack my boyfriend, not that I wanted to risk using him. Quickly regaining himself, Valafar started to speak again.

"This is the story you need to stick to. Lorah and I will be there in about eight or nine hours as long as we don't get hung up on the way there. The rest of the family is now coming. They are mainly checking out the story that I gave them. They will believe Sydney does not have powers once they realize mortals are caring for her and they don't distinguish her from the other patients. I already have her being checked in by a loyal friend of mine. Don't worry, she will be fine. I'll see you soon."

I wasn't given a chance to say goodbye other than to hear the other side hang up. Sitting down on the couch I felt strange. I know it was only pretending for now, but it felt strange. I was supposed to treat Valafar like the others. I've never been afraid of him. I guess if this all worked out it will be worth it for now. I wasn't sure if I should tell Zack but then if anyone questioned him, they would find out he wasn't my boyfriend other than just a friend. Coming back into the living room he did have a rather curious expression on his face.

"That was a rather quick phone call. I would have thought he would have wanted to talk to you for a while unless that wasn't him and from your expression, you don't look too happy." At least he had part of that right.

I wasn't happy because the reality hit me that the others would be here soon. Getting up and grabbing the paper that was by the house phone. I started writing down everything that Valafar said to me over the phone. I didn't want to risk saying it out loud in case anyone was listening. I also wrote in the first line; do not read this out loud. Handing it to Zack, he read it with interest. I could tell when he came to the part about the others assuming he was my boyfriend, he blushed a little, smiling, I knew he liked the idea of them assuming this. Pointing out the line about the others' assuming Zack was my boyfriend, he smiled a bit longer.

"How did he respond to this part?" I knew he would be curious.

"How do you think he responded. Exactly like you if you were in the reverse." As soon as he was done with the paper, I sent it through the shredder near the phone even shaking up the contents inside so it couldn't possibly be found and taped together.

His smile never once left his face as we both walked into the kitchen; we still had two hours before we had to be at the nursing home.

"If we are supposed to be dating then let me get you something for this morning." As he pulled out my chair for me to sit.

I was curious what he would end up making. Grabbing two bowls and two spoons he brought over the cereal. I tried not to laugh; it was too cute.

195

"An expert of the cereal recipe. I see your angle." Smiling I couldn't help it.

"It's even better with more variety of flavors that you mix." As he began to pour four different kinds of cereal into his bowl, I couldn't help but wonder what was going to happen between us once it was all over.

After eating breakfast, I went through his grandmother's closet. Zack said he would explain to her why and felt she wouldn't mind. I hoped it wouldn't bother her even though she might wonder why we were here alone, or why I wasn't over at Melanie's place borrowing clothing from her. Flipping through her closet. There wasn't much to choose from. Many of the pieces were very bright colors with lots of floral print, grabbing the only navy-blue shirt with cream floral print. At least we were rather close to the same size. I wore a pair of loose jeans, and using a pin helped keep them tighter around my waist. I couldn't wait for the shower. The hot water was going to feel good. Zack let me know he was up much earlier before I woke up taking a shower so it would be available for me.

Setting the clothes next to the sink on the small stand with a clean towel on top. I set the water temperature leaving my clothing on the floor outside of the tub. I closed the shower door. It hadn't taken very long for the walls to steam up as I rested my head under the hot water. It felt good standing here until I heard a strange sound. It's not the first time I heard a sound like this before. I always worried when I was in the shower thinking someone was either talking to me or in the bathroom even though any time I had looked or checked no one was ever calling or in the bathroom with me. Usually, the echo in the bathroom plays tricks on my ears. Except this sound wasn't going away, taking a very small peak out the shower door I closed it rather quickly when I saw Zack brushing his hair. I spoke up loud enough for Zack to hear me over the running water.

"Taking the dating thing a little far?" Not that I wanted to be rude, but I almost didn't want to try to get dressed with him in the bathroom with me.

We may be pretending but I knew Valafar wouldn't like this let alone the fact I wasn't very comfortable with it either.

"Actually. If I was taking the dating thing too far. I would strip and join you, but I think even you would knock me out. Besides, I don't want to make you angry. I wanted to change my shirt and brush my hair, unfortunately I left the hairbrush in here. I figured by now the shower would be steamed up and I'm right I can't see anything." He paused for a second before he told me he couldn't see anything.

"I'm sure you can't see anything." I tried to sound as sarcastic as possible.

"I'm sure you will want to come out at some point, so I'm heading out but one last comment, he's lucky. I can't find fault with anything I see." Before I could complain I heard the door shut.

I peeked out the door making sure he wasn't waiting there for me. If possible, I wasn't going to share this with Valafar at all. There was no need to share this moment with him since it was harmless, I felt if I did, it would have given it more meaning.

Getting out of the shower I didn't waste time getting dressed. I hurried as fast as I could in case Zack decided to bring the hairbrush back in to offer for me to use. Instead, I grabbed the comb rinsing it under the faucet with hot water first before I used it on my hair. At least he was sitting on the couch ready to leave even though I was ready. I hadn't wanted to go. I had that quick moment of panic, what if things didn't work out? Trying to remain calm we both got into the car as Zack drove us away from the house now heading on our way to the nursing home. At least I knew the first few hours were going to be fine. I didn't know if the others would come straight in or if they would wait for me to come out? Would they come in to check to see if Sydney was checked in?

I wondered how long she was going to get stuck staying in the nursing home even though I hated to admit it, other than me, there wasn't anyone to take care of her. Her supposed boyfriend she had started dating after her life changed, wasn't much of a relationship. It was purely business-related or at least as she said an agreement between her and Luther. She had become a heartless person. She blamed herself. She made the agreement except, she said to live the way she did and to be around the people she was, she had to harden herself. She chose this not because she had to, but it had been the best way she could see to protect the one she was in love with. I couldn't help it, but I kept thinking of Romeo and Juliet when I thought about her. The only difference in her story the guy who had no clue still lived.

Watching as we came closer to the nursing home, I could see the same stranger standing outside of the building. I was curious if he would say anything to me as I went in which he hadn't, he still pretended not to be watching us as we walked in. I made sure I brought the plastic bag with me that I had left in the car the night before. At least if anything I could try to stay busy with the personal project with the lady, I was going to be spending time with today. Avani was standing at the counter as she was happy to see both of us show up.

"Mrs. Mueller is excited to see you today, you let her know you had a project you wanted to work on with her?" Avani seemed rather happy to see me not empty-handed as I came in.

"Yes, it's all in the bag. I'm looking forward to this myself." Leaving I had walked straight to her room.

She was the first and main person I was going to be spending time with this morning. She was sitting up in her bed instead of the chair she had been sitting in before when I first met her. Pulling the chair over to her bed. I sat down and started pulling out some of the items from the bag. First, we had taken all her pictures out of the shoeboxes and started labeling those that she could remember while we put them in the photo album. She didn't remember going through them before with me, but I sat there listening to her letting her tell me again. It made her so happy to share her memories. We probably spent about two hours doing this. We had the rest of the pictures put in the albums when she told me she was feeling tired today.

I knew while she rested, I could have visited another resident. I felt I needed to stay here. Before she fell asleep, I pulled out the book she wanted to be read. I read it to her as she lay there relaxing until she had fallen asleep. Marking the page to keep track of where we had left off, I set it on the dresser so it would be there for next time. After sitting here for at least two hours still holding her one hand. I noticed it felt limp as a light beep sounded from her bed. A few nurses had come into the room to check on her. The alarm I had heard let them know the weight had shifted in her bed, usually to let them know when a patient was getting out but this time it had let them know she passed on.

I had been so busy with my thoughts I hadn't thought about the possibility that she might pass away. Then suddenly it hit me that Sydney was here somewhere and at some point, she was going to pass away much earlier than she should have. Avani relaxed my hand putting her arm around my shoulder and taking me out into the hallway. I felt more in shock than anything else as she walked me to her office for privacy. I hadn't even been thinking. I let her lead me in. I never even noticed her closing the door behind me other than sitting down in the chair she pointed out for me.

"I hope this doesn't deter you from volunteering in the future. It is sad to see someone pass away but the way I look at it. I would rather have them die with me than to die alone. I know how happy you made her and how excited she was looking forward to doing the project with you. I'm glad she lived long enough to finish it with you." Not even sitting behind her desk Avani pulled one of the other chairs over next to mine.

"I know when we get old, we are eventually going to die, there are so many things that can happen that can take it all away, it just sucks she was still young. How do you do it regularly knowing each one is going to die around you?" I still felt like I was in shock or rather I could feel hot and cold waves shooting through my body.

I had finally felt tears flooding down my cheek.

"I do it because I have the privilege of being one of the few that get to know them before they pass away, and like you, to hear their stories for one last time. I don't regret any of the many people I get to know here or have learned from. I had a patient teach me to knit, I've read many stories, and I've heard so many stories about childhood and growing up. I love people and this place fits me. I can do whatever I possibly can to make the last remaining time they have hopefully a happy one. I don't get paid much; I've been injured many times moving a patient or in other accidents. It's very tiring and yes depressing at times but I think of even Mrs. Mueller and remember her smile and know how happy she was. It makes it worth it. Even our cranky patients are worth my time. I have a few patients to check on before my shift is over today but feel free to stay in here until you feel better. Zack is in room one fourteen if you want to join him." Giving me a light hug, she left closing the door behind her.

I sat in the office almost feeling completely blank, not thinking of anything else other than the pictures we had looked through. When the puffiness from my cheeks and redness had gone down, I got up and walked out of the office. I could see Zack looking down the hallway until he looked back seeing me walking out of the office, he came over right away not hesitating he hugged me rather tightly.

"Let's get some fresh air. I could use it also." Still leaning against him it felt good still being held onto.

We walked outside, not going far, we walked over to the side lawn and sat down at the picnic table while Zack still hugged me.

"I can't believe I didn't notice she was going?" I know she had severe brain damage, but she wasn't old, I wished there was something more that I could have done.

I knew the stranger was watching us now probably wondering who I was talking about. It almost seemed like he was sympathetic to me for a moment from the expression on his face.

"As soon as I heard she passed away I came looking for you. I also checked on Sydney and she's not accepting visitors, otherwise, I thought seeing her might cheer you up. Avani is spending time with her right now, helping her get acquainted with the place. She didn't seem upset when I saw her walking around being shown the different places and things she can do here. She almost looked relieved." I think he was only telling me this to reassure me she was going to be alright here.

I was sure he knew I was concerned about her. I wished I could have seen her. As we sat there, I barely noticed anyone walk up to us as a shadow was now over us. We both looked up at the same time to face the others. Valafar wasn't joking when he said they would all be coming. There had been at least twelve of them standing in front of us. My first panic set in. I was worried about what they might do with Zack as I laid my eyes on Valafar. He almost looked hurt finding me sitting there with him. I wished I could have explained but at least the spy seemed to be doing that for me.

"I think it's time you gave us some privacy. We will leave now to go talk elsewhere. Pointing out a large van I knew they wanted me to go with them. Valafar was already getting in probably to make sure we were both in the same vehicle. Zack held onto me tighter being protective of me.

"It's okay Zack, I will call you as soon as I get a chance to let you know I'm alright. Don't worry. I'll probably be back before you know it." Not wanting to but at least Zack knew how to play it up, as Valafar looked away not wanting to see Zack not only hugged me close but also gave me a rather passionate kiss goodbye and I hadn't fought it.

Oddly enough I almost felt like this might be the last time I would see him. Standing there for a moment. I waited for him to go back into the nursing home before I joined the others in the van. I could hear Angelita whisper to one of her brothers, at least the story of the boyfriend is true, as she closed the door to the van, we drove off. I had no clue where we were going but I almost felt as if for a moment if I were to die, I would be okay with it.

Chapter Eleven
Proof

During the entire trip, Valafar hadn't looked in my direction once. He kept staring out the window. I hoped he wasn't too upset that I was sitting outside with Zack the way we were, not that I had anything to feel ashamed of. I admit the kiss was overboard, but it did make it believable. He was comforting me as a friend should have after something that depressing, not that I normally kissed my friends. Otherwise, all I could think of was perhaps he was trying to hide any connection to me by not paying attention to me, unless he felt betrayed by me or who knows, maybe didn't trust me anymore? I guess I'll find out soon enough what was about to be my fate. I was surprised no one asked any questions of me or even tested me yet, unless they were waiting for us to get out of the town and far enough that if I were to scream no one would hear me? Only two others stayed behind going into the nursing home. No doubt wanting to make sure that Sydney was being looked after as Valafar warned they would. Luther and one of his brothers had chosen to stay behind. He assured me she would be safe. That it wasn't worth it for them to bother with her if she had been human let alone surrounded by so many other mortals, they didn't want to draw attention to themselves.

It felt as if we were traveling forever, I had even checked my watch to see what time it was finding out four hours passed by. That was the longest four hours I ever spent sitting still quietly. If they hoped I would crack, or act scared from all this silence for this long. I probably would have if it had kept going on. Even though I did wonder what they were thinking or if I was reacting the way I should? As we stopped, the side door opened while I was escorted out, I wasn't familiar with where we were now. Looking around it looked like a wide-open field which hadn't made me feel confident at all. We couldn't go any further apparently in the van, even though I'm sure they were happy to get to the speed they were used to. While I watched the others even Valafar take off in a shot. I was wondering if they planned on leaving me here. I stood there for a moment thinking I was being left alone here, which I wouldn't have minded until I felt a tap on my shoulder. Sakarabru wasn't there a moment ago, but I knew what he meant as he stood in front of me, and I climbed onto his back. I would have preferred walking and catching up to the others. I hated traveling this way.

Not that we traveled too far. The path narrowed as we had gone uphill until we came to a rather strange-looking place that was closed inside of a mountain. The pressure from the wind against my face had not only dried out my eyes making them sensitive, but it was also incredibly dark in there. At first, I dared open my eyes as it looked like Sakarabru had chosen to jump over the side of a cliff almost expecting to emerge in several feet of water. Instead, we landed on the other side, being slowed down by a gust of wind. I did my best not to panic and send myself somewhere else even though he would have gone with me because I was holding onto him. I tried to act as purely mortal and human as I used to be before I was given this power. I wished I could have paid attention to what the surroundings looked like in case they decided to leave me here. I would have no idea how to get back. But then looking at their expressions I wondered if they intended on letting me go back. Taking in the sights, I could see a small stream reaching up halfway inside of the cave as the rest of it opened even larger to reveal what used to be a city. The once-grand building now stood with its doors barely clinging to their hinges. Peering inside, it appeared as if bombs had ravaged the interior, leaving the place in a state of ruin. Though I was no expert, the dark, shimmering rock formations that adorned the crumbling walls struck me as remarkably beautiful, hinting at the structure's former grandeur.

A small fountain in the center wasn't working or the only thing that caught my attention. The picture that was drawn on the far-left wall that had caught my attention. It was difficult to make out the whole picture. Something had smashed it. The little parts I could make out were pieces of people. I wondered if someone was trying to get rid of it. It almost looked like three children and others on the other sides of them.

I hated knowing when others were talking about me and not including me in the conversation. I was sure I would eventually find out. I wished I could hear as well as they did so I would know before it hit. If I was going to die, I wished they would get on with it and get it over with unless they were getting some sick thrill knowing I was frustrated by all of this. Maybe they liked playing with their prey first. Even Valafar seemed to get into their conversation occasionally looking angry. As soon as they finished speaking, Angelita stood forward. In a short amount of time, I had known their family. She seemed to be the one taking the lead even though she never went against Sakarabru. He seemed to be the main leader of the group or the final decision-maker.

"To prevent any further betrayals, we have decided if you truly do not have any magic left, we no longer need you, however, you will no longer be a threat other than possible exposure to us. Instead of handing you over to Valafar so that he can keep an eye on you. We will hand you over to someone else if they wish to use your services, after all, there will be no real need for you. We did however promise not to kill you from the test, but we never promised how badly you may be damaged." As she said the last words almost a glint of light crossed over her eyes in delight as she took a quick look back at Valafar.

I couldn't imagine who she would turn me over too? Not that I wanted to be tested after. How would they find out I didn't have any power? If it was going to be detrimental, I almost wished I would die from it.

Before I knew it, they started the testing, and I was already on the ground as I was knocked over by something rather hard that whizzed by me. I felt like I had been hit by a linebacker except for no one from their circle had moved. It felt as if I had water running down my back until I reached back and found it was blood. Feeling shocked by this I had to ask.

"How the heck is making me bleed from something I didn't even see supposed to prove I have power or not?" I didn't even bother standing up.

I directed the question at Angelita herself. She stood silently, pausing before she responded. It seemed she wasn't trying to formulate her words but rather waiting expectantly for something to unfold.

"You're supposed to heal yourself." She stated it as if it was a known fact.

Even Sydney hadn't told me I could heal myself. I would have asked further questions trying to play the stupid card even though I hadn't known how to heal myself. They might think I wouldn't be able to defend myself well if I wasn't fully trained. They were only aware of the physical training I had while I was there. I had been trained by Sophie and the other former guardians in a dreamscape away from everyone else. I stood up, not that I hadn't wanted to but then I also didn't want to get smashed into the ground either.

At least this time I saw the next object coming for me. I would have blocked it long before it would get to me instead, I dropped to the ground letting it fly over me. I wasn't entirely sure what it was but personally, to me, it looked like a flaming bowling ball. This was a rather strange test unless they were trying to see how else I reacted to things. As evil as Angelita was, I couldn't help but feel she was holding back as I had seen the look on her face. I was right. I almost wished I could have been checked in by the nursing home also if they thought humans believed I was normal after being tested. I could be done with this already. The next step I hadn't been ready for. My body dropped to the ground as I was pulled into a dreamscape where only Angelita, Ruby, Damar, and Kristopher were standing. Oddly enough I was still aware of my own body here. One thing I hadn't learned yet was to keep my physical body upright during this. They whispered something to each other before bolts of light went shooting past me. I knew that no matter what happened. I was supposed to protect myself as a human, except never to show the magic or this would never be over. In here they could get away with whatever they wanted and Valafar couldn't possibly object. Sophie taught me that the only people that could make a dreamscape dangerous had been the Lady in black and the old Doc Denthre, except both had been dead. She sadly hadn't known if the Augustus family had that sort of power or not.

They had to know that people didn't die in here unless the person controlling it could. How did they plan on proving it here? The main thing that Sophie taught me had been whether something seemed out of the ordinary or beyond logic. There had to be something they were getting at. All I could think of was to use illusion to make me believe something worse than what was happening to use my power. But then in here, it had at one time helped mortals become as strong as others when fighting vampires. At one time it was only controlled by witches, shades, and a few other classes until it was taken over entirely by vampires.

They simply stood there making it appear as if nothing was happening until it looked like the ground was moving at an extremely fast pace, instead of running. I stood there knowing the ground wasn't moving. It had the illusion of moving. Looking back at them in wonder I was curious about what this was supposed to do. Then the area changed, the whole scene almost as if we were transporting from one place to another. I knew I wasn't doing this, but they were trying to trip me up into believing I was doing it and probably hoping I would try to stop it to prove it wasn't myself doing it? Instead, I simply let each scene shoot past making me dizzier as it went. Eventually, I closed my eyes so that the images wouldn't make my balance worse.

The next thing that happened had been landing in what looked like a lake. I was in the dead center under the water. I had never actually been in the water before so I wasn't sure if I could breathe in this or if it had been the same as in real life so in case, I held my breath for a while. It was starting to get hard to hold my breath any longer. I couldn't tell if they were still here or not, I could only assume I was getting lightheaded from not breathing.

What I hadn't expected as I wondered if I was hallucinating, the water began to get thick. Taking the chance to breathe in. I figured either way I would find out if I could breathe in it or die. Taking in a breath I choked at first but then thankfully I was fine. My eyes started to focus again even though I was surprised by the consistency of the water. It no longer looked like it was deep dark blue, it was now a thick red gooey substance. This can't be good. Concentrating as well as I could on my body, at least I knew I could choose to leave this dreamscape. I learned to do this before I ever had the power. Ignoring all the sounds around me. I almost think they felt they were about to prove their theory correct that I still had the power until they saw me disappear.

Reappearing in their physical bodies. I sat up rather slowly still feeling dizzy from the dreamscape. Looking at my body, it looked as if I was covered with tiny little lacerations, I had no clue what they were doing while I was out of my body but either way, I could see how sick Valafar looked not that he could do anything about it. I was beginning to think it was easier hiding. My body and most of the ground had been covered in blood. I almost felt too weak, so I didn't even try standing up this time. If they had intended on bringing me to the point of breaking, they were not too far. My entire body stung. I felt like passing out from being dizzy. One thing I had to admit to myself. I hadn't panicked the way I thought I would. I think knowing this was going to end one way or another took the fear out of it. But then it might have been the reason they still hadn't believed it. I was free of magic because of the lack of fear probably assuming I would heal myself once it was over and I had to admit I wanted to find a way. With the rest of the group talking between each other and Valafar listening. I wondered what they were going to do next. The ground felt harder than normal until I picked up a small piece. Now I know where the lacerations had come from, they must have shot them at me while I was out of my body. There were tiny pebbles all over the ground around me and their edges were still sharp cutting my fingers. Trying not to rest on them I sat up all the way waiting for the next torture test.

Sakarabru stepped forward motioning for the others not to join him as he walked over to me stopping only inches in front. His expression looked surprised except it hadn't shown in the tone of his voice. I detected neither emotion either way if he felt sorry for me or justified.

"What do you remember as you and Sydney disappeared from our sight? Do you remember any unusual sounds, sights, or feeling?" His tone revealed absolutely no reflection in his voice to show which part of his question he was more interested in finding out.

At least I knew I could answer his question. I hoped he wasn't going to get angry if I didn't answer it the way he wanted.

"It happened too fast, the last thing I had known, I was sitting in the chair and some kind of fast movement then next thing, I was getting up off the ground next to Sydney. It was raining hard so the first thing I thought about was trying to get out of the rain. I probably wouldn't have noticed the shooting star if it hadn't been for the rain that illuminated it so much. Sydney was out for a long time, and she looked massively aged. I didn't know what else to do so I waited a few days in the old farmhouse with her waiting for her to wake up. I didn't know how to contact you, and it took me a while to remember Valafar's number so when I did, I called it." Sadly, I didn't know if I should mention how Sydney wound up in the nursing home or not. I hoped they wouldn't ask. I could tell he was still waiting for more, so I tried to be careful of what I said.

"I didn't feel anything other than the cold. I was worried about getting out of the rain and it's not easy moving Sydney. It's not like I'm very strong, but I didn't have to carry her very far. Someone from the road driving by stopped and helped me carry her in, she was just too heavy. I couldn't move her myself. I don't remember hearing anything at all. There was a lot of thunder." I hoped that satisfied what he was looking for.

As he stood there, he seemed to ponder over what I told him. As he walked away from the others and then turned his attention to me again, I wondered if he intended on testing me any further. Another woman was standing by the far side as she walked up towards him; he hadn't seemed interested in stopping her, not that the expression on Valafar's face looked too good.

"We do not need you without any magic, being a mortal human, but we can't send you back to your old life. If for some reason you cross paths with any of us, it will be accepted that you are in our world but like anyone else, you try to expose us there will be no warnings. You will be killed. I have decided that your new watcher will be Alana. I know this will be in the best interest of all of us." He said as he watched for my expression.

How could this possibly be in the best interest? I swear I must be missing something. I watched as Angelita grinned at me as if she couldn't have thought of a better punishment now. As she left, the others seemed rather pleased with themselves. The only one that meant anything to me had been Valafar, and all I could see him do was mouth the words 'I'm sorry, he couldn't have known it would turn out this way. Every one of them left leaving me here with this woman and two men who accompanied her.

She stood there looking me over almost with a disgusted look on her face as if she had been left with a pile of dung left on her doorstep. Motioning for me to follow them I hadn't seen too much of a choice other than to listen for now. For as destroyed the first part had looked, the far back part of the city had a brand-new

211

look to it as I noticed others were working hard to restore the place. When we made it to the mid part of the city. I was handed over as Alana continued to walk to the further back area out of sight. Apparently, I was going to be part of the group restoring her city. Who knows, maybe after a while she might forget I'm even here and I could wander off? For now, it was better than what I was going through. Not even getting a chance to get acquainted. I was thrown into working, moving large pieces of brick and other pieces placing them in the center clearing out all the mini buildings along the wall that either resembled what would have been homes or businesses. Instead of just being covered with blood-dried lacerations. I now had dust and other pieces that were flying around in the air stuck to my sweat that was now stinging the old cuts. I had no idea how long we were working. There was no way of seeing the natural light in here, even though they had enough lamp posts lighting it up. I was relieved when we stopped, not that I knew where we would be staying. Following the others, we left the area we were working. Several had gone up along the far hill going into some of the homes built into the walls that had been abandoned. I followed the others even further close to the front where we first entered, now going up the steps on that far side of the city where it had still looked untouched or in desperate need of being fixed up. The one in charge stopped in his tracks as he had turned to me.

"When you hear the whistle in the morning it means you are to show up at once to start working, we are restoring this place until Alana gives us further orders. Until then you can pick any place up here that's not already occupied by someone. This is your permanent living space, the areas up further and closer to the cleaner part of the city belong to those that Alana had appointed or has an actual need for. We are workers and nothing more. Learn not to piss her off and stay out of her way and you should live long enough in this crap." As he said that he turned and continued up the steps until I could no longer see him.

I was tempted to back down the steps and wander away from here. I didn't care if I knew where I was, I would find something at some point. Sadly, the entrance was being guarded. At some point, I would find my way out. Halfway up I saw this tiny little place, barely squeezed in it but there was more space once I passed the collapsed part. Sort of reminded me of myself, a spot that just didn't seem to fit in here. Opening the door there was dust and a bunch of other things on the floor. Not that I was in the mood to clean it up. I used the broom inside to move things aside and on the carpet, I banged on the side cleaning it the best I could. I guess if I was going to be here for a while I might as well make the best of it.

Laying down on the carpet I planned on visiting Valafar but sadly I was so tired I simply fell asleep. I wanted to let him know that I was alright. I did not have the strength to stay awake. Besides, I didn't know if he would be home yet, and I certainly didn't want to risk going through all of that again. I know I could pop out of this place except I kept thinking about what happened earlier and I refrained from it. I promised myself I would eventually visit Sydney and let her know that I was somewhat safe for now. I was still worried about her. I hoped the others would leave her alone now. At least let her die in peace since I highly doubted, she had very much time left. At least looking around the room. I had some privacy, no one else was going to be coming in or at least I hoped not, two medium-size rooms and a closet.

At least the night seemed to go slow this time but then in the back of my mind. I kept thinking that at any moment someone was going to break into this relaxed state and do something. It was too hard to believe that after all the hiding from the Augustus family and hiding the fact that I still had magic, it was impossible to believe things were going to settle down and who knows, this might not be as bad as I thought? After all, where else was I going to go now? I guess if I get a chance to get away from all of this. I could go back and see Zack and Melanie. I'm sure Zack's worried about me. Not that I wanted him to see me looking like this. As I thought about them planning on projecting myself out the next day. I drifted off to sleep.

I had already started to wake up when I heard the whistle I was told to expect. Standing at my door watching everyone pass by wearing the same dirty clothing. I wondered once we were done what Alana would have us do, or would she find any need for us herself? Following behind everyone making our way back close to the same area to start work again, I had never worked this hard before but then I never needed to handle construction by hand, let alone do this. I operated a bookstore which wasn't difficult physically. The majority of the time we moved broken pieces of the building and moved them out to the center while others determined if any of the pieces could be reused. Another group was repairing the broken-down buildings. As we worked, I learned we were only fixing the back half of the city. It was so huge that the others were thankful not to be going to the other levels. Apparently the main to the far back area had been the areas that were destroyed. Then I heard the name. I was surprised; Sydney had been the main one who destroyed this place along with another family, and yet one more name I knew came up which was Sophie's. I only had one person attempt to speak to me but then he was more curious about why I was smiling.

"What are you smiling for? I don't think I've seen anyone smile in here since I've been here. It's refreshing." Starting to smile a bit, it almost made working more tolerable.

"I'm not sure you would want to know why." I wasn't sure if I should tell him or not?

"Try me. After being stuck here for so long. I could use something that would make me laugh or smile." Sadly, it hadn't occurred to me to wonder why the others were here.

"The two women who helped destroy this place; I know both. I found it interesting that they were the ones that did this." I know both had a history together.

I wished I could have known more about it. I did like seeing something they had a part of.

"If you knew both then what are you doing here? Seems like you would be dead or being used by Alana? If you have gifts, she likes to put them or anything she can use. Those people are moved elsewhere. My friend had a natural gift and he's in the main palace, but I don't see him anymore." As he spoke, he seemed sad but still working as hard as before not to draw attention to us while we spoke.

"Why are most of the others here? I know why I'm here not that I plan on staying here long." I was still hoping Valafar might find a way out for me.

Unless that was also part of his 'I'm sorry' letting me know it was out of his hands. I think it's time I stopped waiting for someone else to tell me how to fix it. I kept thinking over in my mind what Sakarabru had said that would benefit all of us? If they wanted to, they could eliminate Alana if she was a problem for them. Sydney used to work with them, and Sophie assisted when she was required, but none of them ever bothered her so what is their benefit with Alana?

"Most of us were snatched and forced to work here; others like you have been dropped off by the Augustus family to either work off some debt or trade for still living. There are some here that are not quite normal. They seem to be able to do things

215

beyond normal human beings. Those are usually brought up with Alana to work with her. I had a job at a construction company, and I made the mistake of working late to finish up and this person started talking to me. Last thing I knew I was being clobbered over the head and woke up here. I have no idea how long I've been here." At least I didn't have to wander too much, they did think I was nothing more than an average mortal that might be able to put in some work.

Before I was worthless to anyone. Thank goodness they seem to underestimate how stubborn the human spirit can be.

"Has anyone tried to escape from here yet?" I was curious if anyone had.

"Once, but he was killed before he had a chance to get very far. No one tries now. Not after seeing how they killed him." He seemed to shiver after remembering what happened.

"How often do you see the Augustus family here?" I was curious how involved they were with Alana let alone if Sophie knew about it.

I doubted Sydney knew especially if they both had tried damaging this place. Not that I could figure out why unless they were getting at Alana?

"Do you know why this place was attacked? I only know the two women because they were trying to pass on power to me except it hadn't taken." At least now he could have an idea why I was here without telling him the truth that I was keeping about myself.

"I don't know too much about the attack itself but rumors that there was some fight over power and Sydney, or Sophie had it. Apparently, Alana gets to live simply because she can make something that the Augustus family wants. She also controls whatever it is that goes in the thing to make it. The guy you see coming is the guy you want to be extra friendly too. He's the one that decides if you get food or not. If you die, they won't care. As they have put it, there are always other humans out there to replace you." That seems strange that Alana would get away with using humans unless it's not considered a threat since no one sees us here.

We had stopped talking and kept working until the guy set down a piece of bread for each of us as the second filled our water cup. I could guess why the Augustus family hadn't interfered with what was going on here. All creatures of any kind could do as they wished as long as it hadn't exposed them, the powers, or information about the existence of others. Cruelty was not something they condemned. I only knew about that because it had been why Valafar separated himself from his family. At least it made sense why they were even bothering with Alana. I knew Reyes used to work with her even though I wondered if she knew he was going to cross her. I still couldn't get over what he tried. He must have been desperate to get a hold of the power unless there was something I was missing. Why risk it if he was able to kill Sydney by biting her with the power in her, why would he risk getting the power with so many vampires around to do the same to him? I couldn't help that intuition feeling along with the hairs on the back of my neck as I felt them rise with a shiver. Could it be possible that he didn't die? It seemed like his family would have made sure they finished him off! If I ever get a chance to see Sophie, I was going to ask her a rather grim question. She was the only one I knew of that I could ask other than Nikolai. Depending on how long I'm here, at least I'll walk away from this physically stronger. Any time the guards walked by I tried to listen to their conversations not that they seemed to be talking about anything too interesting.

By the time it was time to stop again. I felt physically exhausted. Not as if we had a choice of doing something other

217

than going back to sleep, until we were stuck doing the same routine again. I couldn't help it. Regardless of how tired I was, or the fact this place was guarded rather well to stop anyone from leaving, there was no way I was staying here. There had to be a way out. Once I was alone, at least I hoped no one would be watching. I sat down leaning against the wall, that way anyone would assume I had fallen asleep sitting up. First-person I thought I should visit and it should be safe to have been Nikolai, no one would ever assume I would visit him. At least I didn't need to know where he was. I just had to think of him, except in case he was with others. I still didn't want to risk anyone seeing me. So far, the only place I learned to create had been the first room I had been trained in. I hoped he wouldn't mind me calling him to me. Focusing the best that I could I thought about him as I started to see a fuzzy image. All I could think of had been that maybe he didn't want to be called in and was blocking which is possible. They taught me to do this myself in case I ever needed it, not that I was able to get it to work every time. Giving up on calling him to me. I stopped and projected myself to him. He stood there waiting to see what I wanted.

"Why did you not announce it was you that was trying to call me, or I would not have refused it?" Simple enough I should have known to do that.

"Sorry, there's so much going on right now I forgot to. I need to ask a question, and it might sound gory when I ask it. What happened with Reyes body when he was killed?" Nikolai didn't seem surprised by my question at all.

"Actually. That happens to be something we are all curious about. Not that anyone has spoken about it. We had witnesses; he was torn apart by different ones but as soon as he had been, the body parts simply vanished in a cloud of smoke. We had no idea if you're safe and that's the first question you ask?" I think he was expecting another question or at least a comment from me.

"Right now, I'm in a city that Alana is trying to rebuild. I heard rumors that Sydney and Sophie had both been here before. For some reason the Augustus family seemed to think my being here would benefit the both of them. So far, they have me working to clean the place. I'm not sure how they are supposed to benefit. But I also found out Alana has something they want which I think is why they haven't done anything with her. I think Reyes might still be alive. No one thinks that I have any power but I'm not the only human stuck here. I hate to say it, as much as I hate being here, I think I'm needed here. I can't leave the others here, there must be a way of freeing them, the only problem I have with that is that Alana will replace them with others." I know at some point I will always come across something I don't like, and I probably won't always be able to do something about it, but feel I can do something about this, I am here after all.

"Don't do anything. Try to blend in as best as you can, I'll talk to Sophie, and we will figure a way of getting you out. I'm positive I know exactly where you are at and there is a way out from inside." I think he was waiting for me to agree to wait.

Just to reassure him I decided that I would say it.

"I'll wait until you speak with Sophie." It was true I would wait to see what would happen, but I didn't promise I wouldn't try something myself as well.

"You're not listening to me, are you? I swear the guardians are nothing like they used to be. You tell them to listen and wait, they did exactly what you asked; now you can see the wheels turning in their minds as they scheme. Just promise me you won't expose yourself. Can you at least do that?" I hated making him plead with me sounding so hopeful.

"Yes, I can at least do that. I'll be careful and blend." At least that I would do.

"Alright, at least I trust you with that part. I'll go find Sophie, pull me into the dreamscape when you're able to tomorrow." Nodding in agreement, I slipped away from him except I hadn't completely left.

I still wanted to see Valafar except I was worried in case there would be others at his home. Instead, I focused on Lorah.

As soon as I was in another room, I started looking around to see where I would end up. I know she had to be here somewhere. I almost expected to end up at Valafar's home still except this living room wasn't his. Much smaller but very nice looking, one large painting took up an entire wall while on the other side three smaller paintings that looked similar covered the opposite side. She didn't need paintings filling her walls. She had something incredibly beautiful, like fine works of art. It was almost as if I was looking directly at a jungle, the large leafy plants with a few colorful birds thrown in. Her real live toucan is in the corner of the room along with several real tropical plants. Her love seat was a dark foam green along with a black carpet and two black chairs. There were a few small pictures tucked in different areas. Now I was beginning to wonder if Sydney and Sophie were related, not that they were both in the same picture. There were several I didn't recognize. I had been paying so much attention that as I turned, I jumped backward. Standing there was a young man watching me without saying a word until I realized he was there.

"Looking for something?" More interested in what I was doing here he sat down on one of the chairs using both armrests.

He relaxed as if nothing was wrong. The only thing I could think of had been that I screwed up. I've been caught.

220

"I was looking for Lorah. I thought this was her place." I hoped he wouldn't ask me too many questions.

I wanted to leave now.

"Do you normally enter people's homes before you find out they live there or are home?" A rather valid point not that I wanted to get into a conversation.

"There's no real good way of answering that one. Do you know if Lorah is home or not? I need to talk to her." I was hoping at least he would let me know.

I don't know how I could have shown up here without her being here herself.

"Depends on who's asking for her?" Continuing to sit there now smiling at me I was getting frustrated.

"I can't exactly tell you who. I think I'll just leave." As I said that he stood and was next to me within a second.

At least I knew I was in the room with a vampire but what was he doing in her apartment, I don't know?

"She was here a few minutes ago but why won't you tell me who you are?" Now he was curious.

I didn't want to explain who I was; it's not like I knew who he was, and he certainly hadn't offered an introduction. I hoped to throw him off a little and at least I hoped Lorah would understand why I was being so secretive about things.

"It's not me but tell her Jess needs to know how Sydney is doing. Can you at least do that?" The expression changed dramatically on his face.

"How do you know Sydney?" Before I could even think to respond.

I felt my body being shaken as I popped out of the living room and back to my physical body. Opening my eyes, I was looking directly at one of the guards. I hadn't heard the whistle and there was no way I could have slept during it. Did they find

221

out what I was doing? Acting as if I was groggy and slept hard, I started speaking slowly.

"Did I oversleep the whistle?" Rubbing my eyes trying to play into the part the guard didn't seem too sympathetic.

"Alana has called for you. I am simply here to wake you and bring you to her." As he continued to stand there, I stood up following him out.

I was relieved that I decided to stay leaning against the wall when I had done this, I hoped my physical body wasn't doing anything while he waited for me to pop back. I noticed a few people around watching being careful not to be seen in case the guard were to look not that he ever did. I couldn't imagine what Alana would want with me now.

Instead of taking the middle part of the city heading back we stayed on the far-right side along the walkway temporarily disappearing from the main area where we worked earlier, which brought us to the far back area faster now heading up to the part Alana had built as her palace of sorts. It was so quiet back here with absolutely no sounds, not even the sound of wind blowing through. Making our way up the long winding steps we passed two more guards before we wound up in a large open room. Three large pillars were near the large balcony that overlooked part of the city down below. Then this woman appeared from the far end door. I only recognized her face from earlier, she had looked so different wearing all black. Many of the creatures that I met so far preferred black because it hid the dirt, or they blended in with the dark better. This time she was wearing a flowing light blue robe with white trim; she looked less threatening now than she had earlier unless that was what she was hoping to accomplish? If so, she did it well. Even her expression was relaxed unless she was more like me and felt stressed having such a powerful family like the Augustus family around.

222

I wasn't going to let my guard down in case she was trying to fool me winning me over with kindness. After all, I knew Sophie didn't care for her and I was sure neither did Sydney. Not that I've been thrust into all of this from the start as being something good, other than I felt I could trust Sophie and after a while I began to understand Sydney also. Nothing in her hands, she waved the guard away as she walked directly toward me.

"I'm sorry about your being put in the labor area, you were never supposed to be down there. I had so much occupied my thoughts the day we brought you back. We have a new room for you. You're free to roam the city as long as you don't try to leave. After all, you're not that free yet. We must make sure we can trust you with our secrets first, besides, most don't wish to be down in that filthy area. Come with me. I'll show you your new room." As she placed her arm around my shoulder trying to act as if she was a close friend, she steered me towards the door I had seen her first come out of.

I didn't have to walk very far until she showed me to my new room even though I liked the one I picked with the others, not sure why it was nothing more than dusty floors and walls. But then I reasoned it had been that the others I related to and trusted in this place. I didn't know what I was going to face in here. Following her into the room she motioned for me to close the door. The floor and walls were completely shiny black with small throw rugs in the lightest blue color. The bed in the room had the old wicker look with light blue bed sheets. If she was trying to use a calming color it was working. I wish the others had this also not that I knew what she wanted with me yet. As she sat down on the only wicker blue chair, she watched me almost as if she was trying to judge my reaction. Nowhere else to sit down I sat at the end of the bed not sure what to say.

"Very nice room, lots of blue and black." I felt naive for saying something so simple except for talking to someone I didn't know or trust I had nothing else to say.

"Glad you like the room. I won't bother you for long. I know you still need your sleep. I'll be back in here in the morning. I have some questions to ask you but nothing you need to lose sleep over. I wanted to make sure you didn't need anything until then?" As she asked that I wondered if she would treat me so kindly if she truly believed I had no magic.

Thinking about how the others were being treated. I highly doubted it.

"I appreciate your asking, I don't mean to be rude but I'm fine, this is more than what I was ever expecting." At least she didn't seem to think I was being rude other than the fact that her expression had never changed.

It was eerie the fact her smile remained the same almost as if it was painted on. Seeming satisfied for now she stood and left me, closing the door quietly behind her. I wasn't sure if I could sleep even if I had wanted to in this new room, it was sad, I knew I could fall asleep in the broken-down room but then I hadn't felt threatened there.

Chapter Twelve
Alana

I had no idea how long I slept in; no one woke me up and neither had I heard the alarm that would normally wake us up. Stretching and getting out of bed for a moment. I hoped all of this was just a bad nightmare until I realized I wasn't home and sadly still living it. Walking over to the door ready to open it, the door was opened automatically for me with a guard standing on the other side.

"Alana is awaiting you in the great hall. You are to meet her there as soon as you are awake." Not that I needed to wake up.

I was already as awake as I was going to get.

"Where is the great hall?" Not that I had been given a tour of the place, it had been rather dark when I was brought to my room. I had been too tired to pay attention to very much at all.

"Follow this hallway as it slopes down, the great hall will be on your left at the very end." As he pointed out the direction in case, I didn't know which way my left was.

Giving him a smile and a slight nod, I started to walk in the direction he pointed. Not that I thought there would be much hope in escaping. I tried to pay attention this time to where I was and any other doors on my way. At least now I could picture this place, hopefully, if I can find an unoccupied spot then I can check this place out more while others are sleeping? At least the guard wasn't exaggerating when he said to follow the long hallway, I was beginning to wonder how many floors down I would be going until I finally came to the end which indeed did open into a rather large, rounded room. I wasn't going to be the only one in the room. There had been a long table with red and black decorating the tablecloth. I could only guess I had been the last one to come since there was only one chair available to sit down at. Sitting down, I could see Alana at the far head of the table with a guard on either side of her. No one else in here seemed to appear nervous other than me.

I wished the others could have been up here, since there had been a wide variety of food to choose from. I felt too guilty to take anything other than a piece of bread and to drink the water that had been poured for me. The others looked at me rather strangely. I couldn't get myself to take anything else knowing the ones I had been with before this were suffering. I was hoping someone would talk so I could get an idea of what we were doing here or at least find something out; no one spoke. Not even Alana who seemed to be observing everyone at the table. Apparently, the others already knew what they were here for as they left individually throughout the course of breakfast, eventually leaving me and two others along with Alana and her two guards. At some point, someone had to tell me what they were expecting of me. I highly doubted she wanted me up here without wanting or expecting something from me. Finally, the last two were standing when Alana had spoken. I was beginning to wonder if I would be left alone sitting here trying to figure out what I was supposed to do.

"Rory and Mason will show you what you will be doing. They are heading there now. I realize you do not have any powers so you won't be able to do this to your full ability, however with the training you have received from an old pupil of mine, you should still work out." Her sugary-sweet tone and forced sincerity came across as artificial and disingenuous.

No smile of hers could cover for the intent she had. As the other two left the table I also got up and followed them out of the room. We hadn't gone up the long hallway as I would have expected us to, instead, we went out one of the other doors leading out of the grand hall leading into a rather simple and small room.

The room itself not only had been small with the ceiling black, but the walls had also been painted a very calming color almost the same light blue that had been in the bedroom. I was meant to sleep in. There were dark green foam mats on the floor, but a mattress also covered in pillows and a soft fuzzy blanket along with a few chairs of different kinds. I hoped to look around the room. I might be able to figure out what we were meant to do in here, but it certainly had not given itself away at all. Mason sat down on one of the mats as Rory chose one of the chairs. Not sure what I was supposed to do so I continued standing.

"Choose a spot where you can relax and meditate. As soon as I find a spot, Mason will explain what we are doing." Rory sounded nice enough, even sincere that I wondered if they were here forced against their will as well or if they were willfully here?

Choosing the dark green mat in the far back corner. I could keep an eye on the door and the others while still being out of the way.

"Simply meditate as you have been taught. On your first day, you will be walking around the grounds becoming familiar with it, however when you are outside of the place remember it so that you can start faster. We are simply keeping an eye on anyone that comes close to the place, as soon as we do, we remove ourselves from that location and bring ourselves directly to a guard inside alerting them to where the trespasser has been spotted. It will be up to the guard to decide what is done with them. Tomorrow you will be introduced to two different guards; they will be the two you will report to. For now, explore but do not try to intentionally contact anyone. We are also watched by Alana while we are in here, she will know." No longer explaining, Mason promptly went into his trance leaving me to watch on for a moment wondering exactly how Alana was watching us unless she was doing the same as us?

I hated the idea of doing this, especially with Mason explaining to be careful that we were being watched. I would have liked looking around. I was going to have to be patient and do it later. I hope I will still have that chance. The only problem with still having the magic would be that my projection would be extremely clear. Before I could only do it with Sophie or Sydney's help. For the next several hours I sat there pretending to practice not that I had been successful at doing anything. I doubted they would keep me up here. Eventually, I would end up back with the others, unless they decided something far worse. If I did get a chance to explore later, at least I had the warning of being watched, maybe that's why they chose to bring me here? They might have known when I projected out to Lorah's home? Halfway through the day, I didn't have to wonder anymore as one of the guards had come in to escort me to another room to meet with Alana. She sat on a rather large impressive-looking chair watching me as I entered. The guard hadn't entered the room only closing the door behind me. Walking up towards Alana. I wasn't sure how close she wanted me to get until she told me to stop.

"I thought you were taught astral projection with your mind and separately with your body?" I could hear the curiosity in her voice.

"Yes, I was taught in case the magic took hold, except I could only project myself with the help of my instructors. I can't do it on my own, it takes me a long time before I can do it." I hoped that would satisfy her at least.

She didn't seem too interested in killing me off yet but then I doubted she trusted whether I had some magic. Instead of keeping me with the others in the palace area. I was moved back down with the other workers, and I felt much more relieved. For now, I had not served the purpose she was hoping for. As I started working alongside the others, I knew I was going to need to be much more cautious with the guards keeping a closer eye on me.

The guards were not the only ones who had a new interest in me, the others who now worked around me watched me as they were curious about what Alana would have wanted with me. Now that I was back on the ground area with them, I did my best to keep up and just work. Not that anyone tried to talk to me. I think everyone sensed how much I was being watched. Not until we were finished for the night, and I had retired to my old room had they even tried to speak to me, with a light rapping sound on the door. Not wanting to leave them waiting for too long, not sure who it was but then I guessed if they were the guards, they would have just come in as they had last time. I felt relieved when I had seen who it was, ushering them in. I had looked both ways outside the door to see if anyone else had been watching. Turning my attention to the others they sat down on the floor in the little room. One of them offered me an extra blanket they had; apparently, they found it leftover in one of the apartments from a previous owner.

"We didn't think we would see you again. Usually, if a person leaves because of Alana, they are either working for her or have some special power she wants, or they end up dead. What did she want with you?" Their question seemed fair enough, I guess I would have been rather curious also.

"Alana wanted to find out if I had a certain power, it seems everyone is obsessed with a certain power, and they seemed certain I would have had it. I was just in the wrong place at the wrong time. I'm only back here now because I don't have what she wants apparently." Not sure how much I wanted to risk sharing with them.

I hadn't wanted to make things worse for them especially if they were ever questioned, but then I also didn't want to be handed over in case they hoped it might win their freedom, not that I could blame them.

"There must be more to it. They would not have allowed you back alive if you did not have something they wanted." As soon as the one asked me that I felt all their eyes on me again waiting for a more solid answer.

"This particular power they want she still believes I have it, I'm guessing she thinks I'm hiding it from her which is why she has the guards watching me even closer now. The group in the palace let me know how heavily guarded this place is so I think she was worried I might contact someone on the outside, so they were in a way warning me not to try. When I do find a way out, I won't leave any of you behind. You all deserve freedom as much as I do." At least by saying this, I hoped they might trust me enough to help me with a distraction or something if I were to ask.

Not that I wanted to put anyone in danger. I had honestly wanted to help them. Over the next few days, it had been the same routine as we would work, being watched by the guards, even at times I could hear them whispering about me so at least I knew my assumptions had been correct. They were waiting for me to slip up. At least my new friends were showing their loyalty to me. To get some privacy and relax I had started to meditate in the little closet in my room not that I was able to concentrate well enough. For some reason ever since I had been up in the palace, I hadn't been able to contact Sophie, Sydney, Valafar, or Nikolai. It felt as if I was being blocked from them.

For about a week I had finally stopped trying to concentrate on any of the others, even Lorah couldn't be contacted. When I had been trying it seemed as if our workload was increased and when I stopped, the workload decreased. We were all starting to feel it however the others still felt encouraged thinking there was still some hope left. Finally, I had decided to contact someone they would not expect, perhaps thinking they were able to block me from those they knew I was familiar with and try contacting. I decided to concentrate on the young man that I had briefly met in Lorah's apartment. With the others out in the main room to slow down anyone that might come in and interrupt me. I sat in the closet again where it was nice and dark. I relaxed the best I could and concentrated on his face. I wasn't sure where I would end up or what he would be doing at the moment that I surprised him. I hoped he might be able to help me. At least if he knew Lorah he might be willing to be a go-between for a while. At least it was what I had been hoping for.

If I had been anywhere else, I would have been able to remove my entire body to where I concentrated except for here. Whatever blocked me from leaving physically at least had not completely controlled my projections. As I concentrated on his face, I found myself in a rather strange area. I hadn't been here before, except it reminded me of a picture I had once seen in a nature magazine. It looked like I was in the middle of a rainforest or some sort of thick moss-covered bush area. Looking around I

231

wasn't sure if I projected myself to him or not. Yelling out "hello" no one responded so I tried again. The next area I popped into looked like the edge of the thick forest next to a stream. I tried this several times. All I could think had been that he must have been moving, and I was not keeping up with him. Then finally the last time I concentrated on him. I still hadn't seen anything other than hear a loud sound behind me. As I turned, there he was standing within inches of me. I guessed I appeared right out in front of him as he skids to a stop to prevent running into me. He looked as shocked as I had felt. At least I finally found him.

"You were the one who was at Lorah's apartment, what are you doing way out here? I almost ran you over!" Curious but questioning why I was here showing very clearly on his face.

"I need to speak with Lorah except I haven't been able to. I keep getting blocked, you're the first one I've been able to find." His expression had changed a slight bit as he looked confused.

"She's been staying at her boss's home waiting for you; she doesn't say much about it except she's trying to find you, why don't you show up at her place physically the way you are here? She should be easier to find than I am?" At least now I understood why he seemed so confused; I would be too if I heard the same thing.

"If I could show up at her place physically then I wouldn't be having the problem that I am. I'm not in front of you physically, I'm projecting myself and so far, you are the only one I'm not barred from projecting to. I hear a noise so I can't stay long. Let Lorah know I will project to you again. I'm trapped here and Alana still thinks that I have the power she is looking for. I'll try again tomorrow night same time; I really must go." As soon as I said that I snapped myself back, feeling dizzy as I stood up.

I walked out of the closet closing it behind and I sat on the floor with the others. There had been a rather loud knock at the door. The others had been playing a dice game with a piece of paper they had drawn numbers on. One gentleman stood letting the person knocking in. Looking at us he didn't seem too upset when he saw us playing a game.

"There is to be no playing games late at night, all of you should be in your rooms." The guard announced, without saying anything else everyone stood.

Apparently, they must have figured I was being protected, if any sounds or person were to come by alerting me. This way I would have to be much more careful doing this on my own and hopefully find a solution to our problem soon. As I watched the others leave for their temporary homes, the guard shut my door. With the slight shadow showing from the other side of the door. I guessed she was going to leave someone guarding my door now. Somehow, I was going to have to find another way of doing this or create enough of a distraction while I did. Not that I could create one every time I needed to do this. Somehow, I was going to have to figure out a way of outsmarting them.

We were rather surprised when the alarm had not signaled us to work yet, from general habit, even I had been able to wake without the alarm sounding this morning. Not sure what was going on, there had been a huge group in the center of the old fallen apart village. It had no longer mattered if we were working by natural light or not, we would be repairing parts of the underground tunnels. Alana was anticipating a need for a quick escape possibly quite soon since she was having us work around the clock only barely taking a few hours to rest before we would start again. After two days of this, we were all exhausted as some would pass out, they would simply be tossed aside until they would awaken and be put back to work. The only way I had known any time passing had been when I would pull one of the bodies back far enough out of the way. I would catch a glimpse of the city. If the torches had been lit it was nighttime, if they had been left alone, I knew it was during the day.

Deep into the tunnel, the torches burned continuously. The tunnels that we were building had been rather long and deep underground. We first entered from the old city which had been built underground to begin with. Blasting through the solid stone from the main palace to the underneath had not been an easy task.

I knew Lorah must have been wondering what happened when I hadn't shown. So far there had been no opportunities yet and I had certainly looked for them. I was hoping I would survive long enough to attempt contacting the outside again. As I stood near the huge rock that lay in our way obstructing our progress, lighting strong and intense fires below and around the rock to heat the stone as much as possible, before we would douse it with ice water hoping to chill the rock enough, shattering pieces of the rock from the extreme temperature change. Moving out the pieces we kept moving forward each time hoping the ground above us would not cave in. There were many explosive devices we could have used to make it much quicker however Alana had not wanted to risk caving in, or attention drawn to this area by regular mortals that may be mapping the grounds activity from a distance away. We were stuck using other rocks or makeshift tools the primitive way.

My eyes were stinging from the sweat dripping into them; it felt as though the further we had gone the hotter it was down here with barely any ventilation. Then sadly I had seen something I wasn't thinking of. One of the others had fainted on purpose to get out of the tunnel to get some fresh air. It was such a clever idea. I wished I thought of it earlier, then maybe I could have met up with Lorah. I could almost feel my hands shake I was so nervous, what if they didn't fall for me passing out? What would they do if they found out? I guess it can't be any worse than what they were doing with me now, other than to kill me, but then they might do that eventually anyway.

I knew I was still being watched rather closely, perhaps it had helped to be so nervous as I kept working moving pieces of stone out of the way, then I had seen the opportunity the second the guard had taken his eye off me. I tripped over a stone rather clumsily falling on the floor with my head near the wall. I managed to make it look as if I knocked myself out by accident. Aaron was the one to pull me to the end of the tunnel slightly leaving me slumped to the side so I would not be bothered. He figured out what I was doing, quietly wishing me luck. I let myself go, thinking of the man who I had no idea his name was, other than somehow, he was tied to Lorah and if she trusted him, then I had no other choice than to trust him also. I could feel that lightheaded feeling come over me as I was about to slip into a sleep except not quite. My body was relaxed even though it took me longer this time since I had been so overheated.

The room had been cloudy at first then it came into focus. I wasn't sure where I was now. Looking around I could only guess he had been in the bathroom. I heard the shower running with hot steam, fogging up the bathroom mirror. I wanted to project myself to him except I hadn't thought this might happen. Not wanting to get caught in here. I reached for the door. Stepping out quickly shutting it behind me. I looked up to see at least ten people staring back at me in surprise. The only comfort I could offer myself at this exact moment had been the fact that I could pull myself away from this place if I needed to. Then I wound up standing there shocked seeing both Lorah and Sophie standing next to each other. I hadn't known they were familiar with each other. Then I wondered if I was seeing Lorah, would I be caught for being here? I guess I will soon find out. Standing up from the couch Sophie

235

had been sitting by a rather nice-looking gentleman who had only let her hand go as she walked away from him towards me. Lorah had not taken her time as she pretty much sprinted across the living room to hug me.

"I was worried when you didn't show up, I was with Lucian for the last few days waiting for you. What prevented you?" Lorah was curious; I couldn't blame her; I would have been worried also.

Several of the others in the room still looked as though they were trying to piece together how I knew both Sophie and Lorah.

"Alana has us building a few tunnels instead of repairing the city. Either she feels the need to possibly escape or plans on using them to get in and out of the city easier. I'm not sure. They don't fully believe that I don't have the power and if I did display it, she's going to go to war with the Augustus' family. They both want the power and if it had worked then they know how to retrieve it from me without needing me to be alive to get it." I guessed at that point when I mentioned Alana and the Augustus' family, the others knew immediately who I was talking about.

Oddly enough I could hear whispering from the others asking if I possibly had the power, did that mean Harmony was dead or rather as I had known her, Sydney. Hearing the door click from behind me, Lucian walked out freshly dried off after his shower looking surprised to see me.

"This is the girl I tried telling you about, the one who keeps showing up." Lucian looked surprised to see me.

"Yes, and she almost saw you in the shower. She transported herself to you, I am curious if she did that in the way Rose can project herself?" The man who had been sitting next to Sophie stood.

"Yes, I swear that's all I did is astral project myself. I couldn't risk anything else, I could but then I couldn't hide it. Lorah, how do you know Sophie? I met her when I was chosen to hold onto the power in the first place, she was training me with Sydney in the room." As soon as I said Sydney, even Lucian became much more interested.

"How do you know Sydney?" As soon as Lucian had asked the others seemed very uneasy.

"She's the one who chose me, she wanted to make sure the power did not go to waste and end with her, however, she also wanted to make sure someone neutral could handle it in case another with the same power became dangerous and had to be dealt with. At least it's the explanation she had given me. Sophie was the one who taught me, and I met Lorah because of her boss Valafar Augustus. He also bought and owned the bookstore that I worked for. That's basically where all of this started for me." I wasn't sure what else to say to them, I hoped Sophie might have thought of something since the last time we had talked.

"I won't be able to stay much longer, they think I passed out, I faked it, or I wouldn't have had the chance to come now. Do you have any ideas yet or do I have to keep pretending not to have this power everyone seems to want?" As I looked from Lorah to Sophie neither seemed eager to answer.

"Valafar seems to think the only way you will get your freedom is if Alana is dead, however that won't prevent others from coming after you. It might be that you will need to live in hiding for the rest of your life to be safe. So far only the Augustus family and those who are with Alana know you were even a possibility of having it. We don't know what to do, other than no one assumes Sydney has it anymore. Her being in the nursing home made her look human since no one there has picked up on it, all her vitals all seem very human and very average. She might not have it even though watching her; the vampire bite is what's causing all the problems for her, the premature aging and such, I doubt she has long." No one was sure how Lucian was going to take hearing Sydney was in a nursing home, he had excused himself from the room.

"We are trying to figure out something. We haven't been able to quite yet, and we know this isn't easy for you except we want to make sure whatever we come up with, you won't have to keep hiding. Valafar seems to think his family for the most part might leave you alone however if they find the need or wish to replicate the power, they might pull you into their group again." Sophie was trying to sound encouraging even though her voice lightened at the end.

Even in the pit of my stomach and the voice in the back of my mind seemed to be telling me I would never be done with this.

"Where did Lucian go?" I was curious why he seemed so upset when I would mention Sydney or when Lorah had.

"He was extremely close to Sydney; they had a rather unique relationship. I'm his grandfather Charlie. He may be handling it except it's still difficult for him to hear about her." Now standing over next to Sophie putting his arm around her.

"I don't understand why I keep projecting to only him, would you know if you're being watched?" I was curious why this was happening this way if he was hurt hearing about Sydney.

I didn't want to continue it if it was going to make things worse for him. I didn't know him however he seemed nice enough.

"We don't know what would be stopping you. To project yourself to someone you don't even know might have to do more with Sydney's connection more than anything else?" Rose had been more experienced than the rest of the family.

Jacob had known how dreamscapes worked however they differed greatly from projections, something he had watched Rose become much better with. The family still held onto the crystals for the dreamscape, keeping them in a safe place so that they would not be misused by others. Not wanting to explain too much. I looked behind me as if I was seeing something they were not. I hated to admit it I knew I was alone on this having to figure something out; except I did want to find out what my connection to Lucian was. After all, today was the first time, I had even heard his name. Leaving the others to believe I had gone back to my body; I went to see Lucian. He was standing outside far enough away from the house resting his head on a tree.

"Lucian, I need to talk to you for a moment. I promise after this, even if I can't project myself to Lorah or Valafar. I won't be following you anymore. You seem very sweet, and I don't want to hurt you if my only connection to you is because of the one who you're hurting over." I wanted to talk to him, except not knowing what to say and never having a real conversation with him or knowing him I was hoping I wouldn't upset him.

"It might be because of her. I only know so much about it. What did you want to talk about?" Turning to face me pretending to be perfectly fine.

"What do you know about Alana?" I could have asked Lorah or Sophie except both seemed to be avoiding it, probably hoping to find an answer themselves.

"You could have asked Sophie about that; I guess that they are trying to protect you from knowing too much especially if they can't do anything. Sometimes there are things beyond our control. You said you were in the city? What does it look like?" I described the city to him, and he seemed to understand exactly what I was talking about.

He even knew the room that I slept in, saying it was once Harmony's room when she had first lost her memory. Lucian was telling me about the secret path in the closet of the old city. I noticed a circle except I hadn't thought anything of it, that it might possibly be an entrance to anything. He continued to explain how to use the pool. Then finally he asked me something I was sure he hadn't wanted to share with his family.

"What nursing home is Sydney in?" Not even taking a second, I explained to him how to get there and why I had chosen that place to take us in the first place.

"If you're anything like Sydney, I know you will figure out how to best do this, after all, the only reason your gift is so coveted is that it's a rather rare and powerful one. If several others had that same gift, it wouldn't be so rare and there would be at least a fighting chance." Lucian said.

I thought of it before except I had the same worry both Sophie and Sydney had with it.

"What if the wrong person had the gift, would you feel safe knowing whoever controlled it could easily kill you or any other vampire?" I was curious what he had thought

"It's no different than the wrong person being turned into a vampire and being unleashed onto the world of mortals. No matter how much power, even creatures that have been around for centuries have the time to calculate every motive or reaction of others, has a flaw, a weakness, or rather an Achilles heel. There is a training room in the old palace basement, it's a great place to sort out problems or rather take care of them. I'm sure you will figure it out, if not, I'll be by there in a few days. I have someone I need to see first." Not needing to explain it to me I knew what he meant.

Watching him take off. I left where I was standing back to the inevitable part of life for now. As I sat up, I looked around, there were three guards apparently who had been trying to get me to wake. When I was in my trance state, I knew it would be hard for anyone to wake me. I was only hoping they would not figure out what exactly I was doing. At least I had chosen a time when Alana was out handling a private business matter, or I was sure she would have guessed. I knew what Lucian said about the training room, except I had thought of even a better place and had hoped if I managed to be successful, Valafar might be close enough to help me. I knew Lorah and Sophie would do anything they could to help, except I also understood their wanting to be careful, not to bring their family into danger, not knowing what might happen. Things were always much more dangerous when dealing with the Augustus family. They had no problems killing something if it simply made them angry or been in the wrong place at the wrong time.

The guards escorted Aaron, Delaney, Alexandra, Audra, and me out of the tunnels. They felt it was rather strange that I was out for so long, and the other watchers for Alana had also alerted the guards when they realized I had been talking to Lorah. Apparently, they did have her being watched. We were locked up in my old room, each with our hands and feet bound so that we would not be able to escape, hoping to hand us over to Alana to let her decide what would happen with us. My friends covered for me or tried to make it look as though I passed out twice, making excuses or slowing the guards down. So now trusting me, they waited to find out what their fate would be. The guards stood to watch outside of the room making sure no one came in or went out.

A message had been sent out to Alana to let her know she was needed and what exactly I had been caught doing. While we waited, we had several guards at different times checking on us making sure I wasn't projecting or doing anything else. After a

241

while, they relaxed realizing I wasn't going to try anything while we were being watched so closely. I knew I needed to be patient long enough before I could try anything. Even though I was glad the others were in here with me, I wasn't sure if they would like what I had planned. I hoped they would not end up hating me. At first, I had to admit I hated Sydney for doing this to me and putting me in this spot, but then after a while I realized she was never given a choice either, she was thrust into an entirely different world she was never ready for either. We both had a lot in common, neither having our parents available for one reason or another and two being separated from those we loved. I hated to admit I was certain my outcome would be far different from hers, unless a vampire decided to bite me as well, then from watching her, I would know what to expect. Either way, I decided to accept what came along in life. For the others, I would have to give it one last fighting chance.

Chapter Thirteen
Taking chances

I wasn't sure how I was going to manage what I had planned; it all sounded great in theory in my head as I ran the plan repeatedly except, I couldn't get rid of that nagging feeling of what do I do if it fails, and I'm left standing there? I guess all I could do is flash out and hope to hide for the rest of my life, never letting Alana or the Augustus family find me? By now the guards came into the room far less often and from the conversations that I was overhearing. Alana already made it back deciding what she was going to do with me. She seemed furious that they even bothered with the others, since they had no gifts other than to further her plans of the tunnels. Apparently now so she would not have to deal with them any longer, she planned on putting them to death as well. For protecting me, it was my turn to protect them. The only way I knew how. I had the gift inside of me right now, thankfully I didn't inherit it physically the way Sydney had, and she gave it to me not by biting me and infecting me which had been one of the tested experiments to fail, I had been injected repeatedly as the last time had been direct with her blood, which worked.

Whatever reason that delayed Alana in coming up here. I was thankful for it. At least it would hopefully give me enough time. I knew once I used the power I would be picked up on immediately by Alana and anyone else nearby. I was hoping this would be the only group that would notice. Perhaps the Augustus family would be far enough away, or no way of watching me perform anything inside of here? I know I was to keep it hidden at all costs, except there was little good for me if I was a prisoner here being used for the wrong reason, or back with the Augustus family taking orders for the rest of my life. I highly doubted Alana would kill me. I had something she wanted, and she knew others would want also. Death at this point would have been a welcomed relief for me, after all, I would finally be done with it.

Focusing now, I could feel my physical body lift and swoosh over so many feet from where I had been sitting. Without needing confirmation of sight, I could hear the restraints that had been on my wrists and ankles clink to the floor as they fell. Looking up the others watched as I performed the simplest of feats. Now was going to be the harder part which I hoped I would be able to do. At least they still had a choice, which is what I was about to offer a chance to, to give them a choice, something I only thought I had until it had been taken from me and decided. Standing next to the others I spoke very quickly as I broke off the restraints from the others.

"I am giving all of you the choice, they are going to kill you, and you have two ways out of here. The first way you can follow me down the tunnel in the closet and go somewhere safe for a while, going to family and friends won't be safe. It would put them in danger and that is if they have not already been touched by Alana and her group. The second choice is to hide for a short time and then join up with me later so that I can teach you how to use your new gifts. I wish I could say it won't hurt except it will, but it only lasts for a short while. It's why you will want to hide where no one will disturb you while your body recovers from it. Which do you wish to do?" As I looked at Aaron, Delaney, Alexandra, and Audra, making their decision, it hadn't taken them long.

"I have no family to go back to, Alana killed them all." Audra stood determined with no looks of worry on her face at all.

Being held here captive for her being presented with a gift was better than any other choice she had in life. When she first came here, her hair was rather short almost a pure white, which now had permanent dust darkening it with calluses on both of her hands. Both Delaney and Aaron accepted as well. They were husband and wife, which shouldn't have surprised me that Alana would attempt to go after those that would not be missed. Neither of them had any other family other than each other, and the same as Audra, they also displayed the same calloused hands that were inflicted upon them.

"Whatever you need to do we accept, just let us know how we can help you." I know they wanted to help except it wouldn't be quick enough, at least this way I would know they could better protect themselves than without.

The best part and to their advantage would be that no one was aware they would have this power.

"After I infect each of you, I have no guarantee that it will take effect. I can only hope it will. It will take a while for it to spread throughout your system, just be careful of thinking of anywhere, especially here or you will end up back here. You won't be in control enough to help, I can barely use mine since I've been so limited in using the gift, and mostly I've done my best to conceal it, hoping others would believe I didn't have it. Once you do have it and can move around on your own, within a week you will be able to concentrate on me and move yourself to me no matter where I am." Now was the difficult part getting them infected before the next guard checked on us?

Writing a note in the dust I hoped it would look as though I was leaving a note for someone else. I would be leading them directly to me. I wanted to make sure I had the others out of the way first.

They seemed confused at first when I transported us to my old room here. Following me into the closet. I could see where the circle had been on the floor that I earlier dismissed as nothing. Doing my best to move it. I wound up blowing it up into tiny little pieces making more noise than I would have preferred. Climbing down the rusted ladder that clung to the wall, we made our way down. As the others were wondering where we were going, they thought for a moment we would be trapped down here only seeing what resembled a wishing well. I told each of a place to think of and try not to be scared by what was inside of the wishing well. I was rather glad that Lucian described it as well as he had. Then slowly we all took a step out into the place I had first chosen. A very old run-down no longer used lighthouse. After no doubt alerting the others, I had to do this rather quickly. Picking up a rather rusty nail. I slit part of my skin letting my blood drain out a little. I didn't have the option of biting them with venom or as rumors had been to be able to scratch them simply to put in my blood, or a few other ways I had heard of. I simply hoped that without having a needle. I could move the blood to where I needed it to go. I concentrated on the splotch of blood then on each person, as I kept the blood running out it would disappear for a moment as I hoped it found its recipient. I had only known it had by their expressions as they doubled over. I hated leaving them like this except they were far safer here than anywhere else. Eventually, I would need to see if they were able to pass on this power or if it was only able to come from me, either from the tests they performed on me or the direct link to Sydney. As the power spread out, I couldn't help but wonder if it would gradually become diluted. Or might it somehow manage to maintain its full strength?

Touching the small piece of water on the floor that we had come through. I wound up back into the well and moved my way out as I could hear the others announce they found where I had gone. I was waiting for the last available moment before I chose to take off. I wanted to make sure they knew beyond a doubt I was down here and for them to follow me. I knew there would be a bit of a cat and mouse chase, if everything worked as I hoped it would, they would still be hot on my heels exactly the way they were supposed to be and hopefully not pick up on the fact it was a trap. From the clue that I left the one person. I knew who was aware of it would pick up on the right place right away, except Alana and her group had no idea, so they had only three in one chance of finding me right away. I hoped they would choose at least one wrong one before they found me giving me enough time to do the next step in my plan, and I knew he would help except he may not like or agree with the possible outcome. Let alone the fact that I had just shared the gift with three others. I kept thinking over what Lucian told me, and he was correct. I had not planned on stopping with just these three.

As they started climbing down, I jumped back into the wishing well moving into the thickest feeling jelly no longer having a top or bottom and no sides to it. I had concentrated on a place moving through the thick jell that clung to me except had not continued to stick or leave any residue on me when I passed through to my destination. I had stepped into a rather large, vaulted room with pristine white making up for the fact that there was very little light in the room. A woman who I could barely make out who she seemed as if she was standing in a shadow that followed her as she moved. Dressed all in black lace, as if she was mourning the dead from the little that I could see from her. I was in awe. I wasn't sure who she was or why she was here, when I was expecting someone else or rather a group of people. Alana's groups of demon hunters were present along with this mesmerizing woman standing before me. I had hoped to do this right except I wasn't sure what power if she had any that she might intervene and destroy my plans. I needed these groups along with Alana to follow me to possibly win my freedom again. I would deal with the Augustus family when the time came.

"How did you get this power? You are not Sydney? Where is she?" The woman asked in such a low tone that I could almost not hear her.

A breeze could have whispered the same message to me as neither sounded different from the other.

"I am not Sydney. I happen to be her student, who are you?" As I asked, she never answered my question other than to give an accusing look at the others angry that they held some information from her.

"What are you doing here?" It was a fair enough question to be asked.

"I was here to let Alana know the power has been duplicated and she can collect it from her main guards in the training room of the Eurubian's palace. I'm heading there now." I was hoping whoever she was she would either stay away, or if she was anything like Alana and fall for the trap since she was aware of the power.

I hated pulling anyone else into this that did not need to be.

"You truly do not know who I am?" She seemed rather curious and amazed at the same time.

"No, I'm sorry I don't." I was even more curious as she had brought it up.

"Simply tell Alana there is another gift coming to the palace. I would enjoy seeing her myself after all this time. Thank you for opening my way out, we've been lost in here for a while." Taking off in the opposite direction the groups of demon hunters followed behind her.

I could barely see her as she left faster than anything I had ever seen before. I didn't even have the chance to agree that I would tell her, except I had the feeling that if this woman wanted to do me in, she had the perfect opportunity right then and I would not have been fast enough for her. Now was the part I was dreading hoping it would work at all. I thought of the training room that Lucian described in detail which had looked like the room the other projectionists had been placed. Even now I wasn't sure what to call them and I was sure they would see me coming.

As soon as I appeared in the room. I dropped to the floor; I wasn't sure what to expect if they would be here all ready and prepared to kill me, or if I would be the first one here. Looking around no one was there. I picked the far corner now to sit and wait for the others to show. At least this way I would see whoever would enter. Not wanting to wait too much longer I had to remind myself to be patient. I was positive they would have understood the clue I left behind, unless they figured it out that I meant to trap them. I waited a while longer before a figure stepped out of the dark. Standing quickly to my feet, it hadn't been who I was waiting for.

"Did you think she was stupid enough to fall for a simple trap such as this? You need to think on a much grander scale, I know for a fact she has." Still not able to see very much of the woman she had been the very one I ran into with the demon hunters.

I was trying to decide quickly if I should disappear or not. I couldn't help but feel I had walked into my own trap.

"If you knew she wouldn't be here then why did you still show up here?" I asked as I was still trying to make out her appearance.

It was almost as if I was being half-blinded by her presence feeling trapped in a bit of a fog.

"I knew you would show up here, and if you wish to think on a grander scale then you will need my assistance. I know her better than anyone else. Why should I ruin my special surprise for her?" She seemed to be rather amused with her comment lightly laughing to herself as I was kept out of much of the joke.

"Why would you want to help me?" I wasn't sure I wanted to risk help from someone else.

I wanted this entire thing over with, what if she wanted to keep using me because of the power?

"Yes, I intend on helping you. I need to make sure this goes right. After all, it's not that often a vampire gets a second chance at this. She should have stayed dead when I first killed her. Unfortunately for her, others helped keep what was left of her alive. Now it's time to correct that miscalculation. Now tell me, do you see what is on the wall?" As she said this, she waved her hand as a picture of a mountain top appeared.

All I could see had been a huge mountain with water all around it.

"Yes, I see it." I wasn't sure how it appeared other than her magic must have made it appear.

"They are already below the mountain; you are to come immediately and join me at the tip of the mountain for when she sees her other gift." As soon as she said that the woman evaporated into thin air.

The longer I associate with this world the more I'm finding I never knew existed before. Concentrating my best, I had to hope this would have an end, even if it was not one I particularly liked. I was almost taken off guard when I felt the gust of wind almost knocked me over when I appeared. Where we stood there were no trees around for shelter, we stood on the edge of a cliff with nothing other than a wide-open space at the top of a hill. We could even see Alana racing her way up. I was curious why she would show up here than where I had left the note for? Looking around I had yet to see any of the demon hunters. The lady was standing next to me as she stared directly at Alana making her approach.

When Alana joined us, her expression went from being self-assured to complete shock. I highly doubted she would have noticed if I had left as she watched the other woman. Then I wondered who the other person was and why Alana would almost seem to shake in front of her?

"You should be dead. Sydney killed you." After hearing that, I didn't need to ask any questions myself other than the fact both had expected the other to be dead.

"Mutual feelings dear sister as you should have stayed dead when I killed you. I know the reason you lived, sadly you don't know how I survived." The mystery woman seemed rather pleased with herself.

"I will make sure when you die this time you will stay dead, I won't share this world or any other with you." By now several of Alana's guards were now standing around her.

"Give it your best shot little sister." As she taunted Alana, I wasn't sure exactly how she thought this was helping me or how I was going to be a part of it.

I simply hoped something would happen soon to get this agony over with.

"I was going to spare your life except I see you're working with her. Too bad for both of you there is no special power between the both of you." Alana motioned for her guards to come closer as she was mentally preparing herself to fight.

I was hoping this mystery woman knew what she was talking about. I only had some training from Sophie and Sydney. I was hoping she hadn't expected me to be an expert with my craft. Except once she took care of Alana, would she do the same with me? Just how long did she intend on helping me?

The mystery woman and I had been knocked off the cliff's edge alongside Alana. The two women were locked in a desperate death grip, seemingly unaware or uncaring of their plummeting descent. As I transported back to the top of the hill, I regretted my decision since they saw me use my gift, for twelve vampires now stared me down. Sydney's fate flashed through my mind - would I suffer the same? Why couldn't I have moved myself to a different place than this? Thinking quickly, I raised my hands and summoned a wall of fire to block their advance. The flames wouldn't hold them back for long, but perhaps the gusting wind at my back could blow the vampires on the other side of the firewall away. I wished I knew what to do.

My concentration was shattered by a series of loud cracks. Lowering the firewall for a moment, I watched as the vampires shoved burning trees aside, climbing up the hill towards me. Even as I struggled with this new threat, the ground continued to tremble with unexplained earthquakes. I didn't know how much longer I could hold them off.

Twelve creatures came charging at me. Thinking quickly, I transported myself down to the fallen tree area as the others raced up the hill, expecting to catch me. From my vantage point, I saw the forest fire and used my powers to draw the moisture out of the air, preventing it from spreading further. Dousing the flames with a surge of water, I made my next move.

I thrust the remaining water forward, smashing it into the group of burnt vampires. Though I hadn't yet learned how to kill with my abilities, the force of the water flattened them. The thought of taking a life sent a shiver down my spine.

Unexpectedly, the cascading water began flooding downward. I was no longer standing in front of the others. If the mystery woman had wanted my help, she should have told me what she needed. I found myself back at the Eurubian city, unsure of why I had thought to do that.

I could hear the others working as a cart was pulled out of the main tunnel filled with stone pieces that were still being brought out. One of the workers looked up at me. I could tell the person was shocked to see me standing there in the center. Not saying a word, he gave the slightest nod of the head and moved the now empty cart back into the tunnel. Looking back, I could hear a few shouts as the guards from the entrance now came running at me. Doing my best, hoping I can lift it. I had never seen how much weight I could lift with this gift. Picking up a rock. I threw it at one of the guards knocking him back into another. The first had not been able to get back up after being knocked out. The second had come running at me as I found one of the things that I could end up doing. I had only intended on forcing the person away with wind, except there had been very little wind flow through here, instead of knocking him into the far back wall he exploded leaving a trail of blood and remnants of himself on the ground where he once stood. After seeing this I couldn't control it. I felt so sick I vomited on the ground. I could feel my head swirl. I was scared I might do this again. At least now I knew why neither Sydney or Sophie had taught me to kill with it. Even though I was positive that if I had been stuck with the Augustus family, they would have me kill quite often. After what I had seen them do. this act I just did was nothing.

253

Walking out to the entrance. I had been rather surprised that I hadn't seen any other guards, perhaps they thought those two were capable unless they had no idea, I would end up back here? Except why would I, other than to free the others? I hadn't been making other plans other than what happened as it came at me. At first, I hoped to torch the entire group with Alana in the training room except that plan failed. I wasn't sure why. I had wondered if they had shown up if it would have worked anyway. After all, how does one kill a vampire, I've only heard stories and legends? Walking over to the tunnel, a few guards were watching the people working hard. Whistling loud enough I hoped to get everyone's attention inside. As soon as I had done this the workers stopped what they were doing as the remaining guards tried to run at me. I stood at the entrance with them only stopping a few feet from me as they were wondering why I wasn't running, just standing there not displaying any expression. I had hoped to figure out my next move as it came available.

Charging at me as quickly as they could. I had been able to successfully force them into the wall knocking them out this time, instead of blowing them up. The workers in the tunnel had been surprised to find out I had power since I hadn't been separated from them working. The others with gifts had been living in the palace working for Alana. As I had done this the others dropped their pickaxes, shovels, or whatever they had in their hands walking out of the tunnels in surprise. Without having to say anything I was either thanked or hugged as each one had left. I watched as they left the city exit. Not sure what I was going to do now. I watched making sure everyone left safely. Turned my attention back to the workers. I could see the one was faking being knocked out as he was slowly working his gun out of its holster. Forcing as much air pressure as I could I made the roof over the men explode with the already broken-down buildings above and rock came crashing down on them covering them.

I had guessed that the guards that went with Alana were the only vampires she had working with her; these were far too easy to take over. Looking around I was trying to figure out where the cold gust of wind was coming from. Not that I could see anything other than the few people I had met coming down through the center of town who worked for Alana, the other ones who could project themselves. I wasn't sure if they had any other gifts themselves or if they had intended on attacking me also. Giving a slight nod of the head they said and did nothing towards me other than to leave. Then the last shiver went up my spine as I looked to my right and there she was. The mystery woman dressed all in black with a light natural haze around her almost as if the shadows followed her. Looking at her she hadn't shown one scrape showing she had gone over a cliff. I was just hoping she wasn't here to finish me off now.

"I knew you would be here and do not worry. I don't kill what might be useful to me later." Barely above a whisper, I had to strain to hear her.

"I didn't know what else to do, there wasn't a plan, so I came back to the only place that came to mind." I was hoping I hadn't failed in what she expected from me; except I didn't know if Alana was dead or if I was going to be dealing with her still?

"You did just fine child. I only needed a small amount of time with Alana without the others helping her." As she said this, she pulled out a cloth bag stained and dripping with blood. Dropping it in front of me it smelled like a rotting corpse.

"I'm not sure I want to know what's in there." I could barely respond hoping she didn't want me to look inside.

I fought the nausea feeling of needing to vomit.

"Unlike myself, my sister won't be coming back from the dead. She was only a mere human turned shade with no real special skills of her own. She could control only what elements happened to be in the air. However, once dead she ceases to exist. I on the other hand. I am a pure vampire and when I die, if there are elements from earth, fire, water, and air around. I will always reform, cursed never to die. I have a note for you to pass on for me and for now it will be the last favor you owe me. Give this letter to Charlie and tell Valafar we are even now." I had to think rather hard, did I know a Charlie?

Then it occurred to me, that Sophie's husband had just introduced himself as Lucian's grandfather. I hadn't planned on visiting them quite yet. I hadn't seen Valafar in so long, every time it seemed as though I might finally be able to be back with him, something kept us separated for a while longer.

"I'll bring it to them now." As I looked up from the note, she handed me she was no longer there.

She left before I ever had a chance to notice her leave. Hoping to get this over rather quickly. I focused on Sophie, at least now there wasn't anything that would prevent me from moving myself to her. I hoped never to run into her at a time she wanted privacy. That was something I wanted to learn in the future, if it was possible after showing up in the bathroom with Lucian getting out of the shower, I needed to find some form of discretion with this gift. After showing up and finding Sophie. I did wonder how much privacy she even had. When it was the three of us, it would only be the Augustus family joining us occasionally, except here where I could only assume was her home, there were always others around.

This time as I appeared in her living room, she was sitting down on the couch with Charlie as they were speaking with each other. There were two other couples in the room with two little girls playing some sort of game on the floor. Everyone looked as soon as they realized they had a surprise visitor, even though they seemed to be taking this much better than I would have if someone had dropped in unannounced the way I have been lately.

"I'm supposed to give this note to Charlie. I don't know what's on it, but I'm supposed to give this to him from someone, sadly I never bothered asking the name. Alana is dead this time." Not wanting to say any more than I had to.

I walked over to Charlie as he stood up taking the note I had given him. Carefully reading over the note, he didn't seem too happy about it. Folding the paper up he put it in his pocket without saying a word about it. Perhaps he wanted to wait until I was gone to say anything?

"If you would like to finish your lessons, I would be happy to continue teaching you, that way you can feel more confident with your gift?" Sophie had offered, however, made it clear it would be a more relaxed schedule so that I could try rebuilding some sort of life again.

"I appreciate the offer. I have to check on a few people first and it might not be just myself joining in the lessons. I will be back, there's a lot that I want to learn, and if you're able and willing. I accept. By any chance do you know where Lorah is?" I was hoping she would be here again.

I knew I didn't need to ask about Lucian if he had been anything like me, he would be checking out Sydney.

"She's with Valafar. She was filling him in on your last visit, are you sure you do not know who the woman was that gave you this note? Did she ask anything of you other than to deliver this?" Charlie seemed genuinely concerned.

"No, she said this was the last favor I owed her for now, not that I know what she did for me other than killing Alana. She wanted you to have the note, she did say Valafar, and you were even with her. I could barely see her; she was always in a fog, or my eyes were just too hazy to see her. She wore a black lace dress almost as if she walked out of an old-time renaissance picture. The men with her called her 'lady' and she seemed rather powerful as she told me, I had nothing she wanted except as she said, she didn't kill what she might be able to use in the future." Once I remembered that I did start to worry.

Perhaps it would be a good thing if I learned how to use my gift better, at least this way if she tried to kill or harm me, I could at least protect myself.

"Just be very careful around her, the woman's name is Katherine Hawthorn and known as the lady in black. According to this note apparently, she intends to visit me sometime in the future as well. I've always had this feeling not that she ever needed to confirm it. From the way she treated me growing up. I was rather her reserved favorite and while I was young, I never understood why. I knew without a doubt who my father was except neither Katherine or Julie was my mother. Maybe someday she will tell me? If you see Lucian let him know not to stay away too long." Sitting back down with a questioning look on his face, I could only assume the note was a rather personal one.

As curious as I had been. I needed to take off and check on a few people. I would check on my friends except I already knew they would be finding me very soon. I hated leaving them in the condition they were in. At least I knew they were safe for now and if they had not found me when and where we planned, I would go searching for them. After saying goodbye, there was one place I wanted to be right now. I just hoped it was safe now.

I was hoping for a breath of silence before anything stressful occurred again. Focusing on the guest bedroom where I stayed. It felt so long ago since I was last here let alone in this bedroom. Everything was the same, my luggage sat on the floor empty with my clothes hung up in the closet. Even my hairbrush with little pieces of loose hair draped over the brush. It felt so good being there, almost as if I came home. Listening first, I wanted to make sure I hadn't walked into anyone in the hallway other than Valafar. After a while of walking the hallways, I found no one was in the house, even his office seemed empty with no signs of him being home for quite some time. Where had he been staying all this time, was he out looking for me or dealing with his family? Either way, I hoped he was safe. Focusing on him hoping I would be able to locate him, for some reason I wasn't moving at all. Before, all I had to do was concentrate on someone and I would be standing next to them within seconds. The next person I focused on was Lorah and I was instantly standing next to her. Oddly enough we were outside of the nursing home where Sydney was now living for her final days.

Chapter Fourteen
Moving on

Zack was coming out of the nursing home when he had seen me with a relieved look on his face, he came over to me rather quickly grabbing a hold of me almost squeezing me too tight. He had been worried from the moment I left. Worried, I might be dead and for all he knew, I should have been. At least they left him alone. He was safe. I could see Avani wave to me from inside.

"I've been so worried about you, I'm glad to see you in one piece, there were people here asking questions about you and your grandmother. Sydney is alright, she's probably sleeping right now. She does that a lot. Despite her advanced years, she appears to be deteriorating at an alarming pace, far beyond what one would expect even for a person of her elder status. I'm sure she will be very happy to see a familiar face again and to know your safe. She seemed very worried about you." I didn't want to admit it, I hadn't even thought about visiting Sydney even though I should have.

"How is Sydney doing?" The last time I saw her; it was clear she wasn't doing well. She seemed to be aging rapidly but now there are others that are noticing.

"She has her moments. We think she's delusional with her old age, and possibly not aware of what she speaks about. The others think she's gone mentally except after what I had seen, what you can do, I'm not so sure. It's hard to know what's real and what's not." I couldn't blame Zack for feeling this way even though I was having a difficult time accepting some things and I was seeing it firsthand.

"What sort of questions were you being asked about me?" I was curious if it had been Alana or the Augustus family that was checking on me.

"They wanted to know how you were related to Sydney, where you're from, what family might still be around, if there was anything unusual about you, they tried to say it was to figure out the heredity of certain illnesses. I just said we didn't talk about those things, that I was just a pen pal for so many years until we recently started dating; I mainly tried to stay as vague as possible. I was worried about you. What are you doing now?" I hadn't realized until now that Zack had yet to let go of me.

It was nice being around someone familiar let alone human, and away from the world I've been thrust into. Lorah finally started making her way over to us with a rather questionable look on her face.

"I was about to leave. I wanted to check on Sydney before I did, also to make sure Lucian was handling it. Valafar is with his family discussing you, he's trying to make sure you have your freedom from them; he's been trying to contact Alana except no one seems to know where she's moved to. How did you get away from Alana? We can try to hide you, so she won't find you." Lorah seemed rather nervous talking to me in front of Zack.

"It's okay. He knows probably more than I should have told him. Alana won't be looking for me. She's dead, and your family doesn't seem to be too thrilled now. Charlie was rather upset over a note that I had to deliver to him, and I think whatever is going on between your family and this mystery woman. I would rather have Charlie or Sophie explain it to you." I wasn't sure how I was going to explain this other than I think I found my way of keeping my freedom myself.

At least if I wasn't the only one with this power, I could have more powerful friends and allies who could come to my aid, just as I would theirs when they needed help. Then they wouldn't have to face the life-threatening trials I've endured.

"How is Valafar?" I had a sudden urge to cry but I did my best to hold it back, that and I didn't want to hurt Zack when I asked.

"Valafar misses you dearly and hates that he hasn't been able to keep you safe. He's watched you endure those painful trials with anguish, and he can't wait to see you again, your all he speaks about. If you'd like, you can wait for him at his home. He's eager for the moment he can be reunited with you." Lorah tried to offer some comfort.

"I'm going to check on Sydney and then take off for a while. I have some other people I need to meet up with in a couple of days. Don't say too much to Valafar, just let him know to keep himself available tomorrow and I'll see him. I don't know if he's going to be able to convince his family anyway." As soon as I said this, I took Zack by the hand and pulled him inside along with me.

I knew Lorah would leave out the part of my dragging Zack in with me by the hand. Valafar didn't need to know that. I had other plans for Zack though.

Walking past the offices, Avani seemed rather busy to notice I had walked in. Heading straight for Sydney's room I could still see Lucian standing by her side talking. I hadn't wanted to interrupt so I stood in the hallway until Lucian looked up at me motioning for us to come in. As I walked in, I couldn't tell if Sydney had remembered me or not from the look on her face. It had only been a few months since I had last seen her, even though her condition seemed to have progressed from the last time. Lucian never moved once while we were in there. I worked my way over to her other side; I hated seeing her like this since I knew how she was before any of this happened. I couldn't imagine what it was like for Lucian.

"Hi Sydney, I wanted to see you again before I took off." I wasn't sure what to say at this point.

I was hoping to find out if she even remembered who I was. It was a good thing I wasn't depending on her getting me out of this mess, but then I think that was sort of her plan all along. She may have been trying to protect me towards the end. She mainly bought me time to figure out what I wanted and how to handle this.

"Are you, my granddaughter?" Sydney seemed rather unsure when she asked me in a low tone.

Lucian said, "she doesn't remember me even though this hadn't been the first time she's forgotten. We were just talking about the garden the nursing home has outside, which she likes to sit in. She doesn't seem to remember much other than she rattles on about a few very strange-sounding things. They could be true; except I wasn't with her when those things happened. She tells stories of vampires, shades, and humans with special gifts. I know special creatures exist except she doesn't seem to be able to distinguish from reality to fantasy." Lucian couldn't hide the sound in his voice when he told me this.

It's difficult when someone you loved doesn't remember you or even resemble what they once were. I wasn't too sure how to respond so I made it simple.

"I'm not your granddaughter Sydney. I'm your friend." I had tried to say it as simply as I could.

A nurse walked by curious why Sydney was getting so many visitors suddenly.

"Another friend, how wonderful, have you met my other friend Lucian here?" She seemed rather happy when she introduced him to us.

"Yes, I've met Lucian; I'm going to give you privacy so you can talk more. We need to get going. Also, Lucian, Charlie said to pass on a message for you, not to stay away too long. I was guessing you would know what he meant." He nodded his head in agreement.

We were going to leave when Sydney reached for my hand. Looking at her she was also holding Lucian's hand. From the words she spoke. I wasn't sure if it was just how she felt or if she was remembering something and perhaps felt it best not to admit to it and let life go on? I tended to overanalyze things and could be completely wrong, either way, her words would stick in my head.

"When you remember someone because you feel sorry for them. It's only momentary, when you remember someone because you care or love them, it lasts more than life itself. I'm tired and taking my nap now." Letting go of our hands she laid back down pulling her blanket over her not waiting for us to leave, she closed her eyes.

"I'm ready to leave anyway. I'll walk out with both of you." Leaving Sydney behind I was sure this was going to be the last time I would see her.

Standing at the front entrance, Lorah was still waiting nearby. I could only guess she wanted to stick around in case Lucian needed her.

"I guess Charlie isn't the only one worried. I should probably go see what grandpa wants especially if Lorah is waiting for any other reason. Do you know what was on the note you were asked to give him, was it from Alana?" Lucian was curious as his voice seemed rather controlled.

264

"No, it wasn't from Alana, it was from someone Charlie called Katherine, or she was also known as the lady in black. He was warning me to be careful around her, she killed Alana, it's the only reason I'm here." Even Lucian had that worried look on his face the same as Charlie did.

"How could she possibly be alive? Where did you see her and what was she doing? How does she know you?" These were the questions I had expected Charlie to ask except he hadn't, which made me think he wasn't too surprised to hear she was still alive.

"I'm guessing partly because of Valafar. She said they were even, and she wanted to kill Alana, so my only guess is that she's been watching me for a while or knew me from some other point? She knows your family and I've been around Lorah and Sophie. She was also involved with Sydney at one point. There were several opportunities for her to find out about me. First and only time I ran into her was when I used the pool at the city, I never would have known it was down there if you hadn't told me. She said she's been lost for a while, I assumed she was stuck in there until I ran into her. I was about to take Zack home and I have another place I need to get to after this." For a moment I almost thought Lucian was deciding whether he wanted to come with us.

"I'm sort of stumped mentally, in a way I'm curious what you're going to do and on the other hand I'm pretty sure I'll be seeing you in the future anyway, so best of luck to you, I'm heading home for a while before we move. I doubt Sydney will remember. I think it's best I don't visit her anymore. Will you be seeing her again?" Lucian seemed almost far off in thought to catch my answer.

"I don't think so." With a nod of the head, Lucian went and joined Lorah.

Waiting until they were out of sight, I looked around making sure no one was watching, still holding onto Zack's hand. I moved us both to his family's farmhouse.

"What are we doing here?" I knew he would be curious.

I hadn't wanted to spring this on his sister if he wasn't in favor of it, and I wanted to make sure I wasn't interrupting anything.

"I wanted to offer you something, you're my best friend and I wanted to give you the choice if you wanted to join me. I have a few other new friends who have decided to follow along. I can share this power with you." Stopping for a moment, I wasn't sure how else to say it.

I had thought it over in my mind so many times and for some reason, it never sounded right.

"I have to admit I am impressed by what I've seen so far. Except what you have said it's supposed to be this massive power everyone wants, and you haven't learned everything there is about it since it's never been contained like this before. How do you know it won't backfire on you? Are you still seeing this other guy?" Zack asked as he watched my expression.

I hadn't known how to answer him. Oddly enough I hadn't thought once of Zack while I was gone, he was a great friend. I just shouldn't have used him like this.

"Yes, I'm still with Valafar even though It's been a while and more complicated then I want to admit to. I think I was only asking you for selfish reasons. I know you will always be there for me. It's not fair to ask you, is it?" I knew at this point I should stop.

"I don't want to exist forever until I meet a fate of death by being bitten. Or watching you for a lifetime with someone else. I would love to protect you. I just can't do it. I like my average life and not knowing this whole other world that's around me. It's

266

safer and I won't risk losing my family." Zack's expression looked rather sad as he looked me in the eyes.

Wrapping my arms around him I knew I would never see Zack after this, not that I would ever forget him.

"I'll miss you." Giving him a kiss on the cheek I had thought of Valafar hoping he would be somewhere I could get to.

I wasn't moving anywhere so I thought of Lorah, just so that I would be gone from here, otherwise, I was going to start crying in front of him. I didn't want to do that. Startling Lorah a little as I appeared in the back seat of her car, Lucian seemed rather relaxed looking back at me almost as if he expected me to show up. It was either that or he was getting used to my showing up unannounced now.

"I have one more day before I'm expected at a certain place. I was hoping to see Valafar, but I can't seem to find him? I've concentrated on him just as I have with anyone else, and I go nowhere. Are you sure he's alright? I can't figure out what would be preventing me from going to him?" I had tried to figure out a few ideas except they hadn't seemed any more logical than the reason why it worked with others.

"I'll call him on his cell phone and see what he's up to." Lucian picked up Lorah's purse rummaging through it searching for the phone. Looking frustrated, he handed it back to me.

"I don't know how you find anything in that thing. I'm a guy and I don't deal with purses." He seemed more frustrated that he couldn't easily locate it.

I wished I hadn't made it look so easy as I reached into the side pocket inside the purse and pulled out the cell phone. Handing it to Lorah to call in case his family was listening, it was safer for her to call for now. Pulling the car over to the side she dialed the number, instead of ringing it had gone straight to his voice mail. Valafar never had it turned off no matter where he was. With the cell phone turned off there was no way of tracking him either to see where he might be. At least one bonus to this gift had been the mode of transportation.

"I'll check back with you. I want to check a place to see if he might have gone there. If I can't find him I will find you again." As soon as I had said it, I disappeared before either could respond.

I could get easily addicted to instant travel. I had wondered what made this gift so powerful or unique. Supposedly I had the power of turning a vampire back into a full-breathing human, not that they couldn't be bitten and changed again. There were so many things that I hadn't even begun to learn yet and mostly because I had been busy trying to hide it. Now I knew how important it was to master it so that I'm not stuck under someone else's control. Not that I wanted to rule or be powerful. I would like to blend in again not that I knew if it would ever be possible. I just hoped.

Checking the house again. I made sure I went through every room. I even searched the pool house, then went into his office which hadn't changed from the last time I had checked it. No one had been at the deserted factory where the party had once been held where Sophie and Sydney had first taken off with me. I had checked every place I could think of that he might have gone. I had even gone to the Eurubian city again in case he had come looking for me. Then I knew where I needed to go. First, I wanted to speak with Lorah again in case she heard anything, then I would risk my last attempt. If he wasn't there I would have to hide until I heard from him again. Focusing on Lorah again she had ditched the rental car choosing to run back, it had been much faster even though she still gave a slight jump as she was about to pass me. Lucian had stopped asking if I wanted a ride, they were almost to Charlie and Sophie's home. I had opted for meeting them there. Not that I had to wait very long with their speed, they were there within the hour. Sophie had been against my going to the compound to check on Valafar.

"I'm sure he's fine. He might need some time. I'm sure if anything would have happened, we would have heard by now. Rumors have a nasty way of spreading fast." Not that I wanted to hear anything bad, which was the only rumor I could think that would be spread.

"I don't understand why it would take this long if he was discussing me with his family, they usually make up their minds rather quickly with things like this. Lorah, do you know what he was going to say about me to his family?" I was curious if he had known about Alana or not.

Maybe they were not letting him leave because she was dead and proved that I had the power, maybe the woman in black said something to them, possibly how she and Valafar were even. Now I was feeling nervous wondering what exactly she had meant.

"How long has he been gone? Lorah, I thought you saw him just the other day?" Charlie was trying to think of any possible reason that we had not been in touch with Valafar.

Both Charlie and Valafar had grown up in the same town when they were little, so he knew his friend's habits rather well. One thing we were all hoping had been for the lady in black not to be a part of it or it would have complicated things more. Before they let me go check myself. Charlie wanted to make sure the other choices were tested out first before I subjected myself to the Augustus family, in case they hadn't heard about Alana yet. And even then, once they had at some point they would try to come after me. I had never been a patient person. For some waiting might have been tolerable except for me just waiting an hour felt like a year. After checking with a few of Valafar's friends. Charlie had decided to go with the direct approach. At least Lorah would have had a reason to call since she worked for him in the world of humans, she would have to keep him current with transactions with his company. Being careful and how exactly she would word it, Lorah called Angelita. I had to admit she was the one who made me feel the most nervous and I was afraid. Not that I needed to. I found myself holding my breath while Lorah called on the phone. Looking at Lorah and Charlie. I never would have guessed they had been an aunt and a grandfather; they looked the same age as Lucian. Even though they were changed rather young some still aged while others stopped earlier on.

"Hello Angelita, this is Lorah. I've been trying to call Valafar except he doesn't seem to have his cell phone on. I know he came there to talk with your family, but I need to bother him for a moment and ask him what he wants to be done with the new contracts on his desk?" At least it sounded legitimate enough.

Pausing for a moment, Angelita hadn't seemed in a rush to answer. I had hoped she would hand the phone over to him, at least we would know if he was alright or even there. Finally, when she had answered it wasn't what we wanted to hear.

"My dear brother is rather busy now, however, you're always welcome to come down here and ask him yourself. You don't have a problem with that do you?" Just from the way she took her sweet time speaking almost with a snide sound to her voice we knew the situation wasn't good.

Valafar had been missing for some time before Lorah went to speak with him about my arrival. Lorah wasn't overly concerned, knowing Valafar often took off for long stretches to handle his own affairs. Now she was feeling responsible for not checking on him earlier. She hadn't realized he had left to consult his family about me as a last resort. Unbeknownst to me, Valafar had been trying for a while to break into the Eurubian city, but an old enchantment spell had been raised again, preventing vampires from entering and the Augustus family from checking on me there.

Lorah kept her voice calm and casual, "no, I don't have a problem with that. I won't be able to get there right away, however. please let Valafar know that I am coming." As soon as Lorah said this Angelita hadn't waited for any other conversation or supplied any herself as she hung up the phone right away.

"I'm almost certain it's a trap; I have no doubt he's there, however, this may be their way of getting Jessica to come for him. It's only a thought; the Augustus family is rather crafty and I'm guessing they know about Alana being dead. Her voice doesn't hide very much." Charlie was shaking his head wondering if Katherine was involved and how this was going to now affect the family.

There was no way of turning their backs on Valafar if he needed them, Lorah was already involved as well as Sophie with her student, so of course, they would have the support of the family. They had been involved in minor problems before except they had never had to deal with another family this powerful and experienced before.

"Jessica. I'm sure you will want to help except you're not experienced enough yet. Our main goal will be to get Valafar out, first, Lorah will go in and the rest of us can wait outside nearby in case anything goes wrong. If he's being held and they let her speak to him then she can come out and we can plan on a way of getting him out of there. I haven't been in the new place since they had moved it, however, I'm sure we can figure out something. Does that sound like a plan for everyone?" Lucian was ready and rearing to get going.

As much as Charlie hadn't liked the idea of taking off hastily, he had agreed I was too inexperienced and hoped with just Lorah going in it might avoid a confrontation or bringing up

271

suspicions. Except everyone could agree none of us liked the idea of Lorah going in there alone.

"At least let me be nearby. I can move everyone in and out quickly if we need to." It was bad enough I was waiting I knew I couldn't handle it if I had to wait for everyone here.

"That might not be a bad idea especially if things get dangerous?" Sophie at least knew I would be fine, not that she wanted anyone to risk getting hurt.

"As long as you only stay nearby and come when we call for you." Charlie was trying to make his point clear.

"I'll do my best to stay out of the way unless you call for me." Not exactly the plan I wanted but at least I was going with it.

Both Sophie and I had been at the new one so at least I knew where to move us all to. Judging from her expression she could tell I planned on doing more if I had the chance. Sophie was impressed because the last time I had been with her. I could only transport with one person and now I was able to do it with all five of us.

Closing my eyes helped me concentrate easier so I wouldn't be distracted. The same familiar feel of air rushing past me with the feeling of pressure and slight dizziness. I had wondered if that feeling would go away after time, not that it needed to. I always preferred keeping my eyes closed not just to concentrate but I hadn't liked all the lights that tended to flash by. I wasn't sure where they were all coming from, it was always a white blur with bright lights shooting past me.

Watching from a distance for a while no one seemed to be coming in or out of the place. They would know something was up if Lorah had gone in right away so we had to wait until she would have normally arrived before she could go in. When the time had come, she went in on her own as planned to act as if it was the normal routine. Being motioned past by the guard at the gates, she walked in with no problems. Not that the guard would have had any indication anything was up from either side. It was rather quiet as Lorah walked down the narrow hallway. They had been working on the decorating since the place had looked far different than what Sophie described it as. At the far end of the tunnel had been a rather large room with a very high vaulted ceiling. A few tables and chairs lined the sides and far end of the room with one main chair facing her. Keeping herself relaxed she knew Angelita had something planned.

"Good to see you, Lorah. I told my dear brother Valafar that you would be coming to see him. He seemed rather distressed that you would." Still trying to pretend that she hadn't known anything, Lorah tried dismissing it or to get Angelita to admit to it herself what was happening.

"Why would he be distressed? It's everyday business dealings unless there is something I should know?" If she was going to be direct, then Lorah had planned on doing the same.

"Come see for yourself, the family would be happy to bring you to him." Smiling as she stood up, Lorah could feel the presence of others suddenly around her.

Seth, Sakarabru, Adhene, Lilitu, and Damar Augustus were all standing behind her as Kristopher, Ruby, and Regulus Vondrak were standing to the right of her while Lucius and Pollux Moretti were standing to her left. Apparently, they wanted to make sure she wasn't going to leave any time soon. Not arguing with them, Lorah simply followed behind Angelita as she led the way. Going down another hallway, they walked for a while going down which felt rather steep when they finally stopped. There had been several doors except we stopped at the one closest to the end. Opening the door, she motioned for her to walk in. As soon as she had walked in, they shut the door behind her.

273

Nothing could have prepared her for seeing the way Valafar had looked. His body lay on the floor rather distorted laying in a bloody mess. He looked so ill Lorah could only assume he hadn't been fed the entire time he had been here. Concentrating on her thoughts she knew Lucian, Sophie or Charlie would hear her, as she conveyed the condition Valafar was in. She was also letting them know she was now stuck in the room or from the looks of it she understood why Jessica could not move herself to Valafar. The room was enchanted to keep her out. This was a ploy to get Jessica to hand herself over assuming she would give herself to free Valafar if she had the gift. They had figured it out that Alana had died.

On the outside, Charlie was trying to figure out what their next step would be, they hoped this wouldn't happen even though he almost felt as if he should have. For a brief second, I had taken off and come back. I worried the others since they thought I had gone inside myself except when I had come back, they were curious about where I had gone. All I could say for now is that they would need to trust me. I hadn't wanted to risk any more of their family. That I had a plan, and I wanted to give it a try. At least this way no more would be putting themselves at risk and the Augustus family may believe they are getting what they want. After all, they didn't know me well enough to know that I would pull anything going on the basic human instincts that I had. I knew I wouldn't be able to draw myself to Lorah and Valafar but if I could get close enough then that would be all I needed.

Walking up to the entrance the same as Lorah had, the guard seemed rather surprised to see me. It was rather mutual since he was one of the hunters with Katherine. So, she might have been here. I only hoped she hadn't set a trap for the others outside while I went in. It was so quiet that the only sound being made had been our footsteps as we made our way down the tunnel. Just as Lorah had been greeted, the rest of the group had been there ready to greet me. Looking me over surprised I had willingly walked in instead of trying to use the gift to pop in and out trying to grab either Lorah or Valafar seemed to surprise everyone.

"I came to see Valafar and Lorah." Making my purpose known and straight to the point they were letting Angelita voice their opinion for everyone.

"We can't let you leave with either, they no longer serve a purpose, family or not they have never fit in, and besides we have what we want now. What do we need with useless bait?" Angelita seemed rather sure of herself.

"Would it help if the bait were dead? After all, if I died you would never be able to use my power. The second I die, it's gone, that is if I still have it, do you want to take that risk?" One of the things I learned when others dealt with Angelita had been to show no fear and to match her threat.

I was a lot calmer than I thought I would be, the strangest calmness had taken over me. Watching the expression on Angelita's face I could tell she was silently conversing with the others.

"We will let you see Valafar and Lorah only; you will be nowhere near him. Then you are to do exactly as we demand of you or both die." Nodding in agreement I walked behind Angelita as she led the way.

Not stopping where Lorah had explained at the door. I could only guess they were going to bring them into the other room we entered. Standing there I noticed there were not any enchantments, Assuming I was the only one with the gift, they likely concluded no further precautions were necessary. They felt satisfied that Sydney would not be capable of helping. Let alone be a part of this anymore. She was of no value to them. Only two of the family members stood behind me, blocking the exit as the others stood in the center probably assuming they would stand between Valafar, Lorah, and me. As soon as I heard footsteps, I turned to see Sakarabru guiding Lorah over to the far side wall away from me as Pollux carried out Valafar. Dropping him on the ground next to Lorah. I could hear Lorah telling me, "I should not have come in," not that she knew of my plan. I had to make sure I did not show any emotion right now or risk messing it up.

"What exactly do you wish for me to do?" I had directed the question towards Angelita since she seemed to be speaking for everyone.

"If you attempt to take off with either of them you will meet the same fate as Sydney. We have plans for you in the morning and until then you can stay in a separate room. You may say your goodbye from where you are standing. They will be put back in the same room as they were earlier, we won't risk you trying to take off with them. We don't fall for tricks. We have been around for far too long." Angelita seemed rather sure of herself until she heard not my voice in response to her, but that of Audra.

Both Audra and Aaron were right next to Lorah and Valafar as they touched them, they took off leaving me with the Augustus family. Delaney and Alexandra had shown up outside already to move the others safely away from here.

"Not to worry. I won't try to take off with them, but I can safely assume you hadn't seen that one coming. Goodbye." Before they had a chance, I transported myself out as they were all lunging at me at the same time.

I was glad not to be in the middle of that mess when they wound up lunging at each other because I had disappeared. I was finally feeling comfortable with my gift, and it helped knowing I wasn't alone with it.

With the five of us, we were able to help Charlie and Sophie move into their new home much earlier than they planned. Opting for a more tropical setting this time, almost the entire family had moved to this area. Rose and Jacob with their daughter Larissa and a second baby on the way and only walking distance had been Anthony and Nichole. Charlie and Sophie were not that far as the five of us built a cute little house dead center of all three of their properties. Lucian helped build our home as well as moved in with us. It was nice having him with us. It helped to have a safe place for Valafar to heal. Sophie's home herbs and treatments helped quite a bit. For several months Valafar lay in bed not able to move. I never once left his side. The others had been receiving training from Sophie, mainly what she had already taught me, so I wasn't missing out on anything new yet.

Sitting beside Valafar, I couldn't help but ponder the pivotal role he had played in my life. If I had never crossed paths with him, would Reyes have succeeded in his attempt to end me? And what of my parents' untimely demise - was it truly an accident, or something more sinister? The what ifs swirled in my mind, leaving me to wonder how the course of my life might have unfolded had events transpired differently. Would I never of had the gift I do now? Even with heartache and the stressful way all of this happened. I was still thankful it had. I had what I longed for and that was true friendship, family, and simply those who truly cared about me. Sitting on the bed next to Valafar. I played with his hair moving it over to the side of his forehead. His hair had been rather shaggy since being bedridden. I hadn't wanted to subject him to any pain. Besides, who would see it except those who cared about him? Kissing him on the forehead, he slowly opened his eyes.

"You shouldn't have risked your life coming for me; I was trying to save you." Trying to smile I could still see he was in pain.

Self-healing or not and even with outside help, it was taking a while to recover from what his family did to him.

"Why should I wait to be rescued. This isn't exactly an old-time fairy tale. Besides, you helped rescue me by stalling them so that I could come to get you." Kissing him carefully on the lips I knew I was happy with my choices no matter what happened.

I chose to take the good with the bad. Jacob and Charlie tended to the expansive garden, their hands busy with the preparations, while Sophie focused her efforts in her own private corner of the verdant landscape. Even a lifeless heart would have stirred at the haunting sound of her voice - a sound none who heard it could ever forget, no matter how faint or distant the echo. The mere memory of it still sent icy shivers down his spine. Not sure what she was physically after this time. Charlie stood up to face her, the woman he had known now not to be his mother finally having it confirmed. He had always wondered why he had still looked so similar to Evangeline but then it might have simply been the vampire traits and the fact she looked so much like a McAllister. Charlie wondered if she was here to drop another bomb on the family. What could she possibly want now? As he faced her Charlie could see that the rest of his family noticed she was now standing so close to him.

"Hello Charlie, I see the family is still rather protective of each other." Had been the first words that Katherine said to Charlie

"We will always be close." Charlie had not wanted to say very much to her.

"You don't seem to be surprised to see me my pet." Katherine had that wicked glint of light cross her eye for a second.

"Nothing surprises me when it comes to you." With no change in his voice, he had truly felt what he said.

"I see there is a new little one I have not met?" As Katherine was looking over Larissa, Charlie had wished she was playing inside except he had no idea when Katherine might show up.

At least this way the family was here to protect each other.

"What do you want Katherine. You know I can't read your mind? You don't make friendly social calls." Charlie wanted to get on with it and find out what she wanted.

The years of stress and family relocations had finally provided the peace and solitude Charley craved and enjoyed the last several years, he just wasn't in the mood for the stress anymore.

"With a wistful tone, she said, "There is a magical person I desire more than anything, someone you should know, find him and you find her, something that will go quite nicely with Jessica later on." She then produced a folded piece of paper, which she handed to Charlie.

Katherine had not come alone as nine others were now standing next to her, most that Jessica recognized as the other hunters. They were no longer demon hunters when Katherine had changed them, keeping them to work for her.

"Unlike last time, I won't waste my time searching for it. I'll keep your grandson until you hand it over, you will know how to find me. I'm sure Jessica will help. She still owes me a favor for taking care of Alana and letting her keep Valafar." As soon as she said this she took off. Her hunters had already caught and taken Lucian. He wasn't the only one missing, Jacob was missing as well.

279